After W
Bran Reborn

Nancy Jardine

Praise for *The Beltane Choice*:

"very human and personal story
with a very believable vision of Late Iron Age society"
Mark Patton, archaeologist and author of *An Accidental King*

"as wild as that untamed land and as sweet
as heather mead"
Kate Robbins, author of *Bound to the Highlander*

"her careful selection of words enhanced the
imagery...ancient-century Romeo and Juliet"
The Reading Cafe

CROOKED
CAT

Discover us online:
www.crookedcatpublishing.com

Join us on facebook:
www.facebook.com/crookedcatpublishing

Tweet a photo of yourself holding
this book to **@crookedcatbooks**
and something nice will happen.

I dedicate this novel to my father because he loved to escape the realities of life by immersing himself a book.

His reading tastes varied a great deal but tales of derring-do adventures particularly appealed, as did biographies of famous explorers and pioneers – men who conquered the earth in some way. At an impressionable age, he introduced me to many of the classics, my reading scope broadened by his example.

In After Whorl: Bran Reborn, the main character has to overcome physical difficulties and get on with a new life. When I was 12 years old, my father suffered serious crushing injuries in an industrial accident. He survived and walked again, even when the outcome initially looked extremely bleak. His determination to live, and his sheer fortitude, was greatly respected by all who knew him.

I hope you'll find something similar to admire about my character, Brennus, in after Whorl: Bran Reborn.

Acknowledgements:

A number of people have assisted me during the writing process of After Whorl: Bran Reborn and I'd like to thank them all. Fellow Crooked Cat Author, Dr. Mark Patton, gave me excellent source suggestions for researching northern parts of Roman Britain. Some of these items I acquired through Inter-Library loans from The British Library, my local Public Librarians being extremely helpful and efficient during the ordering process – my thanks to all involved.

Leanne Ferguson, a genealogist friend I met via a Facebook, gave me brilliant help with the Scottish Gaelic used in After Whorl: Bran Reborn. My thanks also go to Seumas Gallacher, yet another Facebook friend, who double-checked and confirmed my use of Scottish Gaelic. An extra special thanks goes to Sandy McIntosh, from a local writers' group, who beta read my manuscript. His support as a reader of my work has been so welcomed – thank you, Sandy!

I also send my heartfelt thanks to the team at Crooked Cat for publishing my Celtic Fervour books– to Steph and Laurence Patterson and to my editor, Maureen Vincent-Northam.

About the Author:

Nancy Jardine lives in Aberdeenshire, Scotland, with her husband. She spends her week making creative excuses for her neglected large garden; doesn't manage as much writing as she always plans to do since she's on Facebook too often; and has a thoroughly great time playing with her toddler granddaughter when she's supposed to be 'just' regularly childminding.

A lover of all things historical it sneaks into most of her writing, as do many of the fantastic world locations she has been fortunate to visit. Her published work to date has been two non fiction history related projects; two contemporary ancestral mysteries - Monogamy Twist and Topaz Eyes; and one humorous contemporary romance mystery - Take Me Now.

The first in her Celtic Fervour historical romantic adventure series, The Beltane Choice, was published in August 2012 and the third, After Whorl: Donning Double Cloaks, is due for publication in the spring of 2014.

She has been published by Crooked Cat Publishing and The Wild Rose Press

The Celtic Fervour series:

The Beltane Choice
After Whorl: Bran Reborn
After Whorl: Donning Double Cloaks

After Whorl: Bran Reborn

Celtic Britain 71 AD

TARRAS ■

■ GARRIGILL

CRANNOGS ■
OF GYPTUS

WHORL ■   ■ STANWICK

■ QUERNIUM

NIDD ■
SOWER ■
MARSKE
WITTON ■
■ EBORACUM

■ SCORTIN

DEVA ■

■ LINDUM

■ VIROCONIUM
CORNOVIORUM

Chapter One

"*Fóghnaidh mi dhut!* I really will finish you! I have you now, invading scum!"

Another couple of whacks would have the shield gone. The Roman auxiliary's arm already showed signs of fatigue as Brennus slashed below the man's chain link protection, his full power backing each blow of his long Celtic sword. The man was brawny, a practised opponent at the edge of the tight cluster of Roman bodies, but was much smaller than he was and rapidly weakened. Brennus knew the advantage he had. A drained grin slid into a grimace of pain as his sword jarred on the Roman gladius when the soldier's stab interrupted another of his blows, the impact juddering his weakened elbow, an injury sustained with a previous combatant.

"*Diùbhadh!* Scum!"

The gladius flashed upwards. To reach his head the angle of the auxiliary's attack had to be higher than the usual, demanding a different force to succeed, and the Roman just did not have the strength any more.

A cry of frustration emerged from the Roman, the clenched teeth an indicator of the man's tenacity as the gladius prodded forward yet again. Brennus understood none of the man's tongue, the battle ground not the place for meaningful talk, but the intent was clear.

"Come! Come forward! *A ghlaoic!* You fool!" Brennus'

hollering taunts and crude ridiculing gestures gained him a little ground as the auxiliary broke free of the rigid formation, desperate to gain conquest over yet another Celtic adversary, the shorter gladius slashing and nipping at his chest but not quite breaking the skin.

The tight group of Roman soldiers had been almost impossible to breach; their raised cover of shields an impenetrable barrier. He had been toying with and provoking this particular soldier for long, long moments. Yet, even with his superior strength, he knew he could not sustain such weighty combat for much longer either, before he would need to retreat to regain his reserves of vigour – though only a little more wearing down of the man's resistance should be enough. He knew that from an earlier experience. Drawing breath from deep inside he slipped back a pace, and then another as if giving up the pursuit.

"Come forward, you piece of Roman horse dung! You demand the blood of the Celts? Let it be so! Have mine!"

Powerless to resist the lure the Roman soldier surged at his bidding, his shield swinging, his gladius jabbing. One last twisted swipe of Brennus' longer Celtic sword detached the blade-nicked shield from his foe and sent it sailing aside. Abruptly unguarded, the auxiliary pulled his gladius in front of his rippling mail in a futile attempt to cover his chest.

"Too late!" Brennus' snort rang out as he whacked the soldier's fist with his shield when his opponent readied his blade for another stab. It was enough: all the leverage needed to topple his foe. Witnessing the Roman's slithering attempts to right himself he allowed an exultant smirk to break free, knowing victory would be his over this particular rival. "Death to all of the invaders!"

The sounds of battle all around him seemed all the sweeter as he slashed his blade towards the Roman's vulnerable neck, the man's cloth wrap having unfurled from under the chin during the tussle. It was the weakest part of his well equipped adversary

4

that was uncovered above the waist. He knew that a blow to the head was wasteful since the glinting copper-flapped helmet fit tight around the Roman's skull. His first swipe was met with the flailing gladius, the clang and screeches of blade on blade an exhilarating challenge. Triumphant warmth flashed through him, the sweat of the combat a bitter taste in his mouth as it streamed his face. The auxiliary was doomed as Brennus spat through his teeth, "I hate every last one of you!"

The shrieking, the neighing and squealing behind him he ignored, the battlefield noises a tremendous din all around. The stench – of heated combat; of the blood tang and of faeces of man and horse; of the already putrid reek of entrails; of the stale sweat and battle lust essences – he also disregarded. His attention was only on his quarry as he felt the edge of his sword slice in under the man's chin. He prepared himself for the spurt of warm blood that showered on him as he angled his neck away from the first gushes.

What was totally unexpected was the crushing mass that slammed into his back, so powerful it lifted him off his feet and propelled him onto the blinking gladius he had successfully parried.

"By Taranis…" His yell muffled into a spluttering squelch. "*An cù!* The bastard!"

Down he went, onto the slippery blood drenched grass, his sword sliding fully through the auxiliary's neck. His dead opponent softened his fall only partially since the horse that had slumped into him followed on at his rear. As the agonised cries of men and the squealing of the horse echoed around, his fist relinquished the grip on his sword, the blade having snapped on skidding impact with the ground.

The frantic, writhing animal that pinned him to the Roman gladius totally overpowered him. Devastating agony seared at his back; blood filled muck crammed his mouth. A blinding white-red haze gave way to darkness.

Felled by a mighty powerful beast, and not that Roman blade, was Brennus' last thought.

Ineda checked over her shoulder, yet again, as she crept through the forest heading for the rock face at the bend of the river. If her grandmother, Meaghan, was anywhere around it was likely to be near the cave. She would have been sheltering there since fleeing their roundhouse village at Marske some five days past. Meaghan's last word to her had warned that the cave was where she would run to.

The day was early-summer warm, the sweetness of new foliage a fragrant sniff, the sunbeams creating pretty slashes on the ferny undergrowth. Usual forest sounds greeted her as she trod a light-footed pathway over tree roots and avoided the deteriorating debris of winter cold, which still remained a slippery rotting mess in some deeper grooves. It would have been pleasant to hum her way across the last stretch of undulating forest floor before the land dipped down to the riverbank, but it was not the time for such frivolity. Chirping and fluttering chiff-chaffs, and lightly buzzing insects were a fleeting glimpse as they went about the business of pecking and first-nectar gathering. A herd of deer crossed over to her right, their progress a delicate and graceful dance amid the green in her peripheral view, their passage through the trees with nary a sound to be heard. They were a good example to Ineda to remain vigilant – silence being crucial. Her reasons were two-fold. She never unnecessarily disturbed the peace of the forest god, Cernunnos, or his creatures.

More importantly, she did not wish to be tracked by inadvertent noise.

Soon burbling water gently rippled and twinkled in the sun, way down below her, the eddies around the large flat stones flashes of slow movement since the river level was very low at this point on its traverse through the forest. Skittering down the last earthen slope Ineda halted her slide, grabbing a tight hold of the sun-warmed brackens.

The cave was close by. It was a haven often used by her and her grandmother if the weather was inclement while Meaghan was instructing her in the lore of healing herbs.

The light tap at her shoulder had Ineda swivelling in a flurry. Not the touch of a hand, it was the smallest of pebbles that pinged off her shoulder. From behind a tree to her rear an old woman emerged, her voice light and cheerful.

"You still have much to learn, Granddaughter, if you think to surprise me."

Ineda rushed into the bony old arms for a welcome hug. "That will never happen and was not my intention. If I try to evade anyone, you know it is the Roman patrols."

"*Ciamar a tha thu?*" The old woman's inquiring look was intense.

Ineda grinned and answered the question. "How am I? I am fine. All the better for seeing you."

"It is good to see you well, Ineda, but not so good about the persistence of the Roman Army. Come, and give me your news."

Meaghan's gnarled fingers feathering at her braids, to tidy them, was a gesture she had missed so much during the last fraught days.

Ineda had a lot to tell as they tramped their way along the riverbank towards the cave. "The tribespeople of Witton have given us shelter, as Father had hoped they would. We use roundhouses that lay empty after the Roman Army first descended upon the settlement about a half moon ago."

"Were many Witton people slain?"

"Aye. Many from Witton and the nearby villages." Ineda's tongue dripped contempt of the Roman blade. "Anyone who put up the slightest resistance was put to the sword. Men,

7

women and even children."

Meaghan's hand clutched at her arm, halting her stride. "Your father?"

A reassuring tap on Meaghan's bony fingers was returned by a surprisingly tight squeeze from one so riddled with twisting knuckles. She was careful with her reply knowing Meaghan's concern for her only living son.

"Ruarke is unharmed, apart from his earlier foot injury that now heals well. Our trek to Witton was a sore trial for him, but I tended the wound as you instructed. The bindings are kept tight and the sole of his foot has not suppurated, though the injury remains red and angry. Your stitches to the skin hold firm. The crutch slowed our escape, but without it to help him hobble he would not have made the distance to Witton."

"Witton is farther than you expected?" Meaghan tottered a little, grasping the ferns and low twisting willows as she skittered along the narrow strip of pathway right on the river's edge as it followed the curve of the water.

Ineda trod along making sure not to trail too swiftly or she would topple her grandmother. Accepting the pulled-back branches which concealed the cave mouth, she ducked inside, allowing the cover to slap back into place behind her. "Aye! We were two full days travelling before we reached it, though if Ruarke had been fit and healthy it would have taken us far less than one day. Unseasonable marsh mist and cloying rain also sapped our strength."

"I journeyed to Witton some time past with your aunt Caitlin, but the weather was favourable and we were eager to arrive there." Meaghan's tone was wistful.

A deep sadness trickled through Ineda. Stepping closer to Meaghan, who busied herself about the fireside, she clasped her grandmother's shoulders, turned her and buried in for a hug. Her next news was bad.

Meaghan's touch at her hair and the deep sigh that escaped to ripple from chest to chest indicated her grandmother already guessed the worst.

"My daughters have already gone to the otherworld, I know this Ineda. The Roman gladius has struck fiercely and has left me bereft of my family, save you and your father."

Ineda's tears ran freely, soaking Meaghan's woollen dress. "Aye. We three are the only ones left now."

She felt Meaghan's strength of character as the old woman put her from her and gave her a little shake at the shoulders, the elderly voice strong and determined. "Our blood has been drained by the Roman Empire but we will not lay down our lives willingly, Ineda. Remember that! It is part of your future to resist!"

"I do not want to lose you as well, Grandmother!" Her plea met with a small shake of Meaghan's head and a beaming smile which revealed yellowed, yet healthy enough teeth for one of so advanced an age.

"You are the child of my son, but also the child of my gift, Ineda."

Ineda could not doubt the fervour in her grandmother's eyes, a vital life force lighting them with a bright green fire. If she had inherited her grandmother's gift she had also the look of her grandmother in eye colour, height and shape. Another bony hug reassured her before Meaghan put her from her at arm's length, the old eyes penetrating, yet tired at the same time.

"Ineda, though you but realise it, you are also my future! My craft is in you."

"I cannot understand you, Grandmother." She faced Meaghan, asking a further silent question. When no answer came to enlighten her, she added, "Yet."

The soft finger pats to her braids were gestures well learned. Ineda knew it as an unspoken signal for patience.

Meaghan's voice softened to an amused chuckle. "Neither of my two daughters had the power, or the will, that you possess. You will always have me with you in spirit, my girl. My healing force is within you and binds us."

Meaghan's fingers flicked away the tear trickles that still ran down Ineda's cheeks, the tutting and clucking as though they had been a waste of precious spirit, her old rheumy eyes reassuring and endearingly warm with love. "Never fear for me, Ineda, my girl. I tell you this, now. I will not depart this realm with a Roman weapon the cause of it. My passing will come, ere long, but I have more healing to do before then. My next task is important to our Celtic brethren and not just to me alone."

Looking into Meaghan's face Ineda did not doubt a single word. She forced her tears gone. Courage did not come easy but she willed it so, the wobble to her lips only momentary before she found the control Meaghan demanded.

"I will find strength to resist."

The cackle that followed was typical of Meaghan, any weakness put aside and barely worth a mention. Sliding away from their embrace her grandmother almost bent double to poke at the embers of the tiny fire that lay a little inside the overhang of the cave. It was a fire small enough to slowly cook by but not fiery enough to create noticeable smoke. "You will resist, my girl! Now, tell me how your father finds Witton."

Ineda sat down and ate the fish Meaghan handed her, a fish which had been slowly roasting between two hot stones at the fireside. Wrapped in wide leaves the flesh had not dried out, the taste of it reminding her that she had not eaten since the previous day. In between welcome mouthfuls, she gave answer.

"Father is dispirited that we fled so ignominiously from Marske, but he accepts that we had no other choice. We need the shelter, and support, our distant family at Witton affords us. He also accepts the Roman yoke dished out to us at present, though not willingly." She picked a small bone from between her teeth before continuing, shaking her head in disgust. "I could not persuade Father to return to Marske now, even if the Roman scum left it alone."

"You are sure of this?"

"I fear he feels safer at Witton where there are more men to protect everyone."

Meaghan halted her tending of the fire and stared at her, shocked by her words. "Your father has grown into a coward?"

"His fighting strength is gone, sapped away by those moons of Roman threats and attacks. He snaps at assistance, yet rejects any measures of friendship."

"My son feels less than a man?"

Ineda did not answer that question. It needed no answer. "He still strives to protect me but has lost his sense of our village unity. I am not so certain he would defend anyone from Witton against Roman attack, and I do not understand that, Grandmother."

"Ruarke would stand back and allow others to do that for him?" Meaghan's voice was pained.

Ineda shrugged her shoulders, her gaze on her grandmother unwavering. "Perhaps. The settlement is well down in numbers of original people, but it is still very large compared to our own tiny village, now that there are many unfortunates that the Roman Empire have forced to live in it. Though we have not sheltered there for long Ruarke seems befuddled about our future."

"Yet he would not return to Marske? This behaviour does not match."

Ineda knew her words seemed contrary. "Aye. I have no understanding of why he accepts succour, yet resents the friendship tendered to him."

"Guilt must lie heavy on him. My son was always a deep one, not easy to understand." Having picked at a little fish Meagan rose again and stood hovering by the doorway. "Come. I have some healing herbs to show you."

Wiping her fingers on her dress Ineda followed her grandmother, thinking how unalike the mother and son were. Her father was a good man but was prone to making some strange decisions.

They made a slow climb back up the banking. When she crested the rise and was up onto the flatter ground she felt Meaghan's bony fingers plucking at her dress to halt her progress. Dropping onto a raised level stone her grandmother drew hard won breaths before speaking again, her whole torso trembling. "I have crept back to Marske a few times. The Roman Army still sends patrols every day to pilfer more of our stored goods, but they have no notion I have been anywhere near. The past nights I have spent in the cave, but as soon as they have cleared out every vestige of our supplies and tools they will cease to visit our roundhouses. By then, they will have another place to plunder. And I will return to my home, even if your father refuses to do so."

"Grandmother!" Ineda made no mistake about her plea as she clutched Meaghan in a tight hug. "It is far too dangerous to go back. They are still bent on destroying any Brigante who flaunts their authority. We must make no show of being armed now, and groups of warriors of more than two or three are held in suspicion. Any more out on the hunt together incur the full wrath of Rome as they are deemed to be on the attack. I have been tending to some stripling warriors this morn who thought to challenge one of the patrols, though their wounds were not as serious as they could have been. I suspect them having come as more of a warning from the Roman gladius than any other purpose."

"I hear you, girl. I will do nothing to put me at risk. Now, tell me of any risings against these Roman oppressors."

Meaghan put her away from the clutch and looked deep into her eyes, demanding answers she did not have, although her grandmother's gentle hand pats were soothing and reassuring, indicating that she would do nothing rash.

Drawing a deep breath, Ineda related all she knew. "It goes ill for the tribes of mid-Brigantia. I have heard that those from further north congregate at Whorl where they may be battling as I speak. A few Witton warriors escaped the patrols before dawn yesterday morning and headed there."

"Then those Witton warriors will either triumph, or will go to the otherworld knowing that they fought for our Celtic heritage."

"I do not want them to die in vain, but the Roman Empire is a mighty foe!" Ineda could not prevent her anger from spouting forth, her voice strident and scathing as she looked across the river. She could hardly face Meaghan since her next news seemed worse and yet might be the reason for her father's apathy. "More could have gone, I am sure of it, but they chose to avoid the conflict."

Meaghan's reaction was not what she expected. The old woman's laugh rang out over the river noises, drawing back her gaze. "Then they will live to clash with their heart. These battles with the Roman scourge are intended to subdue the warring tribes of mid-Brigantia. The Roman Army floods our territory now, their presence a direct threat. They will drag us into their Roman province – which they did not properly do when Queen Cartimandua made her long-ago treaties with them."

Ineda did not even try to hide her scorn. "Aye! As their client-Queen Cartimandua kept their marauding tendencies at bay, their main presence remaining in southern lands."

"Girl, you do our former queen a disservice. You may not have liked Cartimandua's methods but in her own way, for long moons even when you were a tiny child, she afforded us a form of freedom from their constant presence on our Brigante soil."

Ineda jumped up from the stone and paced around, her temper roiling. "Cartimandua is long gone – dead or elsewhere – but King Venutius still lives! He survives and will continue to rebel against the Roman scum." Shocked at her grandmother's words she dared speak as she never had before, her tone berating. "Do you now give these Roman oppressors your allegiance, Grandmother?"

Unable to look Meaghan in the eye, betraying tears

hovering, she gulped down her anger and frustration as she stared across the water. There were so many people whose actions and speech now confused her.

Meaghan's arm snaked across her shoulders and squeezed her tight to her breast, her fingers a reassuring stroke down her braided hair. "Never will I do that, Ineda, my girl. You tell me Venutius lives, and I believe you. Aye, this may be true, but who is left to follow him and rise up against the Roman Empire's army? "

Lifting her face to view Meaghan, she kept her voice low, the vow in it unmistakeable. "There are still northern Brigantes who will repel the Roman Empire. It may not look that way just now but there are many, like me, who will continue to resist."

Meaghan's arms held her stiffly out at length, fingernails inadvertently nipping into her flesh, before her grandmother's gaze took on a cloudy look, her eyes flickering and rolling skywards, as though seeing an inner vision. "You are only a thin sapling, my oftimes foolish granddaughter, but there is strength to build and grow on…" The old voice trailed off.

Ineda had watched her grandmother trance like this before, and did not fear it. The twists and grimaces at her old cheeks indicated both pain and pleasure, the flickering of her eyes a frightful sight, but the tight grip of her fists remained firm. Ineda watched and waited knowing she could do nothing to speed, or safely halt, the progress of the vision. After some moments, Meaghan came to herself and smiled before she spoke again. It was not a smile of worry, but one of promise: an affectionate twinkle was there in her eyes…and love. Meaghan's love never failed to warm her.

Her grandmother's words were firm. "Ineda, child of my son, you have a warrior's heart – even if you never have proper warrior training. I see your time is coming, though it is not here yet. Do nothing rash. Act according to your clever head."

Ineda watched as Meaghan's bent finger rose up to tap her on the forehead. The old nail was strong and firm as it made contact with her skin. They now stood so close the flesh around Meaghan's eyes was crinkled and worn, her eyelids almost covering her view as she smiled and cackled. Not daring to stop the tapping, she returned her grandmother's smile, sensing there was more to come when the finger drifted lower and pointed to her chest.

"Your heart will know the way you must fight the Romans. Let that knowledge come naturally to you, Ineda, and do not force it. You have a valiant part to play in your future and in the future of those around you. The path ahead for you will have much frustration, hardships and heartbreak, but there will also be equal joy. You must face what occurs with courage. Wear two bratts when that time is revealed, and continue to wrap yourself thus till the sun shines again. The skills of healing I have taught you will rest in your mind, but bring them forth when they are most needed. Bear your future well, accept the difficulties and live through the very bad times. Always work towards the good."

She accepted her grandmother's words, acknowledging them with a nod. Though she did not know what Meaghan meant she knew it was likely to happen. Foretelling was a gift her grandmother rarely used, but when she did, it had always been accurate.

"You have only taught me some of your healing skills, Grandmother. There is so much more to learn."

"Aye. That is true, but you have learned all of the most important. What is to follow will come naturally to you, from the teaching you have already gained. You have the skills to build on, and you are fine and quick. Believe that this will happen."

Meaghan drew her back down to sit beside her on the flat stones as though nothing unusual had happened. "Tell me more of what happens with our Roman overseers."

"I know very little except that many Brigantes are said to be gathering at Whorl where there is a suitable low hill and flat plains for battlegrounds. Many at Witton are rejoicing at this news, yet there are also terrible rumours of every village and settlement around these parts needing to make treaties with the Roman Governor, Cerialis – like Witton has previously done. Some say Brigante delegates have already decided to journey to these parts in preparation for talks instead of engaging in futile battles. If that is so then those negotiators may speak for the Brigantes, but that does not mean every Brigante warrior has given in to the Romans!"

"You are in the right, Ineda. I must remain here for one such as you speak of. He will never give in and accept the Roman yoke."

Ineda looked deeply into her grandmother's eyes. "Who do you speak of?"

Meaghan's head shaking was accompanied by a wan smile. "I have no answer, yet, to that question…"

A sudden flare of metal glinting in the sunshine across the narrow stretch of river set them both fleeing…in opposite directions.

Chapter Two

AD 71 One Moon After Beltane – Marske

"Nay…the blade, not the beast!"

Meaghan moved around as silently as possible, not wanting to disturb the young warrior who lay sorely troubled on her low cot. Her unsteady old feet shuffled across the beaten earth as she collected herbs to add to the concoction bubbling in the pot that dangled above her meagre fire. A quick shredding and the dried foliage were popped in, followed by a whisk of her wooden spurtle to separate them around.

The condition of the warrior was dire, yet she vowed she would not fail him. For many nights now her potions had kept the man in deep slumber, but her stocks of sleep-inducing herbs had run low. It would mean leaving him unattended while she fetched more but she would have to risk that. Without her brew, he would fall into a more natural awareness, and with the change would come the pain. Perhaps he would make a lot of noise and that was too big a danger to risk.

Lifting a second pot from the hot stone at the side of her fire, she tipped the warm water into a bowl before plucking some clean strips of cloth which draped from a beam near the doorway of her roundhouse.

Hobbling to the cot with her items, she placed them carefully at his bedside before checking his injuries, as she had done regularly day after day, and night after night. No fresh blood on the hand wraps pleased her very much. The young warrior's right hand injuries no longer concerned her; and over time, they should heal over. The cleanly lopped off fingers, just above the joint near the nail, were stitched well – considering her shaky hands – and showed no sign of suppuration. There were no other major injuries to the hand, but the forearm had snapped above the wrist, though it had not broken through the skin. The slat of wood, used under her tight wrapping and tied to the cot, presently kept the arm still. The arm was not a worry either.

His right leg was another matter entirely. That would require tending for some time to come. The examination of it needed her close-up attention. Old knees creaked and protested as she knelt beside him. Lifting away the deerskins that covered his lower body, she leaned forward to sniff closely at his leg.

"Good." A second long sniff, to be sure, and she was content. "Aye! Very good."

Her prattling was a mere whisper as she untied the soft leather thongs before slowly peeling back the pad covering the injury. No fresh blood showed to the inside of the cloth, and no bad smell was encouraging. The many stitches it had taken to close the nasty wound were still an angry deep-red but the skin was knitting together surprisingly well. The swelling around the broken bone was receding – another very good sign. The warrior was lucky the snapped bone had been pulled back into place as soon as it had been. It meant the healing process to the torn flesh now progressed as best as could be expected. It was a nasty leg break, though he looked in no danger of losing the leg.

She dropped a cloth into the warm water and then gently squeezed away the excess before using it to clean around the wound. The man mumbled and thrashed, consciousness returning too soon for her. She dried off the leg before plastering on a thick poultice. That done she placed a clean pad of cloth over the gash and retied the leather thongs that remained constantly around his leg.

"Sick…" The warrior's mumble was agitated.

Gently holding his head, she reassured him. "The dizziness will pass. Lie still."

He was hot to the touch, too hot. He must not move yet, but the effects of her last potion were wearing off.

"Remain at rest, young warrior." She had more hurts to tend to.

Till now, by controlling his fevers, she had controlled his movement on the cot. The leg injury required more settled time for best healing, but more importantly for the injuries to his lower back to mend properly, he needed to lie flat for many nights to come.

"Drifting…"

"I know you are," Meaghan tittered, as his free arm lifted a tiny bit from the bed and waved aimlessly around. "You will feel a lightness that is not normal, and a queasiness that makes you want to vomit. But you will not." There was nothing in his stomach to vomit over; his food intake had been limited to sips of water, and her feeding gruel, for days on end.

As she dipped another clean cloth into her warm water, signs of acute pain gripped him and tightened his features. The very act of grimacing had the warrior gasping in pain even more. She knew what he must be experiencing. The torn flesh at his face was stretching with every wince.

"Nay!" His cry repeated as he evaded her grip.

"The jabbing, nipping pain at your face will be worse if you struggle, young warrior. Be still and allow the pain to subside."

She watched his teeth grit together to keep from calling out, but an agonised oath escaped, nonetheless.

"Garrigill. Pool water…"

Meaghan disliked his pallor as the blood drained from his face, though the heat of his body was intense. Dragging a bowl of cold water closer, she dipped cloths in then swiped them over his chest and upwards to his neck, and after that to the left side of his face. Over and over.

Plunging into the chilly pool near the hillfort at Garrigill was what Brennus strove for.

The first cold drips splashed his face, refreshing and invigorating at one and the same time. His mouth opened wide and cool liquid trickled down his parched throat, but he didn't need the persuasive fingers at his throat that forced him to swallow more. He felt free, floating along on a short journey, his feet leading the way. Something was odd, though, because his progress was even swifter than normal. He usually walked faster than most men he knew, his longer stride unparalleled since not many men matched his formidable height, but this advancement was too wonderfully quick. It rendered him unsteady as he made progress to the deep pool near the low waterfall which twinkled in the distance, the tumbling cascade beckoning his feet to glide faster. A few more steps and he'd be there. He already felt the coolness of it bathe him; needed to sink beneath its depths, and perhaps even remain.

"Stay with me, young warrior. You have more to do here."

A harsh voice rebuked at his ear but he could see no one. The bright sunshine made it difficult to see anything, though it was of no concern, he knew his way.

"Stay!"

Brennus did not want to listen to the voice that soothed, yet at the same time berated him. The water sparkled brilliantly white in the strong sunlight, a fine contrast against the pale green foliage of the reed beds that fluttered in the gentle breeze. He relished the refreshing spray, inhaled its freshness. The speed of his journey made the sweat pool at his neck even more, a strange warmth beating down on his brow adding to the trickle of moisture that made a path down his cheeks. Even his ears tingled and itched as droplets trickled inside. That, he found, was very strange since he was only just approaching the water's edge.

Ah! He wanted to smile at the lovely image in front of him, but it hurt too much when he allowed his lip to quirk.

"Swallow again."

He let himself sink into the cooling river as its liquid trickled into his mouth.

"A little more."

Vaguely aware that the water held a brackish tang did not unduly concern him – it wet his throat like ice shards of winter.

Brennus' head felt swathed as he ventured the slightest of neck turns. Nevertheless, even that tiny movement at his cheeks was an agony so he remained still and listened. His head was muzzy as though he had been asleep for a long time, but he was sure he no longer dreamed. The visions he had experienced had mostly been comforting, though others had been alarming – images of broken limbs and maimed bodies, noises of battle and the stench of death and despair.

He sifted through the sounds coming to him. There was a shuffling of feet and low whispering.

"Tch! My hunting times are long over. One measly bird for the pot, but it must do."

The noise of someone close by set his teeth on edge as he lay prone and defenceless. The voice muttered on.

"Still. A good broth will be had from it. Hah!"

The slippery screech of a sharp knife scraping bone made him wince, his hearing seeming unnaturally sensitive to the high pitched noise and to the accompanying hoot. The cackle was familiar, the repetitive tutting also recognisable. He was sure he had heard it recently. Not threatening, though he could not be sure who it was.

Familiar smells of damp brushwood burning teased and pricked at his nostrils, and other everyday smells came to his nose as he sniffed. The smell of clammy, rough wool was strong, the mustiness accompanying it one of an unwashed stale body. Something else permeated the air as he sniffed, some kind of herb, perhaps in a concoction that was brewing rather than something hung up to dry around the space. The tingle of smoke sweeter than normal played around his cheeks as though a draught had blown it in his direction rather than it settling around him. He was in a confined space, yet, that was not where he expected to be.

The battlefield?

His blood quickened alarmingly. He forced his eyelids to flicker yet could not open them. Something prevented it. All was dark. His body was as unresponsive as his eyes when he attempted to rise. He willed himself to move, yet seemed pinned down.

The horse?

"Rest easy, warrior. Lie still."

The softly spoken command made his body stiffen again, something still preventing movement. It was not the horse. No horse stink, dead or alive came to him, the heat he experienced not one of a thriving animal's flanks. Whatever pinned him down was not a direct weight upon his back like the horse had been. He had no idea where he was, but he was not on the battlefield at Whorl.

The searing heat of his body dissipated, replaced by a dread shiver as memories of battle raged around him, resurfacing too well. The battlefield at Whorl was a fearsome place. Used to border skirmishes he had killed a number of enemy tribesmen in the past but had never experienced combat such as at Whorl. Battle with a Celtic enemy was entirely different from engagement with the Roman Army.

No warlike chanting, or usual bellows of aggression, preceded the Roman surge of attack. The sounds heralding an advance were issuing from only one soldier, his whistle and cries echoed by others as they pressed closer, thickly crowded together in little huddles behind their curved shields. Their tight clique was almost impossible to penetrate with his long sword as he swung it above his head, readying it for another lunge. Three shields faced him tightly packed, the javelin thrusts the only menacing movements his opponents were prepared to make.

He risked a glance alongside. His fellow Brigantes were confronted by similar disciplined clusters and none could go closer to him for Celts always needed the distance to wield their longer blades. He jerked his head sideward to avert a javelin thrust that threatened to pluck out his eye.

"Keep your head steady."

He could not stop looking, or moving. One missed manoeuvre and he would be in the otherworld. Whoever gave him such orders to remain unmoving had to be completely witless. No Celtic warrior ordered another during a bloody battle. It was each man for himself; everybody knew that. He shook his head in disgust. How could he obey such foolish commands?

His sword hewed down another hapless auxiliary whose shield was dislodged, the arm lopped off first before he hacked the legs out from under the man. A cry at his left had him whipping around, a lone auxiliary now attacking him. The glint of his helmet and metal mail blinded him, the sunlight stunning his senses. It was impossible to attack the head and nearly impossible to slash through the mail clad chest of the soldier, though he tried anyway.

"Lie still! Do not break the tether or it will go ill for you."

Tether? Panic seized him. He would not be bound by Roman scum!

The voice urged him to do the opposite from his desires, so he ignored it. He felled more of the enemy, his shield bashing more than his sword arm which seemed to be weakened, though he could not work out why. Though, he only brought them to their knees after he had worked out their weak spots. Neck, forearms, knees and shins. He hacked at those places wishing for a Celtic farmer's sickle, rather than his long sword. That would cleave them much more effectively using his left hand. A sideward swipe would use less power since his sword arm was now useless.

"Aiee!"

The unexpected blow to his rear whipped him sailing up into the air. The horse? Breath rushed from him, the light around him even more blinding before a violent darkness descended.

"Rest. I have no more need to turn you. You are clean now."

He thumped down to the ground sending up a silent prayer to his god, Taranis, thankful he had not dishonoured his Brigante tribe. His god would know anyway but he wanted it noted that he had not been vanquished by his enemy. A strange idle thought occurred before he drifted into sleep once more.

Did Taranis account for the fact that the horse was most likely a Roman one?

"If the goddess wills it you will live…"

He knew from somewhere deep inside that the words did not come from Taranis, though he no longer cared. Still, his hatred of the Roman scum continued.

AD 71 One Moon Before Lughnasad – Marske

Brennus allowed the sensation of domestic security to wash over him.

Moving the fingers of his left hand, he felt a rough wool blanket above him. His back ached, but when he squirmed a little he felt the bumps of a thin straw pallet beneath. He was only able to raise his left eyelid, something preventing movement of his right one. The roundhouse was unfamiliar.

A meagre fire glowed near the centre of the room, a steaming pot suspended over it. The wood smoke curling around the iron vessel blended with the cloudy vapour that emanated from the pot, both drifting up to the conical shaped roof where they lingered a while before dissipating. The roundhouse was much smaller than the one he called home, the home of his father – Tully, chieftain of Garrigill. Tully's roundhouse rivalled many others that Brennus had frequented, its roof beam structure higher than most. Many men could be accommodated at the home of Tully, but very few would squeeze into this one.

A movement at the doorway drew his attention away from the stack of herbs that hung in bunches from a hook alongside his pallet.

"*Madainn mhath!*"

Good morning? He did not know if it was.

"So, you stir at last, young warrior." The voice sounded as tired as the old woman looked. "It pleases me to see it."

Brennus squinted single-eyed as the bent figure shuffled her way across the beaten earth towards him, a small bunch of firewood dropped at the side of the blaze when she passed by. A wrinkled smile bared her yellowed front teeth when she halted in front of him. He flinched when her gnarled fingers crept out from under her bratt to touch at his temple, but he was unable to draw his full body away from her.

"Not so hot now, warrior of the Brigantes. It is a good sign."

"Who are you?" His whisper was weak, like the mewling of a new born kitten, but even a clearing of his parched throat could not produce better when he tried again. It hurt too much. "I do not know you."

"Nay. You do not know me, nor I you, save that you came from the hillfort of Garrigill. I am named Meaghan. Now tell me who you are."

The old woman's voice was rough, with age and with fatigue. Friend or foe he did not know, so he remained silent, and watchful. She bent down to a wooden jug which lay at the foot of the cot and raised it slowly, holding it with both hands since the handle was snapped off to two short stumps. A jerky stream of water rushed from it into a wooden bowl that sat on a low stool near his head. The woman's movements were careful, if slow and trembling. Her gnarled fingers dipped a cloth into the water before she wrung and slowly squeezed out some excess water, the words coming louder when she bent to wipe his face. He flinched his head away from her.

"I only wish to wash away your sweat."

He closed his good eye while the cloth was used to gently clear away the stickiness of sleep.

"You do well to be suspicious, warrior of Garrigill. I have heard tell of the hillfort of Tully, it being one of the few larger settlements. I wished for more time with the men who bore you here, to listen to tales of Garrigill, but it was not to be."

Someone had carried him to this old woman? He had no memory of that. She could be lying, but what could she gain by it? He had had time to use his left hand to investigate further. Under the pile of skins that covered him, he lay naked. He had no knowledge of where his clothes were, or his weapons. He was, in truth, defenceless as a new born.

"I mean you no harm, but it may sting a great deal when I remove the binding from your other eye, to cleanse it. I have been unable to tell before now if you have lost the sight of it, but we may be able to test that now that you are at full consciousness."

Alarm gripped and flushed cold down his backbone. Blind? Was the old woman saying his eye was gone? It gave him no pain, though there was an uncomfortable aching on the skin above and below his eye socket and right down his cheek. It took moments for him to comprehend a matter of blindness.

Her wrinkled, weather-browned skin was very close as she removed the cloth that covered his head. It was impossible not to wince when he felt hair tugging away from his scalp. An itch he'd not fully recognised irritated at his temple but, when he tried to lift his hand to scratch, he was unable to move his arm. Something restrained him. A second wave of fright overwhelmed.

The old woman had tied him to the cot!

That was why he was unable to move. A growl built in his

26

throat as he struggled against the bindings to no avail. The old woman gently pushed his shoulder back down onto the straw.

"Not yet, warrior of Garrigill. I tied you down to keep you safe from yourself, not to restrain you as a prisoner. Your body is broken and could take no thrashing around when the fevers beset you. I assure you that you are safe with me but first, tell me your name? Warrior of Garrigill takes too much of my breath."

Even that smallest measure to free himself had depleted his energy. Brennus acknowledged it with a grunt as he shifted into the bedding. The pain that gripped his lower back robbed him of his speech.

"Br…e…aaa…n," That his name came out wrong, he cared not as he willed the agony to subside.

It seemed for now he was powerless to do no more than listen. He felt the last binding being unwrapped from around his eye, her old fingers firm as she held his chin steady. The wet cloth gently wiped at his skin, the smarting stings not something he could suppress. He held his breath as she repeated the movements.

To his utter dismay tears leaked and ran down his cheeks. The more he tried to prevent them the more the breath in his chest hitched, his bones ached, and the combination of pains added to the flow.

"Let them flow freely, Bran. The tears cleanse your eyes better than I can. You have sustained many injuries, young man, and I will tell you the extent, but first tell me what you see when you raise both eyelids."

He struggled to comply but his right eyelid would not obey his command. Only partially open was the best he could do as pain shot behind his eye, up his temple and on to the crown of his head. When he winced in agony, the stretching of healing flesh on that side of his face was excruciating, but he slowly persisted in opening his eye as much as he could bear. The light blinded, yet he knew no flaming brand lit that side of the room.

In spite of the torture, incredible relief spread through him. He may not be able to fully open the lid, but all was not dark.

"It will pain you very much, but I need to know if you see anything?"

Unable to sustain it – the intensity too searing – he closed both his eyes to replenish his fortitude then attempted to open only the right eye. The brilliance stole his breath, the darting sting perhaps less intense, or mayhap he was adjusting to it. Yet, though it was bright – that was all it was. He could not see.

"Painful! Bright and blurred." Though he tried to prevent the despair, he was sure it was evident in every cried word.

A shadow of the old woman loomed close to his face, her warmth and breath now familiar to him. A longer outline was a sudden threat he instinctively knew could harm him. He flinched his chin away, the old woman's cackle of laughter startling in the quiet room as his left eye popped open to check what was amiss.

"Just tell me if you see the edge of the blade clearly with only your right eye, young warrior. I am not going to harm you with it."

Agony shrieked through his right eye, the leaking moisture something he could not prevent. He closed his left once again, to do as she bid, the knife hovering at a reasonable distance. All was as in a deep misty day, no vision beyond a hazy dark shape in a light greyness. A dark desolation gripped him. How could he function as a tribal champion if he was blind? Along with the hopelessness, a wretched anger took hold of him. Why had Taranis so abandoned him? He had always paid due diligence to his god. What kind of reward for his skills in battle was blindness?

"Your answer." The old woman kept her patient tone.

"Nay."

"You cannot see the blade? Or you will not tell me?"

He yanked his head away from her chin grip for he truly had only seen a vague shadow of the blade. The melancholy deepened. Blind? How could he train young warriors if sight was only in one eye? And what other dire injuries had he sustained if she had tied him down? What was there left to strap down?

Forcing himself to focus on the rest of his body, he willed himself to rise. In his head he moved, but when he looked down to his feet his body still lay prone under the blanket. By Taranis! What else was badly wrong with him? His fingers moved the blanket, the blood flowing there, but almost nothing came from his feet. Even tied down his feet should be able to stir the blanket.

His head felt full to bursting with…rage. His misery deepened further. What use was he if his lower body was dead?

No man at all!

He took his utter disenchantment out on the only person available, his tone merciless. "You should have left me to die, old woman."

"Why would I have struggled to keep you alive for more than two moons if I did not deem you worthy of it?"

"How long?" The question was irrelevant; all he could think on was the state his body was in.

"You have been in my care for many nights, Bran. And the men who brought you had tended you for two nights before that."

"The battle at Whorl…?" His one seeing eye beseeched.

"Long over." The old woman's gaze slipped to the doorway, her eyes glistening with the sheen of tears, her tone sharp as a well honed blade. "Unlike you, self-pitying Bran of Garrigill, many of our Brigantes, and other fellow Celts, died at Whorl. It is now long past. We who resist the terms of the Romans are left in hiding. Some have fled to the north, but most of the surviving mid-Brigantes are now under the yolk of Rome."

He closed both eyes, not really listening to a word the old woman uttered. That she now called him Bran was fitting since he was no longer the Brennus of Garrigill that he had been and never would be again.

"I tell you that you have more to do for your tribe, Bran. Spend no more of your life force on self pity and use the power to heal your body from within!"

He blocked out the old harridan. A warrior's end would have been an honourable transition to the afterlife. He exhaled a painful breath he had been holding for too long. Fearless death had been denied him. But, since he lived, he determined that he would become the name Meaghan had just gifted him. A bellowed vow rang in his head. Henceforth, he would be broken Bran.

Pity that he had no notion of who Bran was.

His last thought before sleep claimed him was that Taranis might have given him more glory in the otherworld had it been a Celtic horse that had pinned him to the ground.

Chapter Three

AD 71 Lughnasad – Marske

"Rise!"

Bran was too much in despair. Meaghan had tended as best she could to his physical ailments, but, now, it was more important to tend to his emotional ones. She could do nothing about the isolation he must feel, since none had dared come near Marske, but she determined to rouse him from his melancholy.

"Bran! You must get up."

She knew he was awake, though he ignored her command and turned his head away from her. He had accepted the need for him to be inactive too well, retreating into a dream world where he felt no need to communicate with her. She would not give up on him, though. He no longer required bed resting to repair the injury to his back, but she worried that his interest in getting up and about was now so lacking. She had kept him drowsy with her herbal mixtures for as long as her stocks were able and after her herbs were all used up the languor was not induced by her; he had sunk into a pit of despair and did not believe her when she told him he needed to use his legs again.

"You no longer need to lie on that cot. Swing your legs out and I will help you stand."

His bitter eyes swung her way, his words deadly cold and acerbic. "I will not walk again, you foolish old woman!"

She would not allow his hurtful tones to wound her. She

had seen strong warriors like this one react in the same way; their pride so dented, but patience and persistence would gain success.

"Leave me to my make-believe world, Meaghan. There the images frighten as much as please me, though at least now I control what images they are. Not you! And none of them are of me walking again. I feel nothing in my legs, so how do you expect that I can move around?"

"It is time! I will despair of you no longer. You have been a lazy lie-abed for long enough, Bran of Garrigill. Many a warrior has had an eye taken from them, and a leg besides. After Whorl, I expect most of our warriors wear their scars with pride. An ugly countenance will not prevent you from living a fruitful life. You should be giving thanks to our lady goddess Rhianna that you still have all of your limbs attached and have good sight in one eye! And all of your other parts function perfectly well. You will get off that cot!"

Bran's scoff was loud enough to startle the goat she kept tethered at the doorway; a scrawny goat that she had found wandering on one of the days she had gone foraging in the nearby woods. A goat which had provided nourishing milk for his bone healing.

She knew Bran spoke untruths, knew full feelings had returned to his legs but he would not acknowledge it to her. Knowing why was easy. He must have been a formidable warrior before Whorl, his physique strong, his height exceeding the usual height of tall warriors by at least a half head. Fear kept him tied to the bed now. Not his leg or back injuries, or even his loss of sight – but fear of failure as a warrior.

"You must try the rope pull, Bran. It will help to raise you to your feet. You have plenty of strength in both arms now."

She pointed to the rope that dangled over the high beams above his cot. One end hung free, the other was tied to a rafter at the back wall of the roundhouse. Use of the rope during his restoration had enabled her to turn him over sufficiently to access his back, in order to manipulate the soft flesh at his tailbone, and to clean him.

The need to tend him like a baby was a large part of his problem. Dependence on her continued to embarrass him but the squirms he had been making over the last days gave good indication his movement was no longer impaired.

"Leave me be, Meaghan."

She would not allow this lassitude any longer. Berating him fiercely, she put her hands on his ankles and swivelled his body till his feet dangled to the floor. It took all of her feeble strength, but she would not give in. Yanking on his left arm, she forced him to sit up. Sitting up was not a new manoeuvre, since he had been able to do that now for some days.

"What are you doing, old woman?" His words denied, though his body complied.

"Stand!"

Before placing the rope into his hands, she pushed at his shoulders to get him into better position. Though he did not realise it his resistance showed what he was capable of. She bent down into his face.

"You will help me raise you, Bran of Garrigill, if only to prove to me that you can! Even the once."

Her vehemence must have given the correct signal. When she slowly drew on the rope, Bran extended his arms till they were fully stretched and pulled himself upright.

"I do this to spite the Roman Army – not you, nagging old woman. I curse every last one of them and will see them dead or banished from our shores. If I stand it is because I am a Celt and refuse to remain lying here!"

Meaghan turned away from him, her small smile hidden. She could easily cope with his glares and curses.

The roles had reversed.

Brennus brought in the pile of damp logs and set them down at the end of the fireside, picking out the thinnest and driest ones to slide under the bubbling pot. He shook off the bratt that covered his shoulders and allowed it to slide to the floor behind him as he stretched his damp hands out to the meagre blaze. The sky outside was grey-dark as winter, the wind fierce and the rain a relentless pelt, and not nearly as warm as a late summer day ought to be. The pathway outside the roundhouse had been treacherous to his recently mended limbs, a slippy mud slide but old Meaghan lay abed, too worn to rise and too depleted to care for him.

His limp was pronounced as he dragged himself around the room to organise their food. Constant dull aching darted up and down his back as he bent to collect the remains of the flat bread he had baked under Meaghan's frail tuition the previous day. His broken leg bone was healed, though the surrounding flesh had lost its natural bulk, the wound now an angry dark red gash of shining, scarred, new skin. That was not unexpected and he knew from the injuries of others that in time, with exercise and patience, he might restore most of the mobility of the limb. He would always limp, though, since one leg was now shorter than the other.

Taranis had had many prayers over the last days, and more unworthy curses. It had taken all of Meaghan's patience to make him snap out of the maudlin despair he had fallen into, but he had realised too late that she had run down her own strength to cajole him back to health. Regret sat heavy on him. He had been a sore trial to the woman who had kept him alive so well, and had bolstered him through his wretched preoccupation. He could hardly credit how unmanly he had been. He still felt overly sensitive about his infirmities.

Plans he had formed to leave Marske and return to Garrigill

had been abandoned when her condition became clear to him. As she had tended him, he would now look after her. She had brought life back to him though he doubted he could reciprocate.

"Meaghan?"

He laid the rough wooden platter alongside her cot, the hollowing out of it an unfinished task and the only reason the Romans had not carted it off. Hobbling back to the fireside, he filled the cracked wooden bowls with the porridge he had left bubbling and ready while he did the other chores. Every single task took him a longer time than should be normal. It irked that he was so pathetically sluggish, but he determined to make better headway with his recuperation. If he had shaken off his disgust of himself earlier, and worked harder at recovery, he would have been much more able now. For long days, he really had believed he would never walk again and had ignored his old nurse's denials.

Now, Meaghan depended on him.

"I have food here, Meaghan, and wood to keep the fire fed." He kept his voice as soft as he could while willing her to awaken since she needed nourishment.

The break to his forearm had healed well enough during his lay-abed confinement, his hand likewise. He accepted restoration of two severed fingers at the lowest knuckle was beyond Meaghan's capabilities; the tips were long lost and trampled underfoot on the battlefield, but her stitching of the stumps had been diligent. The fingers remained bound as they were susceptible to harm, the healing skin still very delicate, though having a healthy thumb and the two fingers next to it meant some dexterity was still possible. He had known many warriors who had lost the whole hand to the wrist when such maiming had festered into the blackened state, after the blood no longer flowed in it. Meaghan's skills were impressive, and he had eventually given his thanks to her goddess for them.

Presently, it took some concentration to carry the filled and steaming bowls though, during the last few days of tending Meaghan, he had learned how not to burn himself.

Keeping his voice soft, he approached her cot. "Meaghan. Will you eat?"

He set the bowls down beside the bread on the low stool before lowering himself onto the other free stool. He fell down less often now. A hint of a grin tweaked up one side of his mouth. The amount of times he had missed the stool during his recovery had been many, the resultant falls not only painful but deeply humiliating.

Meaghan had merely laughed, telling him she had helped to birth many bairns and knew what an infant needed to help with balance – while giving him instructions on how to avoid mishaps. Staggers were still frequent, but he had learned how to rectify the inevitable tilting. She was the most amazing old woman he had ever encountered and possibly the wisest he had ever known.

"I have some oatmeal here for you, Meaghan."

Her old eyes opened, a grateful smile appearing. He had grown used to that pleasant smile during his time in her care.

"I should be tending you. Not lying abed like an incapable babe."

It was easy to return her smile while he pushed a pile of padded skins under her back to prop her upright. When she had settled in the most comfortable position, he handed her the bowl and a chunk of bread from the platter.

"*Tapadh leat.*" Meaghan's thank you was weak, yet he could tell heartfelt.

Sitting down on a low stool nearby, he scooped up his own meal.

"Eat. We both need to fatten up."

"Aye! Well said, Bran. You need to restore your bulk if you intend to be a tribal champion."

Through a mouthful of food he laughed – a laugh that stung deeply, though he said nothing of the fact that he had once

36

been Garrigill's champion. "I may never be as strong as I once was." He looked out the open doorway at the rain still plopping onto the path outside the entrance tunnel to the roundhouse and hated himself for even voicing his next wry words, but they needed to be said. "Nor as handsome."

"Fear not. One side of your face is not as it once was, but the other is as fine-looking as it used to be."

The smile only slipped up on one side of his face, the skin of his healing cheek still tight. "Aye, Meaghan, and it is thanks to you that I can see even this blur out of the eye above. You are a formidable healing woman who uses well the secrets of the goddess."

Meaghan acknowledged his praise with a slight nod as she slowly cleared the contents of her bowl. "It was also the skill of your companions who aided your recovery. If they had not brought you so swiftly to me the story would have had a different ending. They had already yanked your broken leg bone back into place, and had bound your leg tightly."

He set down his empty bowl and tore off a chunk of the remaining bread. "Describe them again."

Meaghan's rheumy eyes looked askance as she pondered his question. After a long pause she answered, as though imagining the events. "One warrior – the one with fiery red hair – said they were from the Crannogs of Gyptus. The other warrior's hair was dark as the deepest night, sleek to his head, his eyes also a very dark brown and very large in his eye sockets."

"Go on."

Meaghan closed her eyes, the remembering better that way according to the slight bobbing of her head. "I see the dark warrior clearly now. As well as the star of the Brigantes he also bore another marking high on his arm." He heard a deep sigh as though the effort of remembering was too great. "It may have been a scar, or an ill made branding."

"Grond. It had to be Grond. He has an arrowhead scar above his brand, from an injury sustained many moons ago as a boy."

"I did not learn their names. They knew that Roman soldiers were in pursuit of them and could not drag you any further."

"You say they had strapped me to a makeshift cart?"

"Aye. If they had not tied you on so well you would not have survived the journey they made with you. Though it may be that you sustained your worst back injuries during the rough hauling. Of course, it was inevitable that the warriors had to make haste from the field of battle."

"What more did they say?"

"As dusk turned into darkness on the day of the battle, when the combat was long over, they found you pinned under the leg of a dead horse. The dark warrior knew where he had last seen you fighting. He had seen the squealing horse rear back onto you, though had been unable to do anything to help at that time, engaged in combat as he was with a Roman auxiliary himself. He returned with the other warrior to claim your armband and sword, to return them to Tully."

"I was not gone to the otherworld."

"Nay, Bran. When the horse was dragged aside they were stunned to hear you groan, and not the last empty breath coming from the body of a dead man."

Bran. He still had not quite got used to his new name but Meaghan was into her story telling stride and he would not have her stop.

"The warriors used boards and wheels from a broken chariot, and carted you off the battlefield that night, avoiding detection by the Roman soldiers who scoured the area. They stumbled on for a whole day, dragging you behind them, stopping to find shelter and to avoid Roman patrols. Your friends chanced on this settlement the following day, at first believing it was uninhabited till I showed myself to them."

"How did you conceal me when the Roman scavengers arrived?"

"I did not have to. After your friends got you onto my cot, I tended to your hurts and gave you a herbal draft. You lapsed into a deep, deep sleep after that. We heard the patrol coming and fled the roundhouse. You appeared as dead but they were more interested in pursuing your friends."

Absorbing the information, he picked a niggling husk from his teeth. "I do not understand why the Romans did not put you to the sword."

"The Roman scourge did not find me. I hid in the grain pit, the place I had concealed myself many times before. They were not interested, at that time, in knowing if the pit was empty or full. Our settlement had been ransacked by their scouting forces around the time of the battle at Whorl, during their surge to the north, and most of the useful grain had been acquired by them. Live, fleeing quarry was the only sport they were after when you arrived here."

"Why have the Romans not come back since then?"

"I must assume that they have moved on to terrorise villagers somewhere else."

Though not much more enlightened than before, he was convinced the dark warrior had been Grond from the Crannog dwellings of Gyptus. It heartened him to believe the two warriors had survived, and had made their way home, since Meaghan had told him there was no sign of their hacked-at bodies anywhere near. Yet, whether or not they had managed to get home was not something he could concern himself with at that moment. He was not free enough to check anyone's welfare.

His immediate needs were to tend to Meaghan since the disabling frailty had come upon her so swiftly. He appreciated too late just how hard the old woman had worked for many long days to forage for meagre food supplies, to feed him when he had been too stubbornly resistant to rise from his pallet. Guilt riddled his thoughts.

Her old fingers tapped feebly at his arm.

"I know what you think, Bran, yet you owe me nothing. I

was trained to be a healer of our tribe and it has been my life's pleasure to heal the sick, when I was able. The looking after of you was not as tiresome as you think and my ailment was not gained from tending you. Age creeps upon my bones and my life force is waning. My time to leave this place is coming and I rejoice like a warrior since I have fulfilled my tasks. You are my last. And my most complicated."

"I have not made it easy for you." Regret filled his tone.

Meaghan's weak laugh reassured. "No matter. You can pay it back by singing to me, now."

"Sing?"

Meaghan coughed away the mucus in her throat. "I heard your very fine voice, Bran, when you thought you were alone. Melodious. It is very pleasant. Your whistling too, which you do without realising it."

He laughed, secretly pleased by her words. "You will want me to tell you more tales as well?"

Meaghan's wrinkled fingers reached for his. "I have liked hearing of Garrigill, Bran. You have a fine way of bringing a story to life. You should perhaps have been a bard and not a strapping warrior. Stories for a while will be very welcome…and I will try not to fall asleep."

Brennus started to talk and found it good. He had forgotten that his voice was deep and rich and had been commented upon many times at Garrigill. He had learned many story songs; was good at remembering the words. And tales he had a plenty.

His body may have been broken at Whorl but his voice was one of the few unaffected parts. Some little part of the old Brennus flared to life.

His lop-sided smile beamed as he whiled the day away.

"Rest easy, Meaghan. You have earned a sweet respite."

Brennus no longer needed to care for his old healer, only a few nights having passed since that last meaningful conversation. Meaghan had breathed her peaceful last breath during the dark of night. He held the old woman's hand another time and smoothed down the wrinkles of her gnarled fingers, those fingers that had kept him alive for more than three moons. He vowed that her generosity to a stranger would not be forgotten, his lips feathering a soft kiss at her cold, sunken cheek.

"You kept me alive, so now I really must live this new life of mine."

Rising with stiff jerky movements, since he had been dozing at her bedside for a while after she had died, he went in search of implements to inter her. He knew the perfect burial site. Meaghan had not requested her remains be placed on the summit of the nearby hillock, that was his choice, but he was sure she would approve. Though it saddened him, he would not leave the bones to be picked before placing them in the chamber of the ancients that Meaghan had talked about, many of her long gone ancestors residing there. Nature took too long to work and he had no time to linger. She had requested him to spend no time on her death rites, but he would give her the best burial he could manage.

In one of the abandoned roundhouses, he found a blunt scythe, and rooting around he unearthed a broken adze, the blade so nicked it would not have fashioned smooth wood, the shaft splintered off at half its normal length. They were useless for any real work, without being refashioned, but they were sufficient for his present needs. Trudging up the nearby hillock, he oriented himself with the weak sun that flashed among the scudding clouds, the brisk wind refreshing though it stung the tightened skin at his cheekbone when he bent to his task.

"Useless!"

No one was there to see his awkward handling of the tools but talking to himself helped to relieve his frustration over his afflictions.

"Bran. I am Bran the broken warrior!"

His two fingers and thumb grip was not yet strong enough for a quick undertaking, nonetheless, he unearthed the soil with the point of the blade, mainly using his left hand. He paid no heed to the aches that plagued while he toiled, so determined was he on his task. It took him twice as long as normal before the grave was deep enough, his thoughts planning on how to send Meaghan off as festively as he could contrive.

"This maimed warrior you call Bran has your resting place ready, old woman."

His trek back up was no trial to him, the simple plank stretcher he had made to hold the old healer's rickle of bones sufficient for pulling along her feather-light body. Had he been whole he could easily have carried her the distance to the summit but he was not sure his back was ready yet for such a test. It had taken a little time to lash together the frame but was worth it, and Meaghan was in no hurry. He was not even out of breath when he held a one-sided conversation with her.

"You will like this spot, old woman. Your spirit will fly free from here but will easily find its way back if needs be. Just beside this copse of trees, around the ancient stones, is a very good place."

He imagined her craggy smile, those wise old eyes benevolent upon his gesture.

"*Mar sin leibh*! Farewell, my life giver."

He gave her hand a last squeeze of thanks, warding back the emotion that threatened, guessing what her reaction might be to that. He had come to know Meaghan very well over the last moons, and she him, though he was guilt riddled that he had never disclosed his proper history to her. Though he had exchanged details of his upbringing, and many stories of life at

Garrigill, he had never told Meaghan he was Brennus, son of Tully, the chief of Garrigill.

He could no longer bring himself to name himself thus; it was as though he had never lived before Whorl.

As he looked upon the old woman in his arms, he resolved to be the Bran Meaghan believed in: resolved to live up to the curse made many days ago. The idea of thwarting the Roman Empire made putting one step in front of the other a pleasure, any residual pain ignored. How he could achieve it was a mystery though somehow he would find a way. But he would do it as broken Bran.

After laying Meaghan's mortal remains in the shallow resting place, having added some of her herb-cooking tools alongside, he served up the only prayers he knew of for her safe passage to the otherworld as he fingered the thin silver armband she had insisted he have the previous day. It now dangled from a leather thong and lay against his chest under his tunic.

"Do not send it with me to the otherworld," she had entreated as she pressed the thin silver into his palm. "I wish that my armband be used again, Bran, though the arm it will grace will have to be narrower than yours. It is already very ancient having been given down to me through many generations, and very precious."

His pleas for her to keep it had landed on deaf ears.

"I would have had my only granddaughter have it, but as she is not here, and you are, you must be the keeper of it. You will know when to pass it on to the one woman who will gain your deepest love."

It had taken Meaghan a while before her next words slipped free, her depletion so deep. "Keep it close to your heart till that time comes, Bran. Never lose faith in your judgement of who is the only one for you."

As he looked down at her body in the shallow grave, he ran his thumb once again around the worn patterning on the silver bangle.

"May your generous spirit find a pleasant place to be, old healer and giver of my life. I vow your faith in me will not be in vain. I wish I could say a better leave of this world for you, but the words fail me."

Struggling for the correct farewell his thoughts turned to Garrigill. If only Nara had been around, she would have known how to make ceremony much better.

Nara.

A wry, lopsided grin broke free, memories flooding in.

"Aye, Nara of Tarras! You surely would have had the correct words to send her off festively. Your tongue was good at forming words when need be. Meaghan would have liked you."

A recollection of Nara's pleading, and scolding him to let her go free, made his grin turn to full laughter. Nara had been as red-angry as her dark red hair. His laughter was short-lived though, for it turned to a cry of anguish as the reality of his life hit him, the breath in his throat suddenly stifled. He looked at the partial fingers that gripped the armband and then at his leg. A broken man like him would be no good to a proud warrior-woman like Nara of the Selgovae.

His morose mutterings continued as he back-filled the soil and stamped the sods of rough grass back in place with his left foot.

"I will not live with anyone's pity! I will not."

Throwing down the tools, he looked to the now angrier-looking darker grey clouds that had rolled in from the west, his cry to Taranis as bitter as bile. "You gave me this new life, but Nara deserves better than one such as me."

The weak sun was suddenly engulfed, a very gloomy aspect left behind.

During his recovery, he had not allowed his mind to dwell on the woman who was to have been his wife, though he had lingered plenty of times thinking on his father and on his brothers. His knowledge of all of them was extensive, but he knew very little of Nara. The princess of the Selgovae to whom he had been betrothed was largely unknown to him, the marriage bargain made between their tribes – Brigante and Selgovae – the strangest he had ever heard of, though it was a bargain that had not been fulfilled since he had never returned from the battles at Whorl.

Nara was a lust worthy woman, but even when he had accepted the betrothal he had not loved her, and most likely never would.

Now, with summer waning, the day for their full wedding rites had long since passed. He closed his eyes. Her body had been a temptation he would have loved to explore, but the details of her face were a blur; though he could not forget her fiery deep red hair that glinted in the light from the fire in Tully's roundhouse at Garrigill. Try as he did, he could not bring forward her eyes, or any other of her facial features.

And that was no real mystery since she favoured his brother Lorcan and had rarely looked directly upon him.

His head dipped to the fresh grave, his words solemn, and his head gently shaking from side to side.

"Though you say I am still half-handsome, Meaghan, the Selgovae princess will not deem it so. Yet, without you to berate me for my vanity, I must learn better to put my pride aside. I will return to Garrigill a different man, inside and out."

The concept of living the rest of his life alone at Marske held a lot of appeal, never having to face another living being, although deep in his heart he also knew that would be cowardice. He had to face up to the life Meaghan had made him live for. Her berating words rang again in his ears.

"Your attitude makes me look upon a vain, broken Brigante warrior. Bran of Garrigill, you are ugly as you were not before but that does not mean the children of your loins will be. Your fingers have lost parts but rest assured your manhood is intact and all your daily functions work properly. You will live a good life. One that will benefit those Celts around you. You are destined to repel the Roman scourge from our Celtic lands. I know this!"

Though the refrain had differed, she had uttered those sentiments many times when he had been maudlin and unwilling to believe he could live a purposeful life.

As he looked to her grave, a huge sigh escaped. "I will do it for you, Meaghan."

Battle with the Roman army had been nothing like he expected it to be. However, he knew nothing of what was happening now since he and Meaghan had lived in total isolation. The Romans had forbidden anyone from returning and no one had – except his life-giver.

He did not even know where Marske was. Meaghan's explanation of where her roundhouse lay meant little to him since he had never travelled so far south before the battle at Whorl. Only by using the services of a guide had he and Grond's warriors come to the site of battle at Whorl.

He gathered up the tools and stepped away from the graveside, his future looming as blind as the sight in one of his eyes. He could not see it ahead but he vowed he would find the control to adjust to what would work for him in his new life.

"I will find my way, Meaghan."

She deserved that he get on with his new identity. He raised his head to the sky and watched dark grey clouds pass over swiftly to be replaced by fluffy white ones, some blue sky returning. A fair omen? He wished he could be sure but was not. The morn would be time enough to leave Marske. A small smile slipped free. Maybe his god Taranis would help guide him to his new future? It did no harm to send up a small plea.

Withdrawing his gaze from the scudding clouds, he blinked a few times, and then looked down the hillock towards Marske. A glint of something moving furtively in the brushwood below was so startling a sight that the blood surged through his body, almost rocking him off his feet. Fear of not being ready to face an enemy flooded him.

"Nay!" His exhaled breath whispered through pursed lips.

It was no animal, far too large for that. With awkward movements he dropped to a crouch, the impact sending a jarring ache up his backbone as he frantically considered what action to take. He felt the blood rush to his head, the thumping at his heart almost unbearable till he berated himself for cowardice. Because he had seen no one else for so long did not mean he was a weakling! He willed the panic to subside.

"Who are you?" His whisper tickled his uneven lips, his good eye straining to see more clearly.

He reached for his sword but had none. His grunt of frustration was held in tight, his thoughts whirling. It was so strange to see someone, but the figure below did not stride to the roundhouse in peace.

As the shape darted from one bush to another he saw no signs of the armour of a Roman soldier, no mail shirt glinting. The flash of light brown did not mean the person was not a Roman, though. Meaghan had mentioned that some of the raiders of her village had worn no army uniform, yet they were part of the Roman century – some eighty or so soldiers – that patrolled the area.

So deep in introspection he had been off guard, not properly alert for any signs of infiltration of the area though Meaghan had urged him to be watchful many a time in recent days. Gingerly lifting the sickle he had used to mound soil over the grave, he concentrated only on listening. The figure down below looked all around before darting into the first of the roundhouses; however, he could not tell if he had been noticed up on the hill. His other hand reached for the small knife tucked into his braccae – Meaghan's knife. He would have buried it with her other tools but his need for it was now greater than hers. He had kept it, convinced she would approve.

There was no cover up on the hillock now that he had left the copse but he would not wait for the figure to come to him, and he would not flee. He may be maimed, but his warrior instinct was returning. Rising to his feet, he made his way down to the village, slipping and slithering down through the bracken till he reached the place where low bushes dotted themselves around. It was not stealthy in the least, but it got him down the hill more quickly.

He saw nothing, yet knew the figure had not left. Quickening his pace to Meaghan's roundhouse, he was as silent as he could manage with his uneven stride. Close to it he halted, his ears attentive. The rustling was faint, but there was definitely someone in the roundhouse.

At the side of the wattled entrance tunnel he put his ear to the woven wall. Sounds of raking around the pile of worn tools Meaghan kept to one side of the fireplace made him believe the person sought some particular thing. He peered around the tunnel opening.

By Taranis! He cursed his blind eye. It took a few tries before he settled his head to the task, angled the correct way for seeing what was in front of him. A quiet lifting and laying aside was going on by a slightly-built crouched figure.

Two lurching steps took him inside, his sickle raised high above his head.

Chapter Four

"*Dé thu a déanamh?* Tell me! What are you doing?"

Ineda left off her rifling and leapt upright in a rush, flight uppermost. She lunged the wooden bowl in her hand towards the huge warrior, even though it was no real weapon as it bounced off his considerable chest.

The man had erupted into the small roundhouse like a lumbering bull at Beltane, his expression just as furious as a trapped animal. Or maybe that was her own eyes reflecting in the one shining blue? His bulk ensured she could not injure him, her escape route foiled when he thrust the sickle away and reached forward to snare her awkwardly in his hands. Although she struggled with all of her might, the man well out-powered her.

"Let me go!" To add to her protest she stamped on his foot.

The warrior was not impressed by her strident demand or her ineffectual display of outrage as he continued his baleful staring. Maintaining a neutral tone, he clasped her writhing body. She could not fail to notice the winces of pain in his eyes as she kicked at his legs, but he held her firm.

"You seek something in particular?" His tone was low, a menacing thread lurking though his expression betrayed nothing.

Quelling her disquiet she spat back at him, though her mouth was barely at his mid-chest height. "Aye. I do."

The man waited for more but she gave him no further answer, and instead took in his appearance. He was no Roman, of that she was sure: a Celtic warrior and a recently wounded one. There was the tiniest of flinches when her stare reached his eyes. A shimmer of hurt was followed by a curl of derision at his lopsided mouth. She spent no time working out why since she had a good idea. Pride was a wonderful thing for a mighty warrior, but loss of self-respect quite another. The undamaged side of his face declared him very handsome; the recent wounds marring his other side not so well looking. She guessed he had not yet come to terms with the ravages of war on his flesh.

"Meaghan has done a fine job to keep you alive, warrior. Those scars heal well."

Her words angered him, evident in the black scowl he sent her way, the mention of his afflictions clearly not something he wanted her to speak of. He crowded her closer, hurdling her into the corner of the small room.

"Meaghan?" He only spoke the one word.

Ineda knew she was small and thin for her fourteen winters. Normally it did not bother her but something about this wounded warrior made her want to be all the things that had passed her by. Beauty had not been bestowed on her either; though she had been told she was comely.

When she gave no answer he tried again, his harsh voice grating in her face, his unfriendly mien offensive. "What do you know of Meaghan?"

Her eyes dropped to the tools she had recently been raking through, her voice dropping to a mere whisper. "Meaghan was my grandmother, but I see I arrived too late."

"Too late?" The warrior sounded confused.

She squirmed in his tight grasp, but he held firm. The shake to her shoulders raised her eyes once more. She resented his deep suspicion but could not blame him. She had not seen Meaghan for many long days. "I travelled as swiftly as I could, given the Roman patrols all around these parts. Though the local Brigantes put up no visible resistance now, the Roman auxiliaries of the Legio IX occasionally sweep the area nearby from time to time, scouting for any Celts opposing their authority. Sometimes they snatch hostages to do their menial work in places south of here. I had no intention of joining those."

His snort, warm at her cheeks, gave her an idea of what he thought of her answer, his eyes fierce. "I have seen no signs of Roman soldiers during the many nights I have been here." He held her stare, though she could not tell if he could see anything through the half-closed and dragging right one.

"Nay, they do not come here now. After the Romans chased off my clan from Marske they came back day after day. They picked up more of our stored food stocks until they gradually removed every useable item. Then they stopped returning, deeming it abandoned. During that time Meaghan sheltered in a cave in the forest. I managed to speak to her once, days after our hasty withdrawal, although our conversation was cut short when a Roman patrol came our way. We had to scatter, but I was sure she would return when it was safe." She knew she babbled but could not seem to stop, his stare too intent. Forcing her gaze from him she looked over to the pot at the fire and pictured Meaghan standing there.

"Why did your other kin not return?" The wounded warrior shook her shoulders to gain her full attention.

She could not prevent a deep sigh escaping having no desire to speak of that, except the man needed to be convinced. He still held her, though his grip was somewhat relaxed. Fleeing now was a better possibility; yet she found she did not want to. There was a burning need in her to find out more about this warrior that Meaghan had known she would be helping, to her very last moments. There was no doubt in her mind that the warrior had to be special since Meaghan must have looked after him for a long time. Her answer was carefully given.

"Many men from this area died during the early Roman

raids, and at the Whorl battlegrounds. Even more were vanquished during the skirmish at Wath a few days later, when the bulk of our female warriors also fell under the Roman gladius. Those of us who survived the raids, and the blades, are now congregated at the hillfort of Witton."

The warrior made no attempt to intervene when she broke free and moved to the side of him; to his right side. The swivelling of his whole body following her movements made her sure he had no sight in his right eye.

"Distant kin of my father give us security, which we would lack here."

"Are the other comforts better at Witton?" Though his feet remained firmly planted his one-eyed sight tracked her movements.

The warrior meant their living circumstances, but she could not resist giving the solemn man a different reply. She did not even try to prevent the grin that spread across her face. "Aye. You could say so. My mother died before our last festival of Samhain. My father was lost for a while without her, but Witton has sufficient women to favour him. He has found a new purpose in life."

Ignoring her levity, his expression remained sombre. "You would rather come home, now?"

"I already told you." She wondered if the man was unable to listen properly to her, as well as being blind in one eye. "The Romans have declared this village abandoned. They would kill us if we returned."

***

"Your name?"

The girl looked askance, her shoulders drooping towards the rear of the roundhouse.

Brennus repeated his question, and then awaited her answer. Eventually, her gaze swivelled back to him.

"Ineda."

"Bright Fire." She did not return his awkward smirk, nor did she appear to like his answering remark. "It is a very good name. Your yellow-red hair fits it well, though you have little substance!"

The girl scoffed up at his face before she went to the fireside where meagre embers emitted a deep red glow. Pulling up a metal rod, she stabbed the ash into displaying more life, as though determined to show him better. "Unlike you, I am not built to be strong in body. Nonetheless, that does not mean my courage is weak."

What she stated was partly true. She was no physical risk to him. Any other risk was yet to be determined. Slender as a willow sapling she showed few curves under the stained, checked woollen dress that was drawn in tight at the waist, to disguise its being far too wide for her. Her body held no appeal, but her eyes were another story. Somewhere between a soft light golden and the green of dried birch leaves they were framed with long dark lashes, darker than the thick hair on her head which he now noticed was the colour of ripened spelt as it dried in stacks, each honeyed strand a shade different from the other, in parts with a deeper reddish-gold hue. A younger version of Meaghan's eyes. Meaghan's hair had been grey, but he guessed had probably been the colour of the young woman's in her earlier years.

Those challenging eyes were large, dominating a face that had a small straight nose, wide cheekbones and a tiny chin. Her slightly sunken cheeks were an indication her recent food intake could have been greater; the lack of lustre to her thick waves, and the bones almost poking through at her wrists, even more so. Nonetheless, there was something about her that showed a definite kinship with Meaghan – a confidence perhaps? Or some of Meaghan's determination?

Her boldness he found commendable in one so young. And something else stirred in him. He had not seen the face of a young female for so long. The rush of blood in his loins brought a great mixture of feelings. There was sheer relief that his natural desires still functioned and disgust that they were awakened by such a young girl. A dread shiver shook his head and shoulders, dispelling his now unwanted stirrings.

Still, how could this girl know Meaghan had just passed on? Had she watched his inept burial and not intervened?

Squatting down beside the woven bratt Meaghan had used to sit on, Ineda lovingly fingered it for a few moments, her head bent to the task. Familiarity with the roundhouse leant credence to her story. He decided she did not lie about Meaghan being her grandmother, since what would she gain by any ruse?

After a pause she looked up at him. Her appraisal of him was keen as she appeared to find composure. "I can see my grandmother somehow managed to feed you, unlike the settlers at Witton. We have had to make food stocks spread even thinner than usual."

Her small chin firmed, her lips disappearing into an angry pucker as she winced. The fierceness in her gesture made him smile.

"The Roman Army camps close to our gates and they regularly exact their dues. They have already commandeered more than half of Witton's summer crops." A spit on the dry earthen floor was accompanied by some violent curses, her gold-green eyes flashing with a temper he empathised with, a trait he found he readily admired. "*Ceigean Ròmanach!* Roman turds!"

He bit back another smile. It appeared she liked the Roman Army about as much as he did.

"We can do nothing to prevent it. The dung horde follows the agreements made with our Brigante chiefs, who have settled for a life of the yoke."

Contemptuous laughter was brave coming from one whose body strength was limited yet she had to be praised for it if her words were true. "I know no recent developments, Meaghan had no visitors."

A sigh escaped the girl while she rooted around Meaghan's paltry tool stack. He allowed her searches, needing her information to be freely given and merely watched her movements about the roundhouse.

"They say we are not their slaves, but they lie. They own us; use us for their own purposes. They may claim my toil, wounded warrior, but they will never claim my Celtic heart."

She looked so furious, her pale green eyes sparking their own kind of fire, that he did not doubt her fidelity to their Celtic ways. "Tell me more of what the Romans do since the battles at Whorl."

Quick fingers rummaged through Meaghan's stored herbs that hung from a protruding beam. Picking off stalks, here and there, she filled a leather pouch she'd unearthed from under a pile of torn hides that were stacked close to the entryway as she answered. "The Roman Army mostly leave us unharmed, providing we relinquish our food stocks and give them our general labour. We have no recourse but to accept it, or we die. They have no qualms about us starving through the lean months to come as they chomp their way through our food stocks, even when I have heard they expect their small river vessels and baggage wagons to have arrived by then to supply their bellies with stored winter foods."

From what he already knew of the Roman occupation of other Celtic tribes, long before the battle at Whorl, Ineda spoke true. Roman baggage carts would arrive to keep their food stocks replenished. She gave him important information, but he wanted more about her grandmother. "Tell me about Meaghan."

Her eyes clouded with unshed tears before she whipped her gaze away from him, her chin lifting towards the conical roof timbers. He did not prompt her; he could see her fight an emotional battle as one foot tapped with resigned frustration. He felt a hitch inside, something of her distress affecting him –

Meaghan had come to mean a lot to him too. Eventually she turned back to him.

"I knew in here that Meaghan's last breaths were coming."

Brennus watched her curled fist bang against her small breast, a lone silent tear trickling down her cheek.

"I abandoned her."

The trembles of her lip seemed genuine as she crumpled to the blanket a second time. Now, her fingers drummed on the cloth in between smoothing strokes. Without thought, he found himself sliding to the nearby low wooden stool as he waited for more explanation. He had sisters about the same age as Ineda, though he had not seen them for many winters as they had been fostered away from his home settlement of Garrigill.

He had never considered himself a good confidant of women in the past but found he wanted to let this young slip of a girl unburden herself. Before the battle at Whorl his experience of women was of quick coupling, over and done with before much conversation ever took place. But he was not that man any more. It was a surprise to him that any lustful feelings were easily repressed – the interest in her tale more important to him. He knew that should perhaps worry him though set it aside as he waited for her to speak again.

It seemed a while before Ineda looked over to him.

"I fled the village, along with my father and the villagers of Marske, when we heard the Roman Army was about to raid here. Meaghan refused to leave and my father could not persuade her. She claimed she still had healing work to do here. She had to heal you!"

His start of surprise at her vehemence was unable to be prevented. Her look loathed. "To that, I can only say Meaghan truly did save my life."

A terse nod of Ineda's head indicated agreement. "Aye! I have already said so. My father wanted her to use her skills for our own people, but she said it was more important she bide here and tend to one who needed her more. Father was angry she would not come with us but also acknowledged her will. My grandmother was always steadfast in her decisions. The Romans were almost upon us and evading them meant an exit beyond the hills to the east. Anyone found resisting the Roman patrols at that time was put to the sword; and if we had stayed and remained acquiescent we could not be sure they would not have killed us anyway."

Brennus knew the hills she referred to had to be different from the one he had just come down from, though where she referred to he had no clue of. "What did Meaghan mean by someone who needed her more?"

"I have no notion of what she meant. The last time I saw her she told me that she knew you would come to her. As well as being a healer, Meaghan had times when she could predict what would happen. We did not question her abilities, or her judgements. They were gifts from the goddess."

He sifted through her information. "You say you knew she was dying. Do you also have the gift of foretelling?"

The girl shook her head. "Nay. I do not, but a very strong bond tied me to my grandmother. She sensed whenever I ailed without being told, and sometimes the opposite worked for me – though not often because Meaghan bore her years well and sickness did not often befall her."

"Yet something called you here today?"

"Aye. I felt her life force ebb last night, but I had to wait till dawn light to make the long trek back here."

A soft footfall sounded nearby, followed by a rush of heavier ones.

"Romans!" she shouted.

Brennus lurched from the fireside to pluck the one and only poorly tipped spear from the weapon holder near the doorway, but before his fumbling digits gripped the shaft jabbing metal nipped at his chest, forcing him back towards the centre of the room. The first spear was followed by another, and yet another, as Roman auxiliaries flooded the small roundhouse, encircling him.

"Run, Ineda!"

She rushed to the doorway but was easily overpowered by one of the soldiers, his gladius drawn and ready, menace flaring in his angry dark eyes. The small knife she wrenched from her waist pouch only served to stimulate the auxiliaries even further. They circled her, some cackling at her fearsome glower.

"Get behind me, Ineda!" For a time he forgot his infirmities, thinking himself the warrior he had once been. Searingly sharp spear tips prodded him.

The raucous laughter ringing out and the gestures at his wounded face and dragging leg reminded him too well. Bitter embarrassment swamped him, but he was gratified to find the now taunting Romans allowed the girl to scurry in at his back. The jeering and laughing of two of the younger ones was curtailed when an older auxiliary entered the roundhouse and pushed them aside, spouting harsh words at them in some incomprehensible language.

It was far too late to wish he had paid more heed to his brother, Lorcan, who had warned him that learning a little of the Latin tongue of the Romans might be useful some day in the future – though the man's berating did not sound like the few Latin words he had heard Lorcan utter.

Before Whorl, he had been too full of his importance as tribal champion, too avid about showing off his physical prowess to the younger warriors of Garrigill to pay Lorcan any heed. His neglect meant the only thing he could understand was that the younger ones wanted to assuage their lust on Ineda, and the older one in charge thought differently.

A particularly nasty, raucous order was emitted the result of which was that the four younger men turned about, grumbling their exit from the roundhouse.

He felt Ineda's slight form press against him as she whispered up to his ear. "They usually maraud in groups of eight, sometimes more. There will be more of them outside."

He found no need to give answer since the auxiliary who appeared to be in charge replied.

"The girl speaks true. She has taken note of our movements."

Though coarsely spoken, Brennus understood the man's words since they were similar to his own Brigante Celtic.

The Roman continued, "As we have of her. You will leave now. This settlement was abandoned and will remain abandoned."

The soldier pointed his spear at Ineda. "Return to your people at Witton. And take this spent warrior with you. We will find a use for him."

Sharp metal at his throat gave Brennus no option. The comment about his warrior days being over blocked his craw but Ineda was vulnerable; the taunting auxiliaries still jeered just outside the entrance tunnel. Gathering her hand in his left one he drew his neck away from the spear tip and yanked her towards the doorway. Before she could exit through the short tunnel, the auxiliary whipped the small knife from her hand and thrust it into a pouch at the side of his belt. After a brief glance at him the Roman assumed that he concealed no large weapon, given that the ragged tunic Meaghan had fashioned for him, from tattered blankets, hung loose from his body. Meaghan's blade, in a simple hide sheath, was tucked into the front of his worn braccae and was concealed, though little good it was against a primed, slicing gladius. As the Roman urged him through the entrance tunnel after Ineda, the spear point jabbed around his lower back to make doubly sure no long knife was hidden.

Feeling utterly defenceless, he trailed out after Ineda.

Chapter Five

"Go!" The auxiliary was impatient.

Suspicion flared in Brennus. Was he about to become the hunted when they set off?

Ineda's tone was low and controlled; the tug at his hand insistent. "We must make haste."

The smell of smoke spurred Ineda even further as he watched the soldiers move from one roundhouse to the next, makeshift flaming torches made from nearby foliage raised high up towards the thatched roofs.

Her voice remained a low murmur. "They burn the settlement so that no one can use it again. I have seen them do this to many of the smaller clusters of roundhouses hereabouts. They herd us together in larger groups so that it is easier for them to observe our whereabouts. It is also less effort for them to pick and choose us for their labour when we are sheltered together."

There were many questions on his tongue but the time for asking was poor. He could only delay the patrol for a short while, but the girl could flee. He squeezed her hand tightly to gain her attention.

"Run, Ineda. You will escape them if I become their quarry."

The look of derision she sent him would have been comical in another situation. "Have you seen the long reach of the pila they carry? I see these men train every day and those spears do

60

not fail to reach their targets."

The expression on her face was fierce for one so slight before she stepped ahead; still muttering and shaking her head at what she obviously deemed his foolishness. "I have better things to do in my future and no wish to miss them happening."

Her small fingers tightened around his good hand and yanked on it when he looked back at the auxiliary standing sentinel, observing their leaving.

His angry words came after he whipped his good eye back to her. "They let us go? Why do they not kill us?"

They had cleared the perimeter of the houses and were headed for the now neglected fields nearby before Ineda answered, towing him along like a recalcitrant youngster. "The time for sharpening their blades on Brigantes is well past. Unless you show resistance. Then you will be slain. If you do as they bid they seem satisfied. They no longer have orders to cull the tribes of the Brigantes."

"I am not sure I understand you. They wish to subdue all of Brigantia."

Ineda set a good pace but had no problem spitting her rage to the ground before she replied, her face reddened with temper and fervour. "Aye, they do wish for that, but they need the toil of those of us who are left and able. They want our labour in the fields and in their other workplaces. Like us they must eat. That means we need to continue to tend the herds and the farmlands. But in a location of their choosing."

Brennus struggled to keep pace with her, struggled to absorb the implications of her words. Even though her stride was much shorter than his he dragged his limping leg, an awkward lurch the best he could manage as his arm supported his lower back, his breath short and choppy. "How do you know this?"

Her small pointed chin firmed up, her teeth clench noisy enough for him to easily hear. "People tell me things. The Romans have orders to honour the pact our Brigante leaders have recently negotiated with the man called Cerialis."

"Cerialis? Who is this man you speak of?" He was fairly sure who she spoke of but wanted her to confirm.

Now far enough from the flaming desecration that once was Marske she pulled up short causing him to stumble into her slight form. Spittle flew from her mouth and landed on the bracken alongside the pathway. "The turd will have other names, I am sure of that, but I only know of the one name he goes by. Cerialis is the name of the Roman Governor of Britannia. *An cù!*"

Her violent curse about him being a pig was so loud for one so small that he felt his lopsided smile crack up the undamaged side of his face. "I know this name Britannia. The Romans have named it thus for a long while now."

A noise from behind them told of the pursuit of the Roman patrol. Though some paces behind, it was clear they were set to follow them as the small troop gathered into a neat line, having destroyed every vestige of the roundhouse village that had housed him during his recovery. Too many of those sharp spears to flee from. Escape was not an alternative in his debilitated state, anyway.

"What now?" He was loath to rely on the information from a slip of a girl he had no prior knowledge of, but his options were severely limited.

Ineda's face looked to the sun, as though gauging its daily path across the sky. "Now they will force us back to Witton."

"They will track us to ensure we do?"

"Aye!"

She looked away from him, remorse evident. He wanted knowledge of Witton but needed first to understand her guilt. "What bothers you?"

"Though I did not detect it those soldiers must have followed me. It is the only explanation of why they found me. They are assigned to the Roman centurion who organises the work details in the areas around Witton, and they have trailed my movements before today."

"Tell me more." His words were clipped, struggling as he was to keep pace when the patrol closed the gap between them, not keen for the man who understood Brigantian to overhear their conversation.

Ineda had no problem with striding forward to keep their distance from the Romans and talk at the same time. "A group of soldiers patrol the area around Witton and camp close to our gates, though a much larger Roman garrison is encamped further, about a half-morning's walk away or a short ride. They are building a fort there, though have just started to prepare the trenches."

"Why now?"

She looked confused, and as if such feelings annoyed her. "What question are you asking?"

He gathered in a breath before answering, with no halt to his lurching stagger. "Why build a fort now, and not immediately after the battle at Whorl?"

"Ah!" Relief banished her uncertainty as she sidestepped a boulder that lay across the narrow path. "After the battles at Whorl and Wath, the Romans claimed their own dead – though they were pitifully few in comparison to ours – and then they split into smaller groups. Each group patrolled an area for a few days, cleared out more of the Brigantes and herded them to larger settlements like Witton. Some of the small patrols then widened their territory to settlements at a greater distance from here. Those groups made their own temporary encampments."

"So, a small number of them still camp near Witton and go out on patrol each day?"

"Aye. But others work on the fort."

"They take Witton men with them to help build this fort?"

"Nay!" Ineda scoffed. "They do not trust us for that! They do the building work themselves, but they use our labour to harvest wood from the forests for it, and make our men break stone in a nearby quarry, when we are not reaping crops from the fields, or rearing our animals. At the moment, the Witton men are occupied with all of those tasks, as are the men of the two small villages nearby. I do not know, yet, what happens elsewhere in mid-Brigantia, but I vow I will learn of it."

"What do you think they do?"

"Men are forced further south. They do not return so we have no knowledge, yet, of what they are required to do."

A quick glance behind established the patrol was nigh at his heels since his speed was so limited. He kept his ragged voice quiet. "Do you hear of any resisting Brigantes?"

A cackle was his answer, low but bitter. "When five hundred Roman auxiliaries trample your roundhouse not many Brigantes resist them."

He felt her gaze on him, knew she sensed his disappointment though he had meant to mask it. Her little hair tosses and pursing of lips, were full of bitter regret.

"There have been some but they are no longer alive to regret their foolhardiness."

"Do you say, then, the Romans know every Brigante movement around here?" He did not want to contemplate such a thing but had to know.

A wry smile wrinkled her wan cheeks; the tiniest of head shakes a denial. "Not all. If we are careful some of us still harbour secrets, though most accept the bondage of the Roman Empire."

"Like Cartimandua had done?" He wanted to be sure of her allegiance.

Her words tripped out, laced with disdain and disgust, her ire for their former Queen not upsetting him as she spoke at length, since he had to use all his strength to lurch along.

"For long summers our Cartimandua of the Brigantes accepted the Roman thumb."

Those keen eyes strayed back to his face. He felt every single assessing moment as she took time before her next words.

"Over twenty summers ago must have been around the time

of your birth?"

She needed no full confirmation, his short nod sufficient since her guess was an accurate one.

Her scorn continued. "Aye! Our Cartimandua paid her dues and in return the bulk of her Brigante subjects were largely left in peace. For that I have to be grateful since my childhood was a peaceful one, free of this heavy Roman presence I now feel at my back."

Again she spat at the ground. He was not entirely sure what she tried to prove with the gesture, not sure if it was designed to impress him or if it was a reminder to herself to strengthen her resolve against the Roman usurpers.

"The Roman Army should have remained in the far south of Britannia, though I rejoice that Venutius tried to limit Cartimandua adhering to the conditions she had agreed on with Rome." Her expression remained fierce, her glare snaring his attention in between watching the terrain for pitfalls.

"You must have been too young to be aware of Venutius gathering forces against Cartimandua two summers ago?" he said. She seemed too immature to be so aware of what had gone past.

"My age of twelve summers back then was well old enough to understand what was going on in Brigantian lands. I rejoiced with many of my clan when Cartimandua disappeared, and rejoiced even more when Venutius declared himself sole ruler of the Brigantes Federation. I made it my pleasure to find out about all the many small Brigante uprisings against the Roman scourge after that time."

"So, you would have also rejoiced when I and my fellow Garrigill Brigantes flocked to the cause of Venutius at Whorl?" Something inside him was glad she numbered at least fourteen summers and was not so young as he had first imagined.

"Aye! I did, Brigante Warrior. I would have been there, too, but my duty lay elsewhere."

Again, he wanted to test her truth, though the notion of her puny body wielding a sword was ridiculous. "What could have been more important than fighting alongside Venutius?"

"My training as a healer meant I was busy mopping up the wounds from the skirmish that happened not far away from Marske, a few days before the battling at Whorl."

Her speech halted, her glare now a haughty one since he had been unable to mask his surprise that she was a trained healer.

"Venutius may have lost the upper hand at Whorl, but he still has many followers like me who will rally to him in further uprising, even if I do no effective sword wielding."

Though he said nothing, his head shook at her naivety. The girl knew nothing of real battle with the Roman scourge, even if she had wiped wounds after battle. Unable to look at her further he scanned the landscape. He was in Roman occupied territory. Yet where? Many questions needed answers, but his staying power for trudging along was seriously limited. Yet again, he cursed himself for lingering during his recuperation.

"You will follow Venutius to the death?"

Her green eyes darkened to newly rained-on cropped grass. "You ask if I accept Roman domination." Her harsh whispering was fierce up to his chin on his nod. The indomitable fire in her eyes brightened further, her lips pursed over small gritted teeth before she pulled her face aside and spat into the air. "Never."

He again hid a smile. Her body may not have the substance of the bright fire of her name but her will was strong. A quick glance behind showed the Romans at his heels. One in particular appeared amused as he ambled along, making it seem as though he enjoyed a slow walk in the countryside rather than an enforced march. He wanted to slap the smirk from the man's face but he felt weak as a babe. He could not face any more humiliation if his half-hand failed to hit the mark.

Detesting the Romans in a show of words was too tiring as well, so Brennus put all his efforts into the journey knowing his many questions had to wait, though he managed to answer a few of Ineda's inquiries about Meaghan's last days.

When she asked for his name, calling himself Bran matched the unfit warrior he now was.

The sun was well dipped in the sky by the time they approached the settlement of Witton. Not as large as Garrigill it was, nonetheless, a sizeable hillfort and was a sight that he was so thankful to see.

"Halt, broken Brigante warrior!" The Roman in charge of the small patrol was insistent.

Seething inside, Brennus displayed none of his true feelings as he turned back.

Assessing eyes peered closely before the auxiliary walked all around him. "By some intervention of the gods you still live, limping Brigante warrior, and have got here without collapsing, though you would be a useless Roman Army conscript. Your days of warrior sword-wielding are over."

An cù! Brennus wanted to squash the little Roman pig but had not the strength. An unkind laugh rippled down his aching backbone but he refused to rise to the taunt. He stood impassively, humiliated, while the Roman continued his scathing assessment, the man's contemptuous gaze penetrating as he peered up.

"A one-eyed, hobbling soldier, with fingers missing, is of no use to our armies in Gaul. And you would earn little coin on the slave markets, glowering as you do. But fear not, you can still pay your Brigante due to the Roman Empire."

Though only vaguely understanding the man's purpose, Brennus knew his time in seclusion with only Meaghan was truly over. Wishing for regained strength to kill the Roman scum who herded him was futile at that particular moment, but he vowed revenge would come another time when he was as close to being a whole man as he ever might be.

"When the sun rises you will be in the forest with the other warriors from this settlement at Witton. Even a broken man can be put to good use for Rome!"

At that moment Brennus was so fatigued he was not even sure he would be alive come the new dawn.

Chapter Six

AD 71 A Half-moon After Samhain – Witton

"Decanus Egidius! Your contubernium will remain assigned here. The other will work the forest on the far side of the fort."

Brennus kept his head down and suppressed a satisfied smile as the centurion strode towards him, shouting his orders over the noise of wood-hewing. The speech was fluent and sounded like the natural tongue of the centurion he had only glimpsed on rare occasions during the half-moon he had been repetitively chopping wood. That was excellent since he could understand, it being not so different from his own Brigante Celtic speech.

Still exhausted and surprisingly still alive the morning after arriving at Witton, he had considered attempting an escape but caution had ruled over rash decisions. He had known he would not get far having noted the heavy Roman presence just beyond the Witton gates. Biding his time for a while at the settlement seemed prudent – even if he had to temporarily obey the dictates of the Roman Empire.

The language he generally heard from the soldiers in charge of the Witton men came from a place called Germania, far-flung lands he had heard tell of during fireside visits of journeying bards to his father's hearth. Only one of the soldiers guarding him spoke some Brigantian. That man was Egidius, the one in charge of the small group, and the one who was referred to as the decanus.

"We will have a supply of uprights ready for the principia

each day, but how are we to transport them with only one unit operating here?" Egidius spluttered as he towed after his superior officer, his manner obsequious. Flurrying along his speech continued in tentative bursts. "We have few to guard. Few to organise." His swinging gladius sheath caught on a stack of logs, the topmost one rippling down.

It was the pile Brennus had just built up, ready for loading onto the long, low-wheeled cart. The stack buckled then collapsed, the bottom poles almost tripping him up as he hobbled aside to avoid the tumble. With no fuss made, he set to restacking them since it took him closer to the conversation that had now become more hushed.

He had no idea what a principia was but it sounded an important part of the fort. Learning everything about this Roman fort, and how the place was organised, had become very important to him, his knowledge still scant, though he worked constantly to improve it. If he learned enough about the damned usurpers, he could surely use it against them at some future time? Whether or not that came to pass, the notion of thwarting them consoled him during the hard labour.

Contubernium referred to an eight man unit and two such units were in charge of the hewing in the forest. *Decanus* was the man who gave and took orders for the *contubernium*. In his head, he repeated what he knew.

The centurion's gaze took in the area of recently cleared forest. The trees ran deep but the poles the Romans required had been mainly gleaned from the forest fringes, the trees there of an age perfect for felling. While he restacked Brennus took opportunities to track the centurion when the man pointed to some of the Brigantes from Witton and then barked out his orders.

"Reduce the work force there by half."

Brennus dipped his head as the centurion's finger whipped around to point at him. He would not face the soldier unless forced to. Not out of fear, more that he hated to look directly upon his oppressors.

"This lame one can be used to transport the wood to the fort. He may hobble, but he is not completely useless. He will still be able to ride."

Egidius scoffed. "The man is simple. He obeys orders but does not communicate well."

Brennus bit down on a smile at the contemptuous tones while he re-sorted the pile. Egidius spoke the truth. The soldier had tried to make conversation over the many days that had passed, in halting Brigante Celtic, but he had answered none of the man's overtures. The blank expression he had produced had served him well enough. At first he had not intended to appear simple in mind, he had just been too angry at being required to do Roman labour to make any talk, enforced work for the Roman Empire detestable. When he realised Egidius thought him witless he had quickly embraced the idea. The exchanges had dried up.

"All the better!" The centurion sounded smug. "The fool will serve Rome in his own witless way, then."

When the two soldiers from the Legio IX turned away, Brennus felt a surge of interest flood his body, probably the first for a very long time. The notion of hauling the hewn logs to their fort appealed greatly. It was not that he wanted to serve the Roman scum but such a task would get him closer to this building he could only vaguely imagine. Riding a mule also appealed, just as much, because he had never done that. He had heard of mules, a cross breeding of horse and donkey that the Romans favoured for pulling carts and wagons, but had never before seen mule or donkey till his work in the forest. Realising his attention had strayed he listened to the centurion who strutted around like a male bird during mating season.

"Make those who are left work harder to keep up the trimmed wood you deliver."

Brennus doubted that was possible since the men of Witton already gave all their efforts, the long whip in Egidius' hand seeing to that. The weal produced by it had slashed a river of blood from one Witton warrior the previous day, the tunic he had been wearing no protection since the wool had shredded to rags at first lash. The men of Witton did not do the work tasks in what he would term a willing fashion, but they had recently learned to their cost it was unwise to appear lazy.

As the reddish glow of the sun dipped low in the darkening blue sky he trudged back to Witton, along with his work party, no conversation ever taking place amongst the Brigantes till they were inside the protection of the hillfort. Till then it was a supervised march, the line of auxiliaries in charge of the proceedings. At the entrance to Witton, wooden gates which now remained permanently open during daylight, the two units of Roman soldiers turned away and went to the camp area they had set up within monitoring distance. A whole century of auxiliaries inhabited the temporary camp, the tree felling operation only one of the tasks done by local men and overseen by Roman presence.

In such a short time he had learned a lot about the way Roman soldiers were organised, their numbers being uniform as much as their garb. Around eighty men formed the century which guarded the area around Witton, the number swelled with some others who assisted them. He had not personally seen all of these auxiliaries, but had gained knowledge about them from the inhabitants of Witton.

A few men broke stone in a nearby quarry to be used for road building, though Brennus did not understand yet how that was done. Most of the residents of Witton, male and female, worked the extensive fields around the settlement. The bulk of the harvesting was already done, the days growing shorter, but the soil was being turned over before colder weather set in.

"Bran! Wait."

A few steps inside the wooden palisade Brennus halted and waited.

Ruarke, Ineda's father, caught up to him. "What did that

centurion have to say when he pointed at you earlier?"

"I am given a new task come the morning. I will be used to haul the cart of wood to their new fort."

"Why do they choose you?"

Brennus' lopsided smile accompanied a wink from his one seeing eye. "I am witless. I ask no questions and I make no conversation."

Ruarke's open hand contacted his upper arm, a soft amiable blow. "You are no witless Brigante, though your ploy works well."

"We will see what the morn will bring." He nodded as he headed for his dwelling. The men of Witton had not contested Egidius' assessment of him. Not much conversation went on during the work in the forest, anyway, since they tended to work over a wide area.

"Have you given thought to my request, Bran?"

Ruarke was the only man of Witton that he had, as yet, befriended. The man had bemoaned the fact that he did not know what his daughter would do; she was so rootless; even after many cycles of the moon. He bent his head, acknowledging Ruarke's words, his fingers straying to the arm ring which still hung around his neck yet lay concealed from sight beneath his tunic.

"Aye! I have."

The previous evening Ruarke had come to his roundhouse well out of patience. Ineda was still determined to set up lines of communication with King Venutius, even though her father had directly forbidden her to do anything dangerous. Ruarke had asked him if he would take on the role of foster-son, since he had no living son of his own.

The man was not really in need of a new son. Brennus knew that well enough. And especially one who was less than a healthy warrior. The request had been made for different reasons. As Ineda's foster-brother he would be expected to temper, and monitor, any rash decisions she might make. No fighting force necessary to fulfil that task.

Seriously considering the request had not been onerous. He owed a duty to Meaghan's family since he owed his life to the old woman. More than happy to honour the request to be foster-son, he was also very glad that Ruarke had not put pressure on him to become family by another method. Though still very young, Ineda was of marriageable age – Ruarke could have requested that he become son-in-law.

He had no dislike of the girl, but he certainly did not wish to have her as his hearth-wife. He liked her friendliness very well, sometimes too well, and was constantly amused by her fervour to defy the Romans, but he refused to see her as anything other than still a child.

"It will be no great burden to be foster-son to you, Ruarke. I will gladly take on the role."

Ruarke's delight was evident, his shoulder thump almost strong enough to topple him, and only sheer willpower kept him upright. After a day in the forest, the dull aching at his back and leg was considerable.

"It may be more burden than I have the right to ask of you. The role will mean repressing the excess enthusiasm of my daughter. Are you prepared for that?"

"Again, aye, I am. She is just a slip of a girl."

Ruarke's mouth twisted in a grimace of doubt. "Slight she is, but she has my mother's tenacity and inner strength. My mother trained Ineda as a healer, though the girl has all but put her skills aside just now. Has she told you of her latest plans?"

Brennus felt his smirk widen. "To get behind the turf of the new Roman fort? Aye! Ineda has ambitious ideas, though her latest one is not an idea I discount as totally foolish. I would like to view it myself. Maybe the morrow will bring that plan a bit closer."

Ruarke did not look at all convinced that was a good thing to do. He knew the man fretted because his daughter was so headstrong but was not sure if Ineda shared all her thoughts with her father. "Has Ineda told you why she needs this outlet for her ambitions? Why she does not use her healer skills?"

Ruarke's sigh was deep, his mouth a twisted acceptance. "Aye! I know well the old herb wife of Witton will not have Ineda near any of her charges. Jealousy drives the old crone. Ineda has learned far better skills from Meaghan, but the twisted old woman will not have anyone usurp her position in the tribe."

The old healer was exactly as Ruarke described. Ineda would have to bide her time and await the old woman's death before that situation was likely to change in her favour. He sought to smooth Ruarke's worry. "Ineda must have some task to use up her bountiful vigour. The life of the hearth is too idle for someone of Ineda's cleverness and skill. Perhaps the morrow will bring a reason for me to take her to the fort." His deep-throated laugh was echoed by Ruarke.

"Your new task?"

He stopped at the latrine area, grinning at the prospect of hauling the cart to the fort, his head nodding a couple of times. "Aye, indeed! My new task."

"None of us from Witton have been to this fort, yet. It has not been worth giving up our life to creep along to see. *Màthair*, my mother Meaghan, must have been correct that you are destined for greater things."

Brennus' scoff echoed around, the shared laughter a sound that drew the interest of the women who stepped out from one of the roundhouses. He was not known among the women of Witton as one who laughed a lot: more like the scowling warrior who did not know how to. "Greater tasks like hauling a cart? I think not."

Ruarke's voice interrupted his thoughts of what the morn might bring.

"What name did they give to that Roman who has been strutting around so importantly during these last days?"

Ruarke had previously commented on the fact that he was

absorbing Latin words quite readily and often consulted him at the end of their work day. He had no problem sharing what he had acquired since he knew Ruarke passed the words on to Ineda, who had set herself to learning the Latin tongue as quickly as possible. Her thirst for learning about the Romans was possibly even greater than his own; something which constantly impressed him. She might be young, but she did not get bored with her quest.

"*Agrimensor.*"

Ruarke repeated the word a few times till he got it correct.

During the last days, the centurion in charge of the tented camp had ridden in to the work area. On two occasions he had been accompanied by a Roman legionary soldier whose purpose it was to direct the building of the fort. Brennus had quickly realised the hierarchical order between the two. The fully armour-plated agrimensor, a land surveyor, was a man of bluster and importance who directed the felling, right down to marking off exactly which trees he wanted cut down.

The agrimensor was a man the auxiliaries paid attention to, his assistant likewise. It was through the chatter between the assistant and the decanus who was in charge of the contubernium that he had gleaned his latest information. A small wiry man, the assistant trod at the agrimensor's heels, a stylus and wax tablet at hand which he constantly scribbled onto. He, too, wore the full uniform of the legionary, though his skills surpassed those of writing and recording – he translated from Latin to the Brigantian tongue when necessary, and also to the tongue of Germania in order that there should be no question over the intentions of the agrimensor.

"What did the centurion have to say to Egidius?"

"What I understood seemed to compliment our labours. He appeared pleased at the output from our work detail." He pared his words down. Ruarke would find out soon enough about the recent decisions that had been organised.

Most of Brennus' other Latin had been gleaned from his

keen observations and his listening in to conversations. Since the auxiliaries thought his senses impaired, they had not been particularly careful about the information they bandied amongst each other. He absorbed, and even surprised himself that he remembered every small detail. In his former life at Garrigill those skills had never been polished, his physical actions being supreme over his more cerebral ones.

He mulled over the latest information he had gleaned as he bid Ruarke farewell, to head for his own dwelling.

A flurry of hospitable activity surged around him as women moved food from one roundhouse to another. There was nothing strange about that, the Celts were ever hospitable. Since his arrival at Witton, his acceptance in the village had been easily gained, aided by Ineda's claim that he was her grandmother's last wounded warrior and was deserving of their care. Her word had not been doubted. One look at his infirmities had been sufficient for them to believe her assertion, his state of exhaustion on arrival adding credence to that.

A private place in the deserted roundhouse he headed towards suited him very well, women tending to his daily needs while he laboured in the forest with men like him who had formerly been tribal warriors and horsemen but who were no longer given the freedom to train as before. The horse stocks were poor, so only a few people spent the day at the horse enclosure. It would take some time for new breeding to increase the stock of horses which had fallen during battle with the Romans – just like the warrior count had. Brennus tended to avoid the horse enclosure.

His knowledge of slain horses was still too fresh.

Chapter Seven

AD 71 One Moon After Samhain – Witton

"Bran! Wait!"

Before dipping his head to go through the short entrance tunnel to his roundhouse Brennus heard the rush of footsteps behind him, knowing those quick feet very well. Sorcha had come to visit him so early in the eve? Though exhausted and bone sore, his loins stirred in anticipation, though the feelings faded quickly when he turned around and noted her serious expression.

"Merron gathers late this night. You are expected."

Brennus acknowledged the whisper from Sorcha as the woman dumped newly cleaned braccae just inside his dim roundhouse before she pulled a reed torch from a bracket at the side of the door hangings. He was glad of the delivery of clothing, since the ones he wore were caked-firm from hip to knee with the hauling of muddy damp wood. With efficient movements, she lit two brands and set them back into their metal stands by the door before she added wood to the small fire that glowed deep red in the centre of the roundhouse. Poking vigorously, it made it burn brighter.

Going close, he stroked her shoulder.

Her irritated shrug and sidling away from his touch told him his attentions were undesired as no words could.

Sparks flickered upwards and choking smoke billowed around, making him step back more than her actions. Soon the flames from the newly fired wood licked up the edges of a small pot which dangled from a chain suspended from a swivel hook attached to an overhead support beam. As she stirred the game broth, the rich meaty aroma hit his senses.

His eye caressed her bent form. A welcome heat flooded his groin again. Sorcha was a well made woman – at least her body still was. Older than he was by many moons her face had not fared quite so well. She, too, had suffered at the hands of the Roman army as many of his fellow Brigantes had, the slice at her cheek not much better healed than his own facial wounds. It was unsaid, yet a common bond between them, though neither face mattered in their dealings with each other.

"You should take care not to be late." She threw down the wooden spurtle on the warm stone at the side of the pot.

His one seeing eye fixed on her as she whirled around to head for the doorway. Since his arrival she had tended, on a number of occasions, to more than cleaning his clothing and providing food for him – though her present haste and terse announcement did not bode well for another satisfying coupling that night. Something more was meant by her words.

"What is amiss?"

"A visitor comes. We gather late in Merron's roundhouse when dusk is well gone. Old Agneta has sent you some new baked bread. You should eat first as there will be no common feasting."

Her pointed finger, indicating the bannock that rested beneath a fine cloth, he again silently acknowledged.

Merron, the chief of the settlement, was less hospitable than his father, Tully, had been. Merron preferred to keep his roundhouse quiet and only called for gatherings when something important was happening. At first he had thought the chief of Witton to be a mean host but then learned it was not so. Large gatherings tended to draw attention. New developments were something interesting to the Romans.

Since the battles at Whorl and Wath, and the subsequent

total subjugation of the local mid-Brigantes, he had learned secrecy was crucial at Witton. Apparently, there had been too many instances of information ending up at the nearby Roman garrison about the movements of visitors to the settlement. No one could be seen to support insurrection. No one could outwardly proclaim to be a follower of King Venutius.

Visitors could be friend, or foe, depending on the reason for their travel.

In his own way, Merron was vigilant.

Travelling in Brigante lands was still possible for those who dwelled far enough away from the Roman garrisons, since those Celts of the north were not yet accounted for on a daily basis, unlike the settlers at Witton. However, the presence of a stranger was regarded by some at Witton as an opportunity to glean reports of any resistance to the Roman forces in their domain. What they then did with the information was the problem.

Though Queen Cartimandua seemed long gone Witton provided little support for her ex-husband, Venutius, who still ruled the Brigantes of the north.

"Why am I invited this time?" he asked, Sorcha having lingered long enough to do more for him.

After looking at him for a few moments, she sloshed some warmed water into a wooden bowl from the pan on a hot stone and handed it to him, breaking his concentrated appraisal of her body. Looking as though about to change her mind her lips twisted to the side, annoyed with him, certainly annoyed at something. "This is no time for gratification, except if you make it happen yourself!" Though the only two people in the roundhouse, her voice was gruff. "Tuathal comes this time from the north-west."

Ignoring her rebuttal, he continued to stare. He had recently heard the name Tuathal though had not yet met the man. "That is not usual?"

"Nay. His news is normally from the south-west, from the

Deceangli and the Ordovices."

Sorcha was not one to waste words, and was no gossip. Her duties completed she turned with a swish of her check-patterned dress, pulled back the fur hanging that prevented draughts at the doorway, and slipped out the wattled entrance tunnel of the roundhouse. To her own hearth-husband.

Sighs came easy as he resigned himself to no female dalliance that night. There was no love growing in his breast for Sorcha, but she had restored his faith that he still performed properly as a man. Till she had made advances to him he had not been exactly sure how damaged he had been – even though there were times when Ineda caused blood surges to his groin, urges he immediately suppressed.

He worked alongside Sorcha's hearth-husband in the forest; a man he disliked for being too inclined to chatter on about nothing, his constant grumbling an irritation that was hard to stomach. Sorcha did not deserve such a fool for a mate. Why she remained with the man he had not fathomed, though there were three youngsters at their hearth all less than six winters. They had perhaps been sired by her hearth-husband, but then, again, perhaps not. He sensed he was not the only man Sorcha favoured outside her own roundhouse. She had sought him out the first time as he suspected she sought out other men, though he had not been averse to bedding her. After setting down the water, he yanked off his grubby woollen tunic and sent it racing towards the doorway, washed away the stench of his hard labour and then looked around the almost empty roundhouse. His raised cot lay alongside one wall, the hangings to the small enclosure permanently tied back showing the furs topping the straw mattress. No one shared the roundhouse. Not like at Garrigill.

A great sense of loss engulfed him. It took ruthless squelching to banish his father's roundhouse. Tully had rebuilt his dwelling when Brennus had been at his mother's knee. That had been long before the first wooden sword had been placed in his hand – a hand that back then had all four fingers and a thumb. His eyes closed on the scene, needing no reminders of what had once been. Slumping to his knees his hands cradled his head.

Images of his older brothers, three of them, playing around the new and empty roundhouse of Tully with him clomping at their heels flooded him. The newly built room bereft of furnishings had been huge, the echo quite startling. Their excitement had been high as they whooped and yelled, purposely louder than normal. Even back then, young as he had been, he had realised the importance of Tully, his father, the chief of Garigill. No one had a roundhouse anything like the size Tully had just had built. To a very small boy the new one seemed twice as large as the old one.

That memory was almost accurate. Tully's new dwelling was not twice a normal size, though it was substantially larger than usual. When older he had learned Tully had had men scour the nearby forests for many days to find exactly the right trees to provide the much longer roof trusses that were needed for his higher lodging.

A stack of wooden posts filled his vision. A pile of logs he had rebuilt earlier that day. Poles hewn for a Roman purpose.

"Nay!"

The bowl of dirty water hit the wattled wall with a crash, sending a scattering of water droplets showering up to the rafters.

Disgusted with his temper, he slumped forlornly. Not only had his name changed when he came to live at Witton, the changes to his personality were quite marked and he knew would have been evident to anyone who had prior knowledge of him.

Before the battle at Whorl, he would have named himself a carefree warrior, one who had no problem with talking to people, one who enjoyed life. The battle had robbed him not only of two of his fingers but it appeared also his desire to be pleasant as well.

After yanking on the clean tunic that hung on the hook by his cot, he ladled broth into the wooden bowl and ripped off a piece of the bannock.

He would attend the gathering. A better mood needed to be summoned first, though.

In an odd way, the work imposed on him by the Roman patrols in the forest had aided his recovery, had forced him to regain his body strength more quickly than he might have done if he had been on his own at Marske.

Choosing the darkened paths around the rear to Merron's roundhouse, he was alert to all movements. The roundhouse of the chief lay central in the settlement, unlike the one he had been allocated which was situated alongside the perimeter of the circular defences, the least popular situation, and more vulnerable to attack. The location of it made no matter and did not bother him; he was glad to accept the Witton hospitality. He had survived Whorl and knew Meaghan had spoken true.

He was destined to live longer.

Merron maintained the defences, with guards posted at night after the gates were closed, but it was a half-hearted attempt. If the Roman Army chose to invade they would do it easily and swiftly. The gates were closed for a different reason now. It was not to prevent attackers from entering – it was to prevent disloyal Witton inhabitants from sneaking out. A sadly futile gesture. The will of the Witton settlers was not as it would have been before the battle at Whorl. In essence, Brennus realised their acceptance of the yolk of Roman domination had happened even before Whorl. Cowed by their losses, and constantly threatened by the thousands of auxiliaries encamped within a half day's march, they had acquiesced very quickly.

Having been present at the battle at Whorl, and having seen the disciplined might of the Roman horde, he understood why some chose to collaborate with the Roman Empire though it was not what he would accept.

His northern hillfort of Garrigill had never had physical Roman presence in its close environs, and he vowed he would do all in his power to keep it that way. He would stay long enough at Witton to gain sufficient information before setting off for Garrigill, regardless of the Roman dictate that he be part of the Witton human-toil payment to Cerialis and the Roman Empire. It had taken only a few days of being under the Roman whip for him to have formulated that plan, though first he wanted to know what the fort looked like and how the Roman Army were placed inside it. Warriors at Garrigill would be very interested in hearing about how the Romans administered their annexing of mid-Brigante lands.

On entering Merron's roundhouse, he found it surprisingly busy. The few gatherings he had attended, so far, had nothing like the amount of settlers congregated now. They stood huddled in small clusters, chattering and laughing, an anticipatory hum around the room. His glance alighted on Ineda and Ruarke standing well back from the fireside.

"Where is this visitor who calls for my attendance?" he asked, after squeezing his way towards them.

Ineda's green eyes glared at him, nudging his elbow to make him lower his volume. "He prepares himself." She pointed to the covered stall at the rear of the room. Merron had a mere three stalls at the back for guests to use, unlike his father, Tully, who could accommodate many people.

So. The visitor controlled the proceedings. Brennus knew then the person must be of high status. It took only a few moments of conversation with Ineda before the newcomer revealed himself to the congregation.

"Welcome, Tuathal."

Brennus' eye focused on the fine staff in the man's hand as it tapped on the beaten earth. The cane was needed as a walking support, the figure of the visitor hunched over it, the craggy features of the man looking as weary and fragile as the gnarled fingers that gripped the wood near the carved head. A smile creased Brennus' face.

"A druid?" he mouthed down to Ineda who nudged him again in that impish way he liked well enough to nudge her back.

There were so few druids remaining that the old man was a pleasing sight.

Though the druid wore no robe of distinction, the staff told its own story. Tuathal drummed the tip of it on the ground before he sat down in the honoured place beside the chief, and only after Tuathal had settled on the low stool did the elders of the tribe seat themselves alongside, ranked in order to each side of Merron around the low blaze. Once they were arranged, a middle row of people either hunkered down or sat on the rushes that were scattered over the hard packed soil. Those at the back row remained standing or propped themselves against the interior walls.

Brennus found himself almost directly opposite the druid as he looked around the gathering. As far as he could tell, the elders were all assembled. He had not yet conversed with each one, but Ruarke had pointed them out. An important meeting, then.

Tuathal began to speak of the losses in the mid-Brigante areas, his voice carrying well across the fireside. Brennus knew the risk the old man took in moving about the countryside to convey his information to the many villages and settlements which he frequented. If known to the Romans as a druid, his visits would suddenly cease – since Cerialis, like his Roman Governor predecessor, ruthlessly routed out every druid priest. He had heard tell the Romans had many gods and goddesses of their own but the worship of Celtic deities was not the problem. Druids were the learned upper society and control of them, the Romans believed, would suppress any uprisings.

The old man had news of many places and told all in quick fashion. Many of the hillforts and villages mentioned Brennus had never heard of but the plight was similar. Along the

Brigante borders with the Cornovii and Coritani, the Roman cohorts of nearly five hundred soldiers moved in and dominated, gladius flashing, their sheer numbers destroying any resistance.

It took some time before Garrigill entered the conversation. He was not surprised it was mentioned since there were few large settlements in northern Brigante lands; the area populated more by those living in small villages.

"Garrigill is a shadow of its former glory." Tuathal's tone mourned. His head swivelled around, dark watchful eyes alighting on everyone. The man might be old and worn but Brennus could see he missed little. "Tully, the chieftain who had ruled for many solstices, went to the otherworld some time ago."

Alongside him, Brennus felt Ineda nudge his elbow, her eyes imploring him to confirm the news when he glanced down. All she knew was that he was from Garrigill. His heartbeat rose inside his chest though he made no murmur, his eyelids flickering for a few moments. His father was dead. His throat blocked as he swallowed the sudden rush of spit. Blinking furiously he ignored Ineda and paid full attention to Tuathal.

Brennus felt his damaged hand spasm when his two fingers wrapped around the thumb; the hand that could no longer make the fist it used to be capable of. He fought for control. He wanted to rant and lament, but could not.

"Do the Roman armies oversee Garrigill lands as they do here at Witton?" Merron wanted to know.

So did he. The question made him focus on the conversation and not on his loss.

"Nay." Tuathal hacked up gobbets of phlegm and then repeatedly spat into the fire before resuming his speech. "Small parties of Romans survey Garrigill land but they are not so numerous as here. The armies of Cerialis have not yet settled in such high numbers so far north, though as everywhere else they have already dragged off those they wished to be sold into slavery. By that, I mean those able warriors who survived at Whorl and at Wath and were captured. Only small presences of Roman troops remain in northern Brigantia, till they build more forts."

Brennus had heard of the Celtic warriors, men and women, who had been fastened in chains after the battles, and subsequent skirmishes, and dragged to Roman supply ships. A life of slavery somewhere in the Roman Empire was their fate, and no one knew where they would end up.

Merron persisted. "So, the Romans further north are no longer snatching hapless victims?"

Tuathal's cackle rang free. "I would not say it will never happen again, but for the moment the Roman Empire seems more interested in using its supply vessels for other purposes."

An Elder Brennus had not yet talked to posed a question. "Have there been any more risings against the Roman usurpers?"

Tuathal's nods affirmed though his look was fierce. "Aye, some small skirmishes, but those who have dared have died in the process and each time the Romans claim more land for their Emperor."

Brennus listened as Tuathal recited more details. It was difficult to decide if the druid condoned following Venutius into resistance, or was just extremely careful of what he said in the present company.

He set to ignoring Ineda's sudden clutch at his belt, yet could not banish the stimulation he felt coursing through to him from her curled grip.

"The Roman gladius of Cerialis is brutal to all who resist Roman invasion of their territory." Tuathal's penetrating glare dared anyone to refute him.

"Yet you say Garrigill has not been attacked?" Another elder brought the topic back round to Garrigill. "I have never visited myself, but I have heard its defences are impregnable."

Tuathal's harsh tones rang around the room, those piercing

eyes condemning the elder for voicing such a question. "Nowhere would withstand the onslaught of almost five thousand armed Romans when a legion descends upon them."

"Then why has it been left alone when all Celtic villages around here are saturated with the Roman dung!"

Brennus was startled when the warrior across the fire who had made the comment jumped to his feet and pointed directly at him. A man he had no prior knowledge of.

"You came from Garrigill! Is that not so?" Antagonism leeched from the man's eyes.

Before he could say yay or nay, Merron intervened. "Aye. Bran comes from Garrigill. But look at him!"

It was the first time he had ever seen Merron so fired up with anger. The chief rattled on. "You would never claim Bran has come unscathed from battle?"

As all eyes fell on him he felt any embarrassment easily surpassed by fury at being so exposed.

"What can you tell us?" The warrior was persistent.

Merron's anger permeated the room. "Bran can tell you nothing. He lay wounded for many nights after Whorl and has never returned to Garrigill. The news Tuathal brings is as fresh to him as it is to us. Now, sit silent, and let Tuathal continue!"

The warrior slunk back down to the floor, his attack over, though the glower remained.

Tuathal sounded weary; his tone changing to placatory. Brennus sensed the fine line the druid had to take. He should not show partiality to any particular tribe as the bringer of news to many Celts. That was his function, what he trained for decades to do. Many of those now assembled had no real perception of the distance between Witton and Garrigill since few had ever travelled so far. The Roman Might had not flooded Garrigill simply because they had not yet chosen to march so far north.

As Tuathal placated the crowd, he acknowledged the druid had some skill in negotiation. Like his brother, Lorcan. Lorcan had fast become an expert at diplomacy skills, and had been Tully's eyes and ears around the Brigante federation of tribes. Realising his thoughts had strayed he paid Tuathal more attention.

"Garrigill once housed hundreds of people. Bran will attest to that."

He merely nodded, knowing he was not required to speak.

"Now Garrigill is worked by old men and old women, young women and children and the male warriors who limped their way home. Most of their female warriors did not return."

Brennus swallowed hard, again. That sounded very ill. Ineda's little fingers gently tugged at his belt, her support tangible.

"Who rules at Garrigill if Tully is dead?" Merron's question was a fair one.

"Lorcan, a second son to Tully now leads the settlement at Garrigill."

He hoped his sigh of relief was not visible though Ineda had definitely heard it as she stood alongside. Her small hand relinquished his belt. Instead, her fingers intertwined with his and gave a reassuring squeeze. Looking down at her the smile she flashed him was encouraging.

Brennus found her such a strange mix. Innocent girl blended with warrior woman inner strengths. It was pleasant to have her support though he did not care to encourage her. In truth, he could not tell if she merely pitied him for what had befallen him, or if there was more to her attentions than simple friendship. He disengaged his hand from her grip feeling an awkwardness about it. She knew nothing of his promise to her father. His feelings must remain brotherly.

Merron called over to him. "Bran? Does that information meet with what you knew before Whorl?"

All eyes on him he had to say something. Feigning a detachment he did not feel his answer was short. "Aye. Tully was already ailing and Lorcan was named as new leader during the Beltane rites, though Lorcan was not set to become the chief immediately. As the emissary of the tribe Lorcan was dispatched to Owton on the east coast, the morning after Beltane, to find out about Roman fleet movements. Because of that the elders decided Tully should remain leader till Lorcan's return."

"So, Lorcan of Garrigill survived the battle at Whorl. He was well favoured not to be carted off to be a slave of the Roman Empire!"

The man who spoke alongside him was scathing. Brennus' feet itched to move the short distance to squash the warrior like he would an irritating summer insect. Had it not been for Ruarke's shifting on his feet, and the restraining glare he intercepted from Ineda's father, he most likely would have.

Tuathal was surprisingly firm when he answered, putting a stop to any petty bickering from rippling around the room. "Not so favoured as you infer. Garrigill feared all the sons of Tully had been slain at Whorl. Only the third son, Gabrond, was stretchered back to the settlement across two planks of wood, his leg almost in two pieces. Thanks to the skills of the healer there he did not lose the limb, and slowly learns to walk again."

Brennus swallowed hard, his attention straying again, his eyes trained somewhere above the old druid's head. Gabrond had fared no better than he had from the sound of it. He well sympathised with his brother's pain; momentarily wondered how debilitated Gabrond was now.

Once again, he felt Ineda squeeze his fingers, drawing back his attention. He scanned around the hearthside. The gathering lapped up every detail Tuathal could share.

"But you just said Lorcan is the chief?" The glowering warrior across the fireside had not thawed.

Tuathal had the crowd's interest in the palm of his hand. "Lorcan did not return after Whorl with the survivors. Nara of the Selgovae took warriors from Garrigill to seek him out.

Evading Roman patrols was not easy, but she located him at a village near Owton on the east coast where he lay in deadly fever."

The general outcry was disturbing but it gave Brennus the opportunity to breathe again. It sounded like Lorcan had fared possibly worse than Gabrond.

"Why there? Owton swarmed with Roman soldiers who landed with their fleet, just after Whorl."

The druid's hand rose to cull the clamour. "That is true, nonetheless, Nara of Tarras got Lorcan back to Garrigill, though she fell prey to a Roman pilum along the way."

Chapter Eight

AD 71 One Moon After Samhain – Witton

An cù! Nara had been hurt by a Roman turd!

Brennus felt a cold sweat trickle down his back. The feeling was immediately banished by Ineda's small hand soothing him. She could not know why the news disturbed him but she sensed his heightened feelings every time. Her attention began to suffocate him. If he had had more room to step away he would have but everyone was tightly packed inside Merron's roundhouse. The best he could do was shrug off her ministrations.

"Nara's wound could not have been too bad if she got Lorcan back to Garrigill?" Merron was justifiably interested in the fate of another Brigante chief.

Tuathal nodded. "Bad enough, but not enough to prevent her from marrying Lorcan when they returned to Garrigill. Tully lived long enough to bear witness."

By Taranis! Lorcan had married Nara? Brennus' throat dried up. His gaze snared the floor as confusion engulfed him. His god really had abandoned him.

"Honouring the bargain made between the Selgovae and the Brigantes?"

Brennus' head whipped up again to stare at Merron who knew so much about his family. The chief's fingertips scratched at the scraggy moustache that grew down from his upper lip to his chin as he pondered his question, as though remembering a past conversation.

Tuathal's old head bobbed again. "Aye. In a way, though the bargain was for Nara's marriage to the fourth son of Tully – Brennus – but he did not return from Whorl."

Brennus stared at the floor rushes.

Garrigill believed him dead. Dead. Like Tully. Nara had married Lorcan. Nara, whom he had been betrothed to during the last Beltane rites. She would have been his wife had he not gone to battle at Whorl. What was in his future now?

Returning to Garrigill was impossible.

His body heated like a newly poked fire, a dread sweat trickling down his backbone. His brother Lorcan would be far too honourable if he returned. The bargain had been made with the Selgovae and Lorcan was principled to a ridiculous degree. Lorcan would relinquish Nara and enforce the original marriage agreement. He was sure that was what his brother would insist on.

A creeping shiver prickled at his scalp in opposition to the heat below. He could not put his brother in such a position.

The floor rushes blurred at his feet as he swayed on the spot.

His home was now lost to him. He cursed every single Roman that was on Britannia's soil. *Ceigean Ròmanach!* He hated every last one of the Roman turds!

Ineda's hand tugged at his belt to gain his attention but he turned away, unable to face the concern he was sure to find there.

His thoughts whirled and he lost all track of the conversation in the roundhouse. The new man that he now was needed to find a new home as well as a new purpose in life. He would never be any tribe's champion ever again or train the youthful warriors. What was he going to do? Meaghan's words flashed through his mind; she even appeared to be standing right in front of him berating him for being cowardly.

Anger as great as he had ever felt rippled through him as he lifted his chin. He wanted to cry out to the assembled crowd that he was maimed, but he was no coward! Forcing the temper away he considered the implications. His god, Taranis, had ceased to favour him; yet, he vowed he would make Meaghan proud. She had said he needed to live – not only to be of help to his own tribe but to all Celts. Her fervour had made him believe it would happen, but how?

He looked at the old druid. The purpose of his new life must be in finding a way to defeat the Roman grip on Britannia.

Merron directing the conversation to a new topic stirred him to listen again. "Tell us now of the Roman troops who infiltrate the west. What happens there?"

The druid gave updates of the situation regarding the Celts of the west but Brennus still only half listened, preoccupied with his own situation. He could go north to escape the watchful Roman eye but avoid Garrigill and any other place that knew him well? That sounded like a feasible plan.

"The Roman hand comes down hard on the Ordovices. Night after night, more Roman soldiers encamp near the coast by Mona's Isle, subduing all who dwell nearby. My brother druids remain a constant target."

Gasps of outrage burst around him drawing his attention back.

Tuathal's voice was very weary now. "Druids are now so scarce many tribespeople will no longer have a druid to perform their obeisance to our gods and goddesses, few left to properly perform death and marriage rites, and few to give you reliable information."

Few to give reliable information.

The words rang around Brennus' head – over and over, as the old druid continued to share more knowledge with the assembled crowd.

"The pacts made with Governor Cerialis mean wealth for some Brigantes who will trade with them."

"Trade with the scum!" The outcry was general and all contemptuous.

"Brigantes, I do not talk of the cereal stocks they take from us, or the man toil they requisition. I speak of regular trading of goods. Cerialis has put in their Roman writing that they will pay in Roman coin for carcasses from the hunt and for goods we can give to them." Tuathal now sounded very weary.

"Why would they want our kill? They send their own soldiers to hunt in our forests." An old woman seated at the front spat her loathing into the sparking fire.

Tuathal tutted. "They have many things to do to establish a settled presence in these parts. The patrols sent to hunt are few. The weather turns cool already and they will need plenty of kill to feed their troops come the snows."

"Who would trade with the usurpers?" Scorn flew around in many comments.

"There are plenty of Celts, even fellow Brigantes in the south, who have been trading for a long time already. They will not cease." Tuathal had chosen a fine way to remind the mid-Brigantes who sat around the fireside.

Brennus watched Merron mull over the information, the stroking of the man's beard a reflective gesture before the chief joined in. "What advantage would we gain by trading with them?" His subsequent scowl around the company quelled some gloomy comments.

Tuathal nodded. Just once, but decisively. "There is value to be had in this trading. I do not speak of Roman coin in gold, silver and bronze. I speak of added security for your people at Witton."

A ripple started again, the murmurs a low growl.

Tuathal raised his hand in the air. "Cerialis build two types of forts. There are the huge legionary ones – like the one planned for at a short ride from Witton. That means some five thousand legionary soldiers and possibly extra support soldiers. Cerialis also plans to build many more of their smaller forts; set apart at a distance of a day's walking; and these all across our mid-Brigante territory. I speak of the type like the one that is already close to Witton."

At that point, Brennus decided on a task he could undertake. Blood coursed through his veins in a rush of excitement, of anticipation and of impatience. It took all his efforts to master the smile that wanted to break free and to quell the urge to divulge all to the assembled gathering. It was nothing like his old life but surely he could do this? Even one-eyed and hobbling? He would find a way!

Ruarke spoke alongside him drawing back his attention to the talk. "How will trading with Roman dregs give us security?"

"They will let you live your lives more as you would wish to, and our forests will still be available to us for our own needs."

Another warrior spoke up. "Is it true that more soldiers are expected to arrive soon? Are these the ones who will require the extra food?"

Tuathal nodded in the man's direction. "Most likely."

Merron reclaimed the druid's attention. "I do not see how this trading would work. The Roman soldiers toil just as much as we do, at times. Why will they not hunt their own food, and grow their own crops when they are established in the area?"

Tuathal spoke as though to a youngster who needed more understanding. "They may well do that, Merron, but I know what has occurred in the south. Many seasons ago the Roman Empire made treaties with the tribes whose land they overran. In order for the cohorts and legions to conduct the business of being oppressors, yet also to keep the peace between warring Celtic tribes, the Celts of the south continue to work their own farms. The Roman Empire extracts a duty from those farmers, but if there is a surplus a sum of Roman gold is given to the farmers for the extra crops."

A heckled question came from alongside Brennus, the sound strident and angry. "Aye, but is it a fair price for the labour?"

Ineda's little body nudged his arm, her gaze excited when he responded by bumping her back. Her lively mind was definitely stirred in some fashion as she grinned at him, an eager anticipation flowing through to him from her proximity. He wished she was unable to do that; denied the stirring she engendered in himself, while wishing her enthusiasm was not so catching. More heated thrashing went on around them about the rewards earned till Tuathal demanded silence once more; his staff raised high up to the rafters.

"Whether the pay is fair, or not, the Romans will probably be unable to sustain the supplies for the numbers of soldiers who will be here before winter sets in, without our assistance."

"Let them starve, then!"

It was a valid comment but one Tuathal derided. "We all know that it is not the Roman Army that will starve. They have the might and the power. If you are not prepared to trade with them they will commandeer your crops, perhaps even the hunt that you normally share amongst this settlement, and will leave you starving."

The many grumbles continued till Merron rose to his feet.

"Why the need for more troops at this nearby camp, Tuathal?"

This time it was the druid who spat heartily at the fire. "We believe Cerialis plans to spread his hand northwards. When he is satisfied the Brigantes who dwell close to here keep to the trade treaties he will then send detachments northwards to settle on new land. When that is established he will repeat the procedure, gradually covering and establishing total control of the whole of the north. It is what these Romans do."

"Then if we feed the scum we will be harming our northern brothers!"

That was also a truth that Tuathal nodded at. "Aye. It seems that way. Whatever you do the Romans will advance anyway, but if you are seen to comply with their treaties their move to the north may not have such devastating consequences for our fellow Brigantes."

Merron scoffed. "There is a lot of land to subdue peaceably, or otherwise."

Ruarke growled beside him. "Aye. There is. But faced with five thousand soldiers who will stop them?"

"After the whole of Brigantia the Selgovae, the Novantae and the Votadini – those Celts who dwell beyond the high hills – will be the next target for Roman domination. None of the Celtic tribes of Britannia have so far managed to halt their supremacy." Tuathal's words depressed the congregation but none could refute them.

Yet, instead of feeling despair Brennus' blood surged with an anticipatory excitement. Aiding Nara's tribe, and the others Tuathal spoke of, was what he must do. Brennus was convinced of it. Tuathal was an old man. He himself might be slower than he had been while living at Garrigill, but he was still much more mobile than the old druid. There must be some way he could help Tuathal information gather and work with the tribes of the far north to repel the invading scum. He could never be a druid, but he could surely be the old man's aide.

Though he could not understand how she did it, Ineda knew that the excitement had again surged through him, her fingers tightening again around his belt and her little hand quivering against his side. Without looking down, he knew she was gripped with anticipation too.

***

The following night Brennus sought out Tuathal for private words.

"I will waste none of your time, druid. Though I may look riddled with infirmities I can, and will, be instrumental in thwarting the Roman scum with or without your help. I vow to do anything and everything I can to help my fellow Celts repel the aggressors from our lands. Your assistance would be appreciated but know that I will find a way with or without you."

Tuathal's immediate smile and nod of acceptance was a

surprise.

"I noted you at Merron's fireside, Bran. They call you Bran of Garrigill but you must have them change that form of salutation. You must encourage them to name you Bran of Witton. Your new future will demand you are of Witton...for the foreseeable time anyway."

Brennus did not feel he belonged to Witton, yet was curious about the piercing glares the old man sent him – assessing him in ways he did not understand – though, since he could not return to Garrigill, he might as well be associated with Witton.

The dark of the night passed in conversation into a pinkish blue dawn. Tuathal asked many questions of him and in the process confirmed his parenthood.

"I have heard tell of all of the sons of Tully. I suspected you must be the one thought to have perished at Whorl. You are Brennus, the fourth son? Though, here, I will continue to name you Bran."

After that, Brennus held nothing in secret.

"Apart from your might as a champion at Garrigill, what else were you noted for?"

Brennus was not sure of the answer to that.

"What other skills do you possess?" Tuathal was relentless. "Were you the best to work the horses?"

"Nay! That was my brother Gabrond."

"What about negotiating for Tully?"

The question annoyed him. "Nay! That was Lorcan. You know that already."

"So, people only sought you out to fight them?"

An irritation was beginning to boil in him. Where he used to enjoy such banter it now annoyed and almost shamed him. "People also liked me well as a friend. I was told I brightened their day."

The look Tuathal sent was of disbelief. Brennus scrabbled around for something positive to justify his former character. "I was different then. I wove a fine tale to keep them interested."

Tuathal's beaming smile was completely unexpected. "Sing to me!"

"Now?" It was a pointless question. The old druid needed to be obeyed. He began to hum first, and then put words to the tune.

Tuathal rummaged around in a pouch dangling from his belt. "Play!"

Brennus stopped his song and stared at the wooden ocarina in the old man's hand. His throat was suddenly too restricted. He looked down at his maimed hand, his head denying. It had been so long since he had made any wood burst into a melody.

"You have sufficient fingers left, Bran. Believe it!" Tuathal's harsh order was convincing. "The fingers you have left are much more useful than all of mine are now. My playing days are long gone. This is now yours."

The trembling of the old man's fingers could not be denied as Tuathal forced the instrument into his hands.

Fumbling at first, he worked out how to cradle the ocarina and blew. And blew for a while after that till he had mastered the covering of the thumb hole and the sliding of his remaining fingers over the holes at the front quickly enough. Though it was early yet in the morning, a few people entered the roundhouse to see who made the fine music. It was not long before Ineda burst through the entrance tunnel just as he launched into a well known story song.

"You play? That must be of use to you, Bran! And you sing, too?"

Her delighted smile warmed him deep inside, her enthusiasm and eternal optimism something lovable about her. She did not need to add that it would make people listen to his voice and not look at his deformities.

By the time Tuathal was ready to depart Brennus had knowledge of how to pass on useful information to the forces of King Venutius, information he gleaned about Roman troop movements. A second gift also changed hands.

"You have my ocarina to play to them, Bran, but in case some do not recognise it as mine you must also show this."

Tuathal unpinned the silver bratt pin from his shoulder and held it out. "This will gain you entry to every fireside as no other object could."

Fingering the pin with a fine inlaid amber stone he swallowed, the gesture meaning a huge amount. "What of yourself? Will you not still need this?"

The old cackle echoed around. "You think the people hereabouts do not recognise me, Bran?"

It had been a foolish question. His sheepish grin was sufficient.

"No apology. This will set you into my chain of messengers as nothing else ever could. You know now who to start with so make contact without delay. I am certain you will find a solution which will gain you regular knowledge of our Roman oppressors and you will keep me always informed of Roman developments. Wherever you are."

What Brennus lacked was not courage; it was experience of the land he now lived in. He needed to find a way to ensure safe passage around the Roman held territory near Witton. It was a bitter drink to swallow, but he would never be a successful fighting warrior ever again. There was no point in sneaking off with a sword to join the forces of the King of the Brigantes who amassed in the north, so he resolved to put any such lingering desires from his mind. His infirmities would make him a hindrance to his fellow Celts in any planned battle. Nonetheless, he was determined he would still play a part.

The old man had a few more words of advice for him. "You must first make use of any situation the Roman scourge places upon you. If they send you to their new fort, come the morn, learn what you can. And while you await further developments renew your acquaintance with my ocarina and that fine voice of yours. Hone your skills at the Witton fireside, and if need be that you must travel to other hearths you will be a welcome visitor if you remember to entertain them."

Brennus bid Tuathal farewell, the happiest he had been for quite some time.

AD 71 One Moon After Samhain – Witton

"Load!"

Egidius, the decanus, pointed to one of the stacks of logs that had been trimmed the previous day.

Brennus set to work with men from Witton, their task to transfer the prepared wood onto the long four wheeled wagon and tie them down securely. This job was one he had done many times over the last work days at the forest; repetitive but easy enough.

"You, stay!"

A ripple of anticipation coursed in his blood as he obeyed Egidius' command. Singled out to cart the load proved true as he stood aside and watched the other Witton men being marched off by three Roman auxiliaries – one at the front and two at the rear, the pilum in their hand always at the ready. It had been a few days since the centurion's last visit and disenchantment had settled upon him. Nothing about his work circumstances had changed and it had seemed too foolish a hope he would be doing anything different. Suppressing a grin was not easy so Brennus looked at the trampled soil beneath his leather-clad feet. That was usual enough to not cause any suspicion.

The decanus unceremoniously threw reins and bridle at him, the leather whipping him in the chest and making the silver arm ring bite a dent in his flesh. "Hook those two up."

"*Ceigean Ròmanach!*" His curse whispered through gritted teeth.

Collecting the strewn straps of leather, he nodded. The mules were well used to hauling the long wagon but the task of

102

hooking them up had always been done by one of their men. He was used to driving typical two-wheeled Celtic chariots, the basket-woven sides and light construction often requiring delicate balance, but he had never driven anything like the long, heavy and flat-based Roman wagons that rode nearer the earth on four wheels.

A short while later he wanted to smile, an unconditional smile at the sun which now shone high in the sky almost directly above him. He wanted to whistle or sing but that was not in keeping with his deception as a simple soul: any melodies would have to wait till he returned to Witton.

Closing his eyes, he savoured the warmth that bathed him, the slightly cool breeze that blew nearer the river just enough to keep him from overheating. His back ached, his leg possibly even more so, but he had not walked like this for many days and not since arriving at Witton. Working in the forest had been exercise of a sort, but not pleasure. If he had not been accompanied by Egidius it would have been a joy. The mules were as well-trained as their master soldiers, and responded to every one of his simple clucks and commands.

It had been foolish to think he would be riding one of the beasts, yet drawing them along the rutted path was almost as good, his equestrian escort riding behind determining the pace, keeping it slow and steady. Though the surface of the path had been trodden for many days, it was still pitted, uneven and potentially treacherous. One awkward lurch of a wheel, into a hole too deep, might send the wagon load a-tumbling. He did not wish for delays. Of any kind. He was very keen to see this talked of Roman fort.

After coming through a small wooded area, his awkward stride faltered when he slipped on slimy leaves on the pathway, the reins flying free when he ended on his knees. Ahead lay a curving river, its waters twinkling in the distance, flat meadowland in between. When he swivelled his head he took in more of the amazing scene that lay there. A large tract of land had impressive fortifications on it already. Shadows of a ditch dipped well below high turf banking on top of which sat an impressively straight fence of wooden stakes.

The mules slowed as he righted himself and groped to his feet.

Coming from the hillfort of Garrigill, which was the most outstanding Celtic hillfort he had ever seen, the level-topped palisade was not what caught his attention- it was the shape of the defences. They were not round like most Celtic hillforts. Twinkling in the sunlight metal helmets indicated the posting of guards at strategic places other than the four corner towers built higher than the timber fencing. Activity was high around the outside of the fort, the area teeming with bodies going hither and thither, sparks of bright light twinkling as shining metal glinted in the sun. Some of it weapons, although mostly helmets.

The thud of hooves told him his guide had come forward. The whistle at his ear told him too late the whip had been drawn. Searing pain ripped at his back making him almost lose balance again.

An cù! The Roman scum had flayed him!

"Move on quickly or this whip will sting more times!"

Brennus needed no further urging; it seemed his guide was too impatient to savour the view. The pain was acute but much less than he had endured after Whorl. Biting down a grimace, he refused to give the Roman any satisfaction as he hauled the mules onwards.

A loud blast of sudden noise to his left drew his attention away from the pain at his shoulder. To his side of the river, on a stretch of low field grasses, uniformed auxiliaries tramped up and down, the metal mail they wore a dull grey shine. A strident cry from a centurion called the formation to a halt. Another shout had them turn about and a third raised their rectangular shields, the whole group scurrying into a tight huddle. Some of those shields were maintained flat over the tops of helmets in an instant, the men so snug together that penetrating such a defence would be nearly impossible.

He watched with reluctant admiration. Having seen the Roman Army stand together at the battle at Whorl, he had already had too much first-hand knowledge of their training. And he remembered only too well that little shelter formation. His sword and spear had been unable to breach its strength. What he saw in front of him now proved how different the training field of the Roman army was to that at Garrigill.

He deliberately looked away from the exercise area. He would not bring forth an image of what was going on at the Garrigill training field. As he pulled the mules and wagon forward, he allowed only a few memories of the young warriors he had last trained to linger. That had been his purpose in life before Whorl. Though still not one and twenty winters, as the tribal champion at single combat, he had been given the task as overseer of the young warriors. Were those young warriors alive or dead? His heart tugged. He had no way of knowing, but they had been fierce fighters. They would have faced their fate with valour.

Looking back toward the fort other activity drew his gaze. His brows creased in confusion. Upstream on the river people walked across the water, carrying heavy loads, the file of men heading for a gateway in the turf banking. Close by many men were at work in the water, constructing a fixed walkway. Too far away for him to see the detail it seemed as if they rammed long wooden posts into the riverbed, from a platform that stretched across the water. Noise abounded everywhere. Talking and shouting, hammering and banging. Busy, productive noise. Again, he was reluctantly intrigued by their industry.

Near the water crossing on his side of the river there were many wagons being unloaded. The wood, like he conveyed, was easy to discern but not the smaller items. He would see better if he could get closer. Every piece of information might be useful to know and learn. From the clothing they wore, he guessed the men who teemed around the area were a mixture of auxiliaries, legionaries and a few local tribespeople.

The path he trod led to a bend in the river where wooden barges were in use. A few were moored on his side of the river, more on the far banking, and one in transit across the water. All of the barges were loaded with log piles. Many logs were clearly needed for this fort.

Around a hundred paces from the river Egidius halted his progress.

"No further!"

Brennus slowed the mules and brought the long wagon to a standstill. A small queue of vehicles lay up ahead, a trio of men swarming around them. They all bore a wax tablet and sharp stylus similar to the one the agrimensor's assistant had carried in the forest near Witton. All seemed to be talking at the same time, shouting instructions at the drivers when they had made decisions, after which they scribbled furiously onto their tablets. Wagons peeled off to the left and the right, the contents swooped upon by a horde of soldiers who unloaded with frightening efficiency. No time was wasted, and these were not men who had an overseer breathing down their backs with a biting whip. For reasons he could not understand they worked with a will that was commendable.

"Wait here till you are called forward."

Dismounting, the decanus strode past tossing the reins of his horse in his face, his folded whip a warning at Brennus' torn shoulder. Disregarding the insult Brennus caught the leather and controlled the still ambling horse. As he soothed all of the beasts now showing signs of restlessness, he watched Egidius approach a pair of sentries who blocked the pathway.

While he waited, he took note of the activity directly on the river now that the detail was clearer. The bustle at the river crossing in front of him made him smile since he understood it better. A line of simple dugout boats, each bow pointing upstream, had been lashed together; the whole row sitting tight against the banking to each side. Across the top of the boats a wooden walkway of logs, similar to those on a crannog causeway, had been laid. A scurry of figures crossed back and forth, carrying materials in large baskets slung over their shoulders, the traffic swift in both directions.

Laden baskets were ferried across to the fort and returned emptied. He watched the unfilled baskets being laid down in serried rows, the carriers wandering off to stretch the kinks from their necks and shrug their shoulders, with noise that seemed like teasing going on amongst them. They all wore similar light coloured tunics, though not the same as the uniform of the auxiliary soldiers, and they wore no mail over their chests. He could not quite place the men. They were not garbed like any soldier he had ever seen, yet they were not Celtic tribesmen either.

As he memorised all movements around him the gentle flow of river water butting against the boats threatened to move the whole bridge downstream, the scurrying transporters halting occasionally to find balance as it swayed before settling again. When he looked closely, he discerned the strong ties tethered to stakes on the banking that prevented the bridge from breaking free. Further upstream there were more of the flat barges moored against the bank, though all at present were unused. He wondered why. Wondered what they might be waiting for.

"Move the wagon over there," Egidius barked out on his return, pointing to an area where oak logs similar to his cargo were already stacked.

Turning the mules around he backed them up, manoeuvring back and forth and ignoring their noisy protests and their snorting till the wagon was exactly in the spot required by the tablet wielding officials.

"Unhitch the beasts and be quick about it!"

Brennus did as he was bid; his temper held tight inside for it was not the time to exact revenge on Egidius. Another day. Another place, he vowed.

What went on behind the ramparts of the fort across the river was not visible, but he wanted very much to know what lay beyond as Egidius mounted his horse and ordered him to do likewise on one of the mules. The other mule he led by the rein to a waiting place while the logs were unloaded in a blur of light-coloured movement.

"Wait here while I speak with Benignus."

In no time at all Egidius returned, followed by Benignus, the centurion's scribe.

Once again, the whip threatened at his shoulder. Brennus hid a sarcastic laugh for only the whip could reach his shoulder – not the mean little Roman scum. "From now on you alone will take the wood supplies to Benignus, and you will follow his instructions. You will speak to no one else and deliver only to him. Is that clear?"

Brennus' nod was scant but just sufficient. Inside his smile was triumphant. He would learn to ignore the taunts because his task was begun in earnest. There were many things he could pass on about the new fort to his contact. He was sure of it.

Another thought made him want to grin.

Ineda would be so jealous of what he was seeing right in front of him. The tiniest of smirks managed to break free and stretched his scarred cheek. He found himself wanting to hurry back to Witton to share what he had learned with her, to enjoy her company. He squashed on further imprudent thoughts. She was just a child, his foster-sister, and he was a grown man.

On the journey back he had too much to think on. His curses were quiet enough not to be heard over the trundling of the empty cart but they vented his frustration. Ineda could not be banished from his thoughts. As he hauled on the reins, he looked around to distract himself. The day was cold and crisp, the sky azure with an approaching dusk making the green of the evergreen trees tinge with a lighter more vibrant green as they blew in the light wind. A green like Ineda's eyes when she was riled.

His harrumphing was as noisy as the mule he was still riding. He had to stop thinking about her and curb the errant thoughts that turned to physical evidence in his braccae. His needs were surfacing too often lately; in her presence and it seemed when she was at a distance as well. He had lusted after women in the past but had not wanted to share secrets with them, or spend time having fun, or just talk.

He knew the solution, though. If Sorcha did not seek him out, then he would find some way to encourage her to visit more often.

Or some other woman who would look past his infirmities.

Chapter Nine

AD 71 Two Moons After Samhain – Witton

"Leather?"

Bran looked amused as he looked up at her from the pile of rugs he lazed on. Ineda bristled at his doubtful tone and his attitude; she had found him so before with other ideas she had thought of, but she had to win him round to the plan. Convincing him would not be easy yet she needed his cooperation in such a risky venture and he was the only man she would trust to aid her.

"Why not leather? The Romans use leather just as much as we do."

She paced around his small fireside her agitation a physical dull ache inside her, her blood churning in her excitement though her stomping gait was intended to spark some positive reaction from him. The words spilled quickly from her lips, her hands fingering the leather belt at her waist.

"In fact, they use far more leather than we do, Bran. Our harsh weather means constant repairs to those large tents each contubernium uses." She enjoyed her wicked thoughts on Roman discomfort, her smirk one of great satisfaction. "Wait till they experience our snows and crackling frosts! Can you see those tents hoar-rimmed and thick with ice?"

Bran's laugh rang free. She knew his experience of winter snows was far greater than hers since they had discussed his Garrigill hillfort. He had satisfied some of her curiosity about what it must be like to live in a very large settlement; had told her Garrigill was well sited on a natural raised area of a valley floor, yet that meant much sharper frosts, and longer cold and snow spells in winter than they had at Marske and Witton. Stopping in front of him, she dropped to her haunches, her hands performing wringing motions on the pouch at her belt to keep his thoughts on leather.

"And the leather under the breastplates of the legionaries cracks too readily. The rust from our wonderful rain has them constantly polishing the metal, but they cannot get enough of the fat they use to keep their leather strapping supple, and they have to replace it."

He looked unconvinced by her words, his smile changed from amusement to derision, but he did not even move from his lounging position as he sipped from his wooden beaker of barley beer. Casual observation was not the reaction she needed from him.

"I tell you leather and wool is the answer, for now! And later we can trade them the wool wax from the wool supply, and the special cloth that comes off the looms."

"Ineda."

She had tolerated that same flat tone before. Too many times he had brushed off her plans for thwarting the Roman scourge in their midst but she would not have that happen this time – something deep inside told her it was far too important an idea to allow it to fizzle away to nothing.

"Ineda." The repetition of her name set her teeth to grind as she focused on his next words, his head shakes so exasperating. "The Roman Army is well supplied with all the leather they need from those supply wagons which arrived recently and from the animals they slaughter themselves. I am certain their stock of cloth will also be replenished."

The man vexed her, a lot, but he was the only one she would rely on to help her in her venture. There was some special thing about Bran that set him way above all other warriors in her esteem. He was crucial to her plans to thwart the Roman enemy and deep in her heart she knew Meaghan had kept him alive for a great purpose. It had to be him who helped her. In spite of knowing his reticence and attitude her sarcasm seeped free.

"You have such a high opinion of yourself, Bran the all-knowing."

His irritation rose at her snapping tones, his eyes flashing a warning she chose to ignore. She had fallen foul of his quick temper a few times during the last moons but he did not intimidate her. The foolish man still treated her as a child but time would change that. Mostly he remained calm when she presented her ideas but sometimes, as now, his affable approach wore thin when she bristled right up close to him like she was now doing. She bent her head, lowering her face right into his, her words slow and deliberate, the emphasis on some of the words intended to provoke him.

"The leather you think arrived with that last wagon did not come. Neither did a delivery of cloth."

"And you will tell me how you know this?"

The subtle change to his expression was heartening when his eyes dropped to her lips, even though only one eye really watched her talk. He was coming round to the plan, but she knew him well enough now that he would toy with her first before agreeing. He always enjoyed teasing her as though a troublesome sister.

No matter. So long as he did eventually agree.

She rose to her full height and stretched her body, right in front of him, on purpose, though it had little effect on him. As usual. Her womanly wiles never worked on him. She seethed inside before pacing around the fireside, and then changed her approach. There was one thing she knew of that always got his hackles to rise.

"I have been busy while you were carting those log supplies. Madeg, from the village of Sower, tells me interesting things."

Bran was slow to answer, the scowl that had whisked across

his brows quickly smoothed out. He never liked to show much emotion; nevertheless, she knew he disliked her friendship with Madeg. It had taken no effort to know why Bran resented the younger man. Only a little older than herself, Madeg had the reputation of being far too interested in laying any woman down. In fact, she had first hand hearing of his boast that he needed no instructions in bedding females. Madeg was arrogant, that was true, but he was also a resourceful young man who could be very useful to her. She could handle his inclinations so long as he helped her in her quest for information.

A coupling with Madeg was not in her immediate plan, but she did not rule it out. Bran might not think of her as a woman, but she was and she had a healthy curiosity about the mating ritual. Madeg was not the only young warrior who had made advances to her and soon she would make her choice. Bran was her preference for first lover but she could not bear the rejection she knew she would receive from him. Yet, though he did not want her, Bran seemed reluctant for her to dally with any of the young warriors around the area.

"What kind of things?"

She ignored his ease of tone, her stare deliberate when she answered. "He takes the extra hunt to the new fort."

"I know of this, already."

Another flicker of impatience. He was irritated, as she now intended him to be, since she was annoyed at him, too. Bran disliked the idea of her dallying with Madeg, but did not deny himself a woman. He had barely arrived at Witton when Sorcha had lifted her skirts. But then, Sorcha lifted her skirts to almost any man at the hillfort. She drew her errant thoughts back to her ideas. "The Roman trader he deals with was furious two days past when Madeg delivered a deer, and a brace of pheasants."

Bran's eyebrows rose, a mute inquiry. Deliberately misinterpreting her words.

"No, he was not furious with Madeg's delivery. His anger was directed at his own Roman suppliers. The last wagon of the season did not arrive with stored goods and their skilled hunters had been sent elsewhere, to provide for another cohort.

A soft sigh escaped as Bran eyed the doorway. "Why do you believe I would find this important? If they lack anything and we have it, the Romans will seize our supplies. They would take the clothes from our backs if it were not for the fact that the Roman army prefers plain cloth. I do believe they will freeze come the hard frosts rather than wear our patterns. What should I be fretful about?"

Bran's shrug of indifference stirred her temper further. Further sidelong glances at the doorway to his roundhouse were even more telling. She had come to his dwelling uninvited; she acknowledged that, nevertheless, he did not need to be so agitated now by her presence. That he wanted her to leave as soon as possible was perfectly clear in his attitude, no doubt because he expected the imminent arrival of Sorcha. She could not hate Sorcha, the woman was kind enough, but she sometimes wished her elsewhere. Removal to another village would be perfect.

She also wished on herself the allure that Sorcha currently held.

"What do you think to achieve by your plan?"

Bran's sudden prompting her for details was so obvious she wanted to rage. He had used this tactic before, as well. Ask the questions after toying with her at length, get the answers and have her leave. In a hurry. But she needed him to listen, and the morrow might be too late to put her plans into action.

"Bran. The immunes, those Romans who are not ordinary auxiliary soldiers, already know you from your wood delivery this past while. Though that duty has now ceased, and they have told you that your due has been paid to Rome – for the moment – they will soon find other tasks for you. Your movement around the villages will again be curtailed. They will have you breaking stones at the quarry, or some such task and you will have no recourse but to obey."

She knew Bran could not fault that information since the very same had happened to other men of Witton. Once one work detail had been accomplished, the Roman centurion found their labour was required for some other task. Bran said nothing, but his expression encouraged her to continue.

"You will easily gain their passage to the bridge to make trade with a cart of leather. If you are in useful, regular dealings with them, they will not acquire you for other work. After a time, you will gain entry across the bridge, and after that all the way into to the fort. I know you will! You must at least try, Bran."

It was a bone of contention that neither of them had yet crossed that bridge, nor entered through the fort gates, even though Bran had been delivering wood for nigh on a season. The fort was very rigidly restricted to soldier only entry which meant Bran still had no idea what it looked like beyond the palisade. And she had never been near the fort at all.

"Your scheme with wool? Why would they want raw wool?"

She knew he had not been listening properly. Guarding her easily lost temper she made her words calm. "Not raw wool, Bran. They have no need of that from us. We will produce the finest, softest cloth they have ever seen to keep their toes warm."

"Their toes?" A small smile quirked and stretched his scar. Though he did not say it she could see he disregarded her idea already. "Tell me. You know I am not easily persuaded."

Stopping in front of him, she pulled a small piece of material from the pouch at her belt. Shoving the cloth at his face, she wafted it across his cheeks then held it up right in front of him. "Instead of making our usual weave from sheep wool we will make this much finer, softer cloth, in smaller portions from goat wool."

Having grasped the material she allowed Bran to let it ripple through his fingers as he stared at the weave. He was no expert with cloth making, that was solely a woman's work, but even he should be able to tell the piece was different from the weave of his braccae and tunic.

"How did this come about?"

She was sure he was intrigued now, though he maintained that bland expression. "Our best weaver puts more than her usual amount of strands and loom weights on her frame. This was made from goat wool that was washed free of wool wax, much more washing than usual. It takes longer to comb and spin the wool to a thinner string but it produces a softer touch, as you can feel, in addition to ending up warmer and very durable. Normally her effort is so great and the amount produced so small that the weaver does not spend the time on it."

Bran looked disgusted. "Yet you would have her spend the time on it to trade it with the Roman Empire?"

Forcing more power into her words, she persisted with persuading him. "It can be made quickly if enough women are assigned to help. Though the Romans do not know it yet, they need this cloth."

He still remained unconvinced, his scoff hurtful when he tossed the material back at her. "You want me to trade leather and small pieces of this soft cloth to the Romans, even though they have no idea why they need it?"

Keeping her teeth from gritting together was so difficult, her exasperation spiking to levels she could barely control. She moved close-up to him, bending to almost being plastered to his chin, so much so his breath heated her forehead. "Nay! You will do the trading of leather, and I will sell our usual cloth, at first. Then, when stocks are high enough of the soft material I will make trade with the special cloth."

"Ineda. It cannot be done." He stared at her as though the notion was ludicrous and drew his head back when he realised how near she was, his throat swallowing awkwardly.

She knew well the Roman Army would not trade with a

woman, but was not yet defeated. "I do not mean I personally will trade the coin, Bran." Bracketing her hips with her fists, the cloth of her dress drew tight across her breasts, her breath coming in spurts of agitation. When he turned away after a look askance she pulled him back by the elbow. "You will make the money transfer. At first, I will go with you when you deliver the leather and our usual cloth, though it will be of plain weave with no checked patterns. Later, when the goat cloth is ready I will demonstrate what they can do with it. They do not know it yet, but this softer goats' wool will make them withstand our winter more easily."

Bran still looked derisive. "You want the Roman Army to be more comfortable when winter's harsh bite comes?"

Throwing her hands aloft, she stalked away from him. "I despair of you sometimes, Bran. Those auxiliaries, and immunes, who daily check off your log haul think your abilities are lacking because you do not converse very much with them. I begin to think they are correct."

"Tell me…and be done." Now his tones were so placid she wanted to cry aloud. Of course, he wanted her gone. Sometimes she hated him. Hated Sorcha even more.

"I do not want them to be more comfortable, but we need something credible to trade with them. We must give them something different that they really need. In doing so we gain their trust as reputable traders and in gaining their trust we gain entry to that fort that still keeps us guessing! You have been unable to send word to Venutius because you know nothing of what happens within. I will not remain unsuccessful any longer. I, too, have made my vow."

Though Bran had never talked of it with her she knew what he had been doing. If anything was set to rile him, it was knowing that her intentions to help the forces of King Venutius had not been thwarted. The anger flashing from his good eye was not unexpected.

"Information gathering is not an occupation for you, Ineda.

I have told you many times it is too dangerous with the hundreds of Romans we have surrounding our area."

Now Bran really did look fierce. He was forever telling her the same thing, belittling her determination, but she had been sworn to her cause long before she had ever set eyes on Bran of Garrigill. Even though Tuathal had visited three times since Bran's arrival at Witton, the numbers of Witton tribespeople working towards the cause of Venutius were pitifully few. She had to get inside that fort and needed Bran's help to do it.

"Have you a better idea to put forward that will gain us entry?" Her challenge was met with a wry smile. She doubted he had conceived any other plan. Like a tenacious hound she persisted. "Trading with them is the only way. You know that sneaking in to the fort, under cover of darkness or in full day, is impossible and it would not give us the continual updates we need to inform Venutius of new developments. Regular trade will gain us that knowledge. I am sure of it."

Ineda suppressed a smirk. She was wearing him down. Though still exasperated, he now looked slightly more convinced that her idea had merit.

"I will think on it, and give you answer come the morn." Rising to limp to the entryway he deliberately looked outside.

Ineda did not need to look to know darkness had long fallen. Flouncing across she confronted him one last time. "Sleep well on my idea, though I doubt sleep is what you look forward to at this very moment. If you will not aid me with this plan, I will find a way to make it happen myself."

"The Romans would not entertain you as a trader." A flat and final response.

Her blood surged in angry reply. "I know that. It will take a brave man to help me do it. But that is not a problem, Bran, since I know some other men who will help me without putting forward such resistance as you do."

Stepping past him into the entrance tunnel she whipped her head back, not even trying to bite back her bitterness. "Madeg will help me!"

Her boast was likely true, though it annoyed her, at times, the way the young man trailed her, like a dog after a bitch in heat.

"You have till the sun is high to decide whether you will be my helper or not. I will get inside that fort, Bran."

Now he looked furious. She had achieved his full focus. He would not like her next statement either, but her resentment was fierce.

"I fully understand that you will be busy with other pursuits before you sleep, this night, but give my proposition at least a little thought. I doubt Sorcha has any ideas to help you get through those gates."

Her last glimpse of Bran's face was typical: fury repressed in stone-like impassivity. Stomping through the entrance tunnel her anger was high. With, or without, Bran's help she was determined to get across that bridge and beyond the gates. With the onset of winter the Romans would not advance much – they always waited till they could break ground properly, ground free of frost, when they surged northwards into new territory. Somehow she was determined to relay the Romans' plans, before the spring thaws, to Venutius. Why Bran was so resistant to her ideas she could not fathom, because he wanted to thwart the Roman Empire as much as she did.

Perhaps Meaghan had stolen away the man's emotions when she tended him to recovery.

Only a roundhouse away she spied Sorcha heading towards her. Turning aside she darted between the nearest homes, unable to stomach meeting Bran's lover face to face.

Chapter Ten

AD 71 Two Moons After Samhain – Witton

"Ineda. You do not need to come with me to the fortress at Nidd when I talk to Benignus, the immune who deals with the wood supplies. I only seek an introduction to the scribe who organises supplies of leather and wools."

Ineda had tracked him down at the horse enclosure. He had been sure to be there early, hoping to borrow a mount and leave the settlement without her knowing his whereabouts. But, like a little hound, liking to be at his heels, she had tracked him down before his departure. It was a trait she employed regularly which irritated and endeared her to him in equal measure. Tenacious and teasing, she snagged his attention too often. He wished her to be properly grown up so many times he had lost count, but most of all the general frustration he felt in her presence only increased as time progressed.

Her snort of derision was clear. "I need to go with you. Those foolish Romans need to see we are both doing the trading. Your face may be well known already, Bran, but mine is a new one. I must be seen."

She would not be persuaded to stay. He faced down the temper he had provoked, crossing his arms for good measure.

"I must talk to the horse handlers some more just now but if you dare to leave without me, I warn you that you will rue it, Bran. I have something you must see!" Her green eyes darkened and purposely spit fire, the little chin below them turned up the tiniest bit as her lips pursed together, her strong nose twitching.

He liked to get her heated in such a way, had noticed it was something that livened up his otherwise dull days. He liked to delude himself that it would have been a similar situation if she really had been his sister, a sibling rivalry setting off the same warm sparks between them. "You are so sure I will like your surprise?"

"Aye! You will!" Her words were flung back at him as she stomped off.

Suppressing a guffaw at her sounding so fierce he refolded his arms across his chest and waited, amusement guaranteed when Ineda was riled. She had stirred his curiosity; her surprises often highly amusing. He thought her reasoning to be with him a good one, but had no idea how the talk would go with Benignus if she was there. The man might not be as friendly as he hoped him to be. So far any talk between them had been very limited: a combination of his reticence to speak to any Roman and the lack of fluent Latin.

The sight of any woman at the camp of the Romans was also rare enough to stir interest, the kind of attention he did not want Ineda to engender. She had grown into a beautiful girl and would draw attraction despite he still thought she looked young. He knew that would not matter to the coarser natured soldiers in the camp. Her protection was paramount. Resolved to work out how that protection might happen, when surrounded by hundreds of Romans, he temporarily put aside those thoughts as he watched her return.

Towing behind her was one of the horse handlers who hauled along a horse and a small dray. In her bustling way she had wheedled the use of it, though from its bedraggled state it had seen better times. Two wheeled like a chariot it had a small flat bed for carting goods and a central pole for harnessing it. As yet, they had only a few pieces of leather and cloth as samples so it would be sufficient and the horse that pulled it was better than the nag he would have been given. For that alone he was grateful.

"So, you do like my surprise?"

He refused to answer her mischievous taunt, and merely gave a simple nod to acknowledge her achievement.

The frisky little filly got them there more quickly than had he been carting a load of wood from the forest, though he ended up doing more walking than he had initially envisaged. Sitting beside Ineda on a mat of piled up skins was too unsettling since she squirmed and twisted, her chatter continual. Keeping his distance, avoiding contact with her side had become a chore that being on foot solved, though he made sure to join her again as they approached the fort. It was just as well that his leg barely pained him now and that he had acclimatised to his uneven tread.

They met with only a few Romans on patrol as they rumbled along the beaten earth pathway. Though their purpose was not yet established, his face was well enough known for their safe passage when he named Benignus as the person with whom he wished to speak. Close to the wood pile area he was stopped by the first set of sentries who were clearly amused that he brought such a tiny cart and was with a comely young girl.

He forced a blank look. "Benignus. Talk with him."

Benignus ambled over a few moments later.

"Bran. What is this?"

The man's gestures indicted the small cart, and especially Ineda who set a nervous smile to her face. A flood of words followed that he had no hope of understanding. He nudged Ineda and nodded at their trade goods. As she leaned back to lift them up he looked all around. It seemed his presence was so usual few were bothered by his appearance.

Benignus looked puzzled as he fingered the cloth and leather Ineda mutely held out to him.

"Trade." He repeated the word a few times more. "For Roman coin."

Benignus caught his meaning, his raised eyebrows a good

sign before scurrying off with their cloth and leather, to disappear into the throng of workers who trimmed the logs and fashioned smaller pieces of the wood into vessels and bowls for eating from.

"*Buachar each*! Will that piece of horse dung bring our leather back?"

Ineda's fierce whisper was given with a sidelong glance. Like him she tracked Benignus' movements. He was aware of her slump against his arm when she noticed Benignus return with the man he had learned to be the centurion's scribe. Whether or not she was genuinely alarmed, her warm little body squirmed in at his side. Sliding his free hand around her back was a natural thing to do.

"Who does he bring with him, Bran? He looks very important."

"Nay! The man only thinks he is important, though he is generally well respected. This is good!"

Ineda's fingers nipped his leg, her whole body bumping cheekily in closer to him. He decided she was not so alarmed after all, was putting up a good act as she whispered furiously against his bare arm. The tickle it made would have been more pleasant under other circumstances, though he forced the thought away knowing that as foster brother he had no right to harbour such arousing notions.

"Good, you say? We sit here weaponless. That man is in full armour and striding towards us with such purpose, Bran, and you claim it is a good sign?"

"Fear not. He is the centurion's scribe, the one who translates on occasion. He will be useful to us." He straightened up as the scribe halted in front of them.

"I am Eolus. I know you well. You have been carting wood for us, though why do you now bring pieces of leather and cloth?" Though guttural, he spoke Brigantian well enough.

"We wish to trade our leather and cloth for Roman coin."

The cackle that followed drew attention to them. Ineda's

fingers tightened on his leg, perhaps startled by the man's attitude.

"Do you indeed? I am no expert but the leather seems tanned well enough. Dismount. You will follow me while I find someone who will attest to its quality." His busy little hand waved Benignus off. "I will see to them now. Their cart will remain here. See it is not disturbed."

Ineda's hand grasped the sleeve of his tunic and held on, as he hobbled behind Eolus. Though none stopped their progress they were watched closely as they passed through the clutch of wood workers. He had never been able to see beyond that area and did not know what to expect as they moved on past the tented village of the legion. Some soldiers strutted around wearing full armour, but most of those he passed by wore only the breast chain mail of the auxiliaries, though there were many more in the area who only wore pale green tunics. They appeared as beasts of burden who called out to each other as they moved hither and thither and yet he suspected them to be the more skilled soldiers in some way or another.

Eolus halted at a large tent near the riverside. Many baskets lay scattered around its outside ground tethers. Some were empty and some held spilled-over cloth.

"Wait here!" Eolus scurried inside the open flap to return almost immediately with another man.

After only a brief fingering of their leather and woollen cloth the immune official seemed satisfied. Eolus translated for them.

"Onesiphorus asks if you can supply pieces of this size." Eolus held a large untrimmed piece of leather up in front of him.

Brennus looked to Ineda to answer since he had no idea. Those vivid green eyes of hers masked the triumph he could feel through her pinching fingers, her excitement stirring his very blood.

Her head nodded vigorously as she answered. "From a medium sized deer. Yes, it is possible. From a stag, also, if bigger is wanted."

After a brief exchange Onesiphorus nodded in affirmation. More rapid Latin was exchanged.

Eolus turned back, this time holding up a length of cloth about the size of a bratt, enough to make a tunic to knee length. "Your woollen cloth can be this size?"

Ineda was quick to respond. That was just as well since, again, he had no idea of the answer that was needed. She had been correct: her knowledge of cloth making was necessary. The excitement that continued to flash across her expressive little face as he watched her careful answer warmed his insides.

"Aye! And in that shade."

She pointed to a pile of wool that had been dyed the colour of pale birch leaves, the colour worn by those who scurried around conducting the deliveries. She added that she knew which root plants were likely to produce that hue along with some strong grasses that grew on the hillock near Witton. All things he had no idea of, and had not thought the knowledge would be important, though it seemed so as Onesiphorus and Eolus jabbered together.

He could understand very little of their conversation with the exception of the amount of coin they would be paid. He looked at the two coins in Onesiphorus' hand. It was very clear that the man wanted to dupe him into accepting a low fee for the goods. He had to suppress the laugh that begged for freedom. Being thought witless was perhaps not so useful after all.

"Not enough." He startled Eolus by making a statement rather than waiting for them to proffer an amount, his head shaking quite vigorously. He had heard the auxiliaries' moans about not being able to properly feed themselves on less than two of their shiny coins per day. Though the coins were large, and bright like the sun, he knew they were not gold, knew they were the coin that was mostly traded amongst the Romans although very little of it actually changed hands. Only a few days past he had heard an auxiliary complain about his tunic having been ripped so badly during training that he could no longer mend it and that a new tunic would take half a moon's worth of daily coin.

Though he and Ineda were only supplying the cloth, and not a sewn tunic, he needed more than a couple of those coins for each piece. The weavers back at Witton, and the other two villages, would spend a long time making the cloth for them and he had to make it worth their while. He would not disappoint the tribespeople though they had no idea that he and Ineda had a deeper purpose to the trading.

While he pondered what to do next Ineda intervened, her expression tearful and her voice shrill with distress.

"We cannot accept only two coins. That is not a good bargain."

He hid a grin, purposely looking askance, her silent tears looking very genuine for the official who became alarmed by her growing anguish.

"I beg you. I will be beaten, sir. The tribespeople of Witton will not accept this for their labours. We cannot deal with you for such a low amount. They will blame me." He felt her gaze fall upon him, her eyes flashing the tiniest of warnings as she petted his arm like she would do with a tiny child. "They will blame Bran, too. He is very good for hauling the cart, sir, but not so clever at handling coin."

He could have happily strangled her, mischief dripping from her tongue that he could do nothing about. But was it effective enough?

The Latin translation that followed he could only assume was good, his own understanding not yet fluent enough. When Onesiphorus wavered, Ineda made fresh tears fall.

"I beg a moment with Bran, sir?"

On their nod she dragged him behind the cart out of their sight, her delighted smirk for him only. Her exhilaration spilled over as she clutched him tight and grinned right up at him. He quelled his own smiles and encouraged her talk with a hearty nod.

Mouthing the words he squeezed her back. "Slowly tell me what to say!"

She repeated as though he had not grasped the import of it, the glint in her eye warning him not to laugh. "Bran. You must listen very carefully. We cannot go back to Witton with such a small amount of coin. They will say we are not good to represent them. They will choose another person to haul the cart, someone good at talking. You must make the Roman official understand what we need."

He ensured his words were heard, suppressing a smile that wanted to develop into a full bellied laugh. "Ineda. You know I am not quick at thinking. What should I do?"

From that point on it was easy. She instructed him in what to say to the Roman official – cunningly setting the amount of coins to five for each piece of cloth – a bargain even Onesiphorus would not overlook.

They could ask for more coins later on, once they had established the trade properly. They personally did not do it for the money, and when all was said and done it was much more important to ratify their presence every few days.

Rounding the cart he confronted Onesiphorus. Holding up his hand he repeated Ineda's coached phrase, his voice as dull and repetitive as he could make it. The chortled laughs from the Romans halted him. Realising he no longer had four good fingers and a thumb on his right hand he grabbed Ineda's and held it aloft.

"This amount of coins for each piece."

The tingling from her wrist that flowed right through his fist he put down to the exhilaration he felt at the success of their bargaining. He would not acknowledge her touch moved him in any other way, though his loins stirred anyway.

When they were on their return journey, well away from the fort and with no Roman troops in sight he broke into a happy song. Ineda's happy chortling and tuneless humming alongside him warmed him as much as her arm sliding though his, the camaraderie only broken when she squeezed his arm even tighter and reached up to peck him on his damaged cheek.

"I would love to have had you for my older brother, Bran. Neither of my brothers were such fun and they were both as discordant musically as I am."

As soon as he could he detached himself from her grip. Brother?

Ineda was accepting him as foster-brother, but did he want that? He wished he could be sure of what he did want.

Regardless of their mock sibling relationship, their trade began and regular visits were made, the Romans accepting Ineda as the spokesperson for both of them, though he was always the one who received the coin.

Chapter Eleven

AD 72 One Moon Before Imbolc – Nidd

"It will happen this day, my too doubting foster-brother! I tell you, we will get all the way into Nidd."

Brennus wanted to shout some very fine oaths. Foster-brother! He had been hearing those words far too often lately.

Ineda was so eager, her fingers slapping at his leg. Though he could not understand it when she declared in such fashion he believed her. A sunny positive attitude every journey was usual for her; her determination much better than his, but crossing the bridge all the way into the fort's interior still remained elusive after many trading visits. He was losing patience, thinking access inside Nidd would be forever denied them.

He held back his answer, still liking to tease her to the point of irritation. Though, lately, he found he desired to toy with her too much and was irked by his constantly wayward urges.

"What makes you so certain?" He shifted along the cart seat, away from her body and her tapping little fingers which were too tempting.

"We will see more today, I am sure of it," she repeated, as though he needed the reassurance, the grip of her fingers opening and closing in a squeezing caress on the leg he had just slipped away from her. A caress his body could not cope with without showing signs of stimulation.

She brazenly sidled along towards him, purposely provoking further reaction, knowing he had no board left on which to escape. She was becoming too adept at these gestures, as if she knew how she affected him, though no words proclaiming it ever passed from his lips. Or hers.

Forcing his thoughts to the task he had set himself he quelled his lust. He was becoming proficient at that, Ineda giving him plenty of opportunities for practise.

He had already passed information to Venutius regarding the supply wagons that arrived on a regular basis, and the amount of new Roman troops who swelled the numbers at the encampment. That had not been difficult since the Roman Army was extremely organised and their tented villages were so well constructed, an accounting of the rows of tents was a straightforward matter.

Knowing a contubernium of eight to ten men shared a tent gave him a very good idea that the numbers encamped were now closer to a whole cohort – a gathering that numbered close to five hundred men. By listening here and there, he had learned the lately arrived troops were from the Legio IX and had come from a large fort at Lindum, well to the south. That they were deemed to be sufficiently well trained now for venturing further north in the lands of the Brigantes, possibly even to be dispatched as far north as Garrigill, was worrying. Useful information to send on.

More small forts – like Nidd – were being built at regular intervals across mid-Brigante land.

"I feel it deep in my chest."

Brennus did not want to contemplate Ineda's chest that now burrowed into him, the mounds of her breasts rubbing against his arm. He had no idea how she transferred her conviction to him, yet her squeeze of reassurance was sufficient. He could feel her very heart beating against him, the sensation only halted when she let go of his tunic to greet a group of workers nearby.

He immediately missed the intimacy.

Much of the labouring work for the construction of the fort, and background tasks to keep the soldiers functioning on a daily basis was the purpose of the soldiers named immunes – the trained force that was part of a Roman legion. The immunes did not appear to engage in combat practice; at least he never saw any of them do any regular training, though he expected that if attacked they would fight well enough.

"These immunes are duped already."

Ineda's comment seeped into his arm as the horse plodded towards the bridge. She had already greeted many of the workers they'd met with along the path, addressing some by name. Her ploy worked extremely well, her friendly, lively manner drawing the men like bees to honey. They would never have greeted him in such pleasant fashion had he been travelling alone and it gave him time to make more observations.

They needed the security of being accepted in the Roman midst but attracting their attention in such fashion was not something that sat well with him, in fact Roman reactions to Ineda increasingly irritated him. Her freckled paleness and light hair seemed too appealing to the men along the trail. A sense of innocence still hung over her, though how innocent she really was irked him: he was no longer sure. He wanted her to be more mature, could barely wait for that to happen yet felt a need to allow her more time to grow into womanhood. The thought of her already having crossed over into womanhood with another man disturbed him greatly, though it should not because Celtic women made their own choices.

A responsibility for her welfare was all he should feel.

"Duped about what?" he asked.

He fixed his thoughts on their trading but that lasted only a small amount of time since her squirming and wriggling had restarted, her arm doing some more waving. A soft breast jiggled against his arm when she reached across him to see better.

She had gained flesh during the last moons, real curves appearing where none had been before, as maturity settled upon

131

her. It was natural growth and not overeating, since the food stocks at Witton were barely adequate for the settlers.

The farmers had reaped an abundance of autumn harvest. The hunters of Witton and the surrounding small villages hunted sufficient from the forests, and the men who fished the river constantly caught a good supply – even when the first cool winds and rains of autumn had come. Yet, the more the local Celts produced the easier it was for the Roman centurion to requisition their stocks. He came and went with Eolus, his scribe, who continually scraped on his wax tablet. Followed, of course, by his auxiliaries who carried off the food stocks they had just commandeered with the promise of Roman gold as a reward.

"Are you listening to me, Bran?"

Her fingers nipped at his middle, forcing him to answer. It was clear she concocted some new plan and until he knew her purpose it may not be good. Turning his head he asked, "Tell me then. What puts that rosy glow to your smile?"

The day had a nip in the air but that was not what animated her. Awaiting her answer he concentrated on negotiating a bad section of the path. The ruts were deepened by the overnight frost, and subsequent melt: their first real frost of winter. Snow could come any day.

"I have confidence today will be a good step forward."

Though she claimed she could not predict like her grandmother, Meaghan, there had been some instances when her declarations had been accurate.

"To what?" His words were low. Gossip was something he was careful not to make visible. The immunes and auxiliaries around them still thought him simple. He spared her a quick glance.

She was the only woman he knew who could talk without moving her lips, when she chose to. Her smile still in place she answered. "To us getting across that bridge and into Nidd. Oh, look. The very person to help us!"

His eye swept the area as they ground to a halt at the end of the inevitable queue.

Dulius.

Brennus groaned as he gathered up the reins. He hated the sight of the man, had hoped he would not be around, but there he was striding importantly towards their cart from the haggling area at the side of the path. His high pitched voice rang clear, drawing attention as he always intended it to.

"Ineda! Your smile brightens my day."

Before he could dismount, Ineda greeted Dulius, her beam as cheerful as he had ever seen.

"Good day, Dulius. The sun god favours us though the day is chill." She hesitated a moment till the man was right up close to the cart. "Or perhaps you are the favoured one? Does your name mean sun?"

Ineda had learned to string Latin words quicker than he had, though she insisted on teaching him all her newly learned language as they travelled back and forth. It was a pleasant and useful way to spend the journey time, and kept his thoughts on something other than the unwanted desires that sneaked in.

Dulius preened like a bird cleaning its own feathers. "No, indeed. Dulius means war."

Brennus coughed down into his tunic to prevent the grin that threatened to break free. At least that was until he saw the immunis reach forward to help her down.

The man was almost as short as Ineda and too familiar with her, his touch too blatant on her body as his hands cradled her torso. He had taken note of that same too-long-holding during their last visit.

Ineda seemed charmed by the man's attentions, but it was not the wool she brought to sell that drew the fool. Tempering his resentment he had to trust that Ineda knew what she was doing.

"What have you brought to us this day?" Dulius's question was accompanied by a quick rake through the hides that lay atop the pile of goods on the cart.

Though this self-important man was ridiculous he was a useful Roman to cultivate since he was second in command to the Roman in charge of all supplies. By gaining Dulius' trust he knew Ineda hoped it would give them passage over the bridge. No Celtic trader had done that yet, as far as he knew. Some of the local women favoured soldiers with their attentions, but that did not happen behind the turf walls of the fort either.

Only the forces of Rome entered through the fort gates.

There had to be a way for him to see what lay beyond the imposing entrance on the far side of the river. Realising his attention had wandered he forced himself to listen properly to Dulius.

"As before, the quality is good."

Ineda's laugh held a smile in it, never failing to charm. "We only bring you the best."

Dulius's smooth tones kept up what appeared like a one sided conversation with her. Ineda was clever, though, in her insistence that any new word be thoroughly explained.

"Dulius!" Her chide was soft. "You speak too quickly. You know I do not understand. You expect too much of me. I need your scribe, Varius, or Eolus to tell me what you have just said. I cannot possibly agree to what I do not understand."

Dulius' assistant, Varius, was never far from his side and was always happy to oblige her.

Varius translated. "Dulius says the leather you trade is the best quality anyone brings to him."

"Then tell him I have something exceptional to show him."

Ineda always had a knack for picking out the perfect words. It was a facet that he never ceased to admire about her. As usual he noted her enthusiasm was infectious to all around her, their raised eyebrows posing their own questions. Patient when necessary, he was pleased to see Ineda waited for the exchange of words before continuing.

"Tell Dulius that the commander of the fort will be very

interested in what I have today, and he should have the honour of seeing it first."

Some raucous cackling rang around the area as her words were shared.

Dulius's fingers grasped her hand. Brennus noted the squeezing as the man preened and gave a slight tilt of his head. Squashing Dulius into a grimy mess would be pleasant, but the time was not right. Instead he allowed Ineda to continue what she had started.

"If that is indeed the case then I should be the one to tell him of this."

Ineda's most charming laugh trilled. "Dulius! I am impressed. Are you now in charge of all the supplies?"

Brennus acknowledged how she played Dulius like a bard plucking at harp strings. She knew the man was far from being in charge but was testing the Roman's honesty. A cunning young woman was his Ineda, her tactics setting a heat to his heart as he silently applauded her skills.

A dull flush coloured Dulius' skin while her words were translated.

"My superior directs work in the principia, but as usual, he leaves the arrangements of all trading to me." His self importance dripped.

Though he did not look in Ineda's direction as he controlled the restless horse Brennus admired her tenacity.

"That is very good, Dulius, though I would so like to see how happy he will be when he sees what I bring him today. Is it possible for me to see him in person just this once?"

While Dulius blustered he took in the surroundings. The usual trade went on. He now knew the names of the various traders, both the local Celts and the Roman immunes alike. Those who dealt in hunt-kill were now as familiar as those who handled the supplies of wood which continued to be delivered from the forest on the far side of the fort.

Ineda's teasing laugh distracted him for a moment, almost

making him forget to concentrate on Dulius' reactions as she showed the Roman her special weave.

"You can cut it down to strips and use it as foot wraps inside the leather banding you wear across your feet."

Harsh laughter from Varius greeted her statement.

"Watch and take note!" she chided.

Both Dulius and Varius were intrigued when she slowly drew a pair of thin leather thongs from her belt. She stretched them on the ground before laying down a piece of her special warm cloth. Making a fuss of removing her boot, and calling attention to what she was doing increased the growing crowd around her, her entertaining spectacle a welcome respite from daily repetitive tasks. Raising her dress a little, to ensure all could see, she placed her bare foot onto the piece of material. Drawing the length of the strip over her toes and upper foot it took only a few deft folds at the sides and she had fashioned a snug wrap tied in place by her thongs in similar fashion to the way a Roman sandal was tied.

Bran knew this was a necessary manoeuvre for her to make but wished she did not parade herself in such a way.

"What is new about this?" Varius guffawed, his howls of derision drawing an even greater crowd.

Bran gave Dulius his due. The little puffed up Roman made an attempt to soften the mockery around them. "Roman troops in the harsh winter lands of Germania already wrap their feet, Ineda. As we will do here."

"Maybe, so."

Bran sensed Ineda's blood beginning to boil as she responded, but she held temper in check. In fact so well he greatly admired her dismissive smile and cajoling tones.

"However, they would not lose toes with my material as they do with the cloth they presently employ!"

"The winters in Germania can be very cruel." Dulius maintained his mollifying tones.

"You have no experience, yet, of our damp winter bite. Give

me your sandal!"

Ineda ordered in an imperious manner without thinking. He watched as Dulius stared at her in disbelief. Her insistent repeat drew muttered comments to ripple around. That a woman should confront Dulius in this way was entertaining, but a rash measure since he was an important man. He was on the point of intervening when he realised her smiling exuberance was winning them over, her hand gestures adding to her convincing nods. "I will show you how my cloth surpasses all you have ever used in Germania."

Under the jocular laughter that hovered around them Dulius complied, slowly untying the thongs that bound his sandal.

Bran hid a chuckle. When Ineda placed her wool wrapped foot in the man's sandal it fit the space quite well. Tying the thongs in Roman fashion she held out her neat covering for all to admire – a seemingly perfect fit. Dulius was a small man indeed. Ineda covered any possible embarrassment by patting the man's hand in much the same fashion as he did to hers.

"Now you try for yourself!"

She handed another piece of cloth over for Dulius to feel. He slid the soft weave between his fingers as though indulging a recalcitrant child while Ineda strutted around, displaying her wrapped foot to all and sundry.

As Bran looked around he noted the crowd had increased even more, many of the traders and soldiers clustering to see what the fuss was about.

Ineda whipped off the sandal and handed it back to Dulius, instructing him how to wrap his own foot to try it out. "Just like that. Warm feet now! You will endure the freezing days much better. And when the snow comes this will keep your feet snug and dry when you use our leather, or skins, to the outside. We have many more bites of frost to come yet before the weather turns back again to warmth."

He knew Ineda had already wormed out of Dulius that this was his first campaign in Britannia. The man had no true idea yet of how harsh and damp the winters could be, only hearsay from veterans who had campaigned in Britannia.

Anyone who was important in the congregated crowd clustered around to feel the pieces of soft cloth Ineda pulled from under the fur skins on the cart. In no time at all one of the guards from the bridge called over to Dulius. As far as Brennus could understand the commotion had been seen by the guards at the fort gateway and word had sped to the commanding officer.

"You are requested to take your cloth to my superior." Dulius sounded surprised.

Ineda looked smug, though only seen by Brennus when she turned, mouthing soft words. "Did I not say it was a good day?"

"Take only the special cloth in a basket. The cart remains here."

Dulius's order was to be obeyed. Suppressing a smirk Brennus had no care about his transport. Entry to Nidd was eventually at hand as they were escorted towards the temporary pontoon bridge which was still used for goods traffic. The first two steps onto the bridge made of boats lashed together were unsettling, the dipping and swaying of it something he had to become accustomed to, the basket on his arm bumping against the rope sides as he awkwardly steadied himself. He sourly noted the extra concern Dulius was taking over helping Ineda to cross, the arm tight around her waist not needed for Ineda was as nimble as a goat from Witton's upper fields. Once over he was not surprised to be led along the pathway which snaked around the left side of the turf banking. He had already noted it was mainly legionary traffic which used the main entrance. It mattered not to him which entrance they used – all he desired was to get inside the turf walls.

A real surge of excitement had to be squashed as he reached the large wooden gates. Presently they stood wide open since traffic was high, baskets being constantly delivered, and a steady stream of wooden poles being carted in. The whole view was a hive of industry, areas already set out for various purposes. Well to the left of him, and down to the end walls were row upon row of dark leather tents. To his right, and near what he had learned to be the main entrance, were horse enclosures and animal pens – some of the beasts sheltered under thatched roofs supported by tall posts, though open sided to the elements. Horse handlers fed the animals, their long double pointed hooks scooping up the hay. Carts with fresh fodder were being unloaded alongside. And even more tents were pitched beyond the horse enclosures.

Straight up ahead of him was a huge wooden building unlike anything he had ever seen. As Dulius led them towards it he took in the details. Stepping closer he realised it was not one building he was seeing but a covered walkway, behind which was a long wooden wall, openings cut out at regular intervals along its length. Tall posts held up the overhang that was covered in grasses but these were not tightly woven in the same way as his fellow Celts would weave them. The grasses were thick and more loosely bound together. Yet, though the roof structure was different from his own roundhouse the purpose was similar: shelter from the inevitable winds and rain.

Dulius chattered on to Ineda as he led them along an already well trodden pathway, around the end of the walkway and in through an impressive arched wood entrance. An empty area spread in front of them, wooden buildings to all sides. At the far end was a very large structure that was higher than any roundhouse he had ever seen, much higher than his father Tully's roundhouse roof.

"You must wait here in the principia."

Dulius nodded to the inevitable two-man guard who flanked the entrance arch and made some sort of announcement. Having given a quick reply, one of the guards hailed a soldier who stood sentinel about half way up the area. When the man trotted down he was given further orders. Brennus had no doubt Dulius' superior officer was being warned of their arrival.

So, now he knew what the principia was. The huge open space was a gathering place where soldiers could assemble. He could now see why so many poles had to be garnered from the local forests. It had taken many of them to construct the principia, the plain wooden buildings set around it built in a fashion he had never seen before. From the scurrying to and fro between doorways and entrances he worked out they must house the principal officers at the fort. The tall building at the far end had a columned walkway in front, yet not the same as he had seen around the exterior of the whole area. He listened as Dulius described their surroundings.

"Which one is your home?" Ineda asked Dulius.

"None of them. These are not houses." A tight smile flashed across Dulius' face before he rattled on.

Ineda's interest was not feigned, she really was interested, as he was, but Dulius spoke so quickly. Varius waited patiently till he had stopped talking before turning to them.

"The principia here is the main part of the fort where all important business happens. The officers do not live here; these rooms are for organising the fort and the legion. The main supply officer uses the one near the end, over there."

Brennus followed the man's pointed finger to the far left corner.

"The basilica, our great hall, is down there." Varius indicated the huge building. "Only the outside is completed properly at present, but the tribunal will be in there."

At Ineda's lively prompting Dulius explained more of the tribunal, Varius translating. "There is only a small wooden podium, a raised platform, in there for our legate, our commanding officer, to stand on but soon we will build a better one with an impressive arch around it. It is where all news is imparted to the cohort commanders and other important personnel."

Brennus stifled a smile. He knew full well that without

Ineda's feminine wiles none of this information would be passed on.

While they waited Dulius continued to prattle. "The basilica also holds our aedes, our place of worship."

Varius pointed to the far right corner as he explained. "Our shrine is still only a shell but it already houses the main cult statues for the men of the legion. We are similar to you in that we have many gods and goddesses who receive our obeisance."

A soldier emerged from the building at the far corner, hailed them and gestured them to come forward. Striding importantly in front, Dulius completed his little tour, pride rimming every word. "Our legionary standards remain in the aedes for all our soldiers of Rome to bless – legionary and auxiliary alike."

"Standards?" Ineda sounded confused though Brennus knew better.

Varius gave quick explanation of what the standards meant to the ordinary soldier – the significance of the insignia absolute, the sight of the signs held aloft on a high pole important for soldier morale.

An even more struttingly important man emerged from the last building.

"What is all this commotion about, Dulius?"

***

"I was correct, foster-brother! I knew my plan would work."

Nidd was well behind them and the road to Witton empty. Talking was now possible without being overheard as Ineda smirked and nudged Bran. She did not even attempt to keep her excitement from breaking free. Her whoop startled a few thrushes in the nearby hazels setting them into alarmed flight as they headed into the woods.

"Did I not tell you I could get us over that rickety bridge! Was that not a sight to see behind the walls?"

Bran's wry expression was hard to interpret. He was just as

excited as she was, she knew it, but in his usual fashion he let little show, his words calm. "And what knowledge do you think we have gained? That may be our only time in through those gates."

She would not let him dampen her triumph. "We have seen what the principia is like, Bran. We can now explain what happens inside those walls." Twisting around on the bench she looked away yet continued to list. "We now know what is directly behind those gates. We know there is a cleared area behind and below the rampart where they patrol. We have seen all those tents the legionary soldiers sleep under and the few wooden buildings that house some already. Now we know that in a short time they will all be housed under wood rather than leather, the reason for such a lot of wood hewing."

"Aye. I'll grant you that. But can we tell Venutius that they prepare themselves for fresh battle against the northern Brigantes?"

"No. We cannot be sure. Not yet, Bran. But we can send word that it looks as though they entrench themselves for the coming winter."

Though they had not been allowed free wander she had seen the transportation of goods going behind the principia to areas that looked like temporary storage. Shelters, similar to those at the horse enclosures appeared to be used for stocking goods, many immunes scurrying around hither and thither with full and then empty baskets. From what she did manage to see they were preparing to feed many men behind those walls for the coming moons.

"How many does Nidd hold?"

Bran was the only man who could so set her blood to boil with so few words. "I could not tell, and neither could you, though the number in and around the fort is large."

"All legionary forces?"

She studied his expression. He was checking what she had noticed. "Not many, though some of those we saw inside wore full legionary armour. Most were auxiliary forces and many were immunes. Since the immunes wore no armour we have no way of knowing if they are legionary or auxiliary troops. Why do you ask?"

Bran flicked the reins to encourage the horse over an uneven stretch of ground. "Not all the ground outside the principia was covered in tents."

She pondered what he did not say. "Are you thinking those empty areas will be filled with other soldiers, soon?"

"It is possible. The area behind those walls is very, very large. Did you note the walkways?"

Ineda allowed herself to dwell on what she had recently seen. "Do you mean the wide beaten earth pathways, or the areas under the roofed overhangs?"

"The wide edged paths."

She had taken note of them. There were four main ones leading to the four gated entrances to the fort. "They were pounded hard and very flat, men could easily march eight abreast on them."

Bran nodded in her direction before he took the horse over the low ford across the brook not far from Witton. "And enter the fort very quickly."

"Enter?" Ineda was not sure whether he meant Romans or Brigantes.

"Nidd does not yet hold all of the soldiers who could be garrisoned there. It will be good to know if more arrive before winter bites really hard."

Before the winter bites?

Ineda answered more questions, her snapping answers showing increasing annoyance. Bran did plenty of biting of his own. He was even more irritating in recent days. At that moment she wished that the winter would bite him hard. She wished she could swat him out of her existence, at times, but at others did not know how she would survive her days without talking to him. Though, as far as Bran was concerned she was just a nuisance to be amused by.

Turning away from him she was relieved when they drew closer to Witton. She had had enough of talk with Bran.

"What is that little...doing there?" Bran's frustrated grunt barely passed through his gritted teeth, the oath bitten down on.

A little smile broke free. The raising of her hand to vigorously wave made Bran sidle away from her proximity.

Madeg awaited her near the doors to Witton.

Chapter Twelve

AD 72 Imbolc – Near Witton

The shadowy figure slid out from behind the tree as Brennus approached the meeting place. Neither he nor Sorn wished to linger longer than necessary, their information customarily passed on with no unnecessary exchange of words.

"The cohort commander is not at Nidd?"

Brennus shook his head. "Not expected back for some nights and perhaps not until the moon wanes."

"A good time, then, for Venutius to attack?"

"Nay!" He was scathing of the interest flaring in the eyes of the messenger. The man was a trusted courier of Venutius but over eager for new battle without full regard to the consequences. "In his absence they have doubled both guard forces around the fort, the soldiers on the inside palisade, and the auxiliary guard by the riverside. Venutius would gain no advantage from an attack at present."

Spittle shot from Sorn's mouth, his face scrunched up in hatred. "How many are presently inside?"

"Only half of the cohort left to ride east with the commander. I believe at least two hundred are presently inside the fort."

"Venutius could take them easily."

Brennus leaned down to speak directly into the courier's face. He knew full well the man disliked his sightless eye boring down at him, but it was an effective measure of intimidation.

"He could. But the time is not ripe. We need to know more of the plans of Cerialis before an attack is made, and you forget the hundreds of immunes who are also camped both inside and outside. They may not daily bear arms but those men will also fight any Brigante who dares to become aggressor."

Sorn was not done. "Venutius can summon plenty of men to crush that amount."

"Aye! Venutius could gather enough warriors but what would be gained – apart from spilling the blood of Roman underlings who must follow orders from their superiors? Would it halt the plans of Cerialis to subdue and control all of Brigantia?"

AD 72 Two Moons after Imbolc – Nidd

"Your tongue has been cut out?"

Brennus waited for some retaliation but Ineda only huffed and looked away from him. She had been stubbornly ignoring him since they had set off for Nidd, but that was a state of affairs that happened often now, and especially when they had had an argument over some matter or other. In such cases silence greeted him more often than irritated replies. He disliked the distance that now existed between them but knew his comments did nothing to improve the situation.

"Is today going to be another of those good days?"

He thought his words more conversational but Ineda clearly did not think so. Her one glare was very telling. From experience he knew if he let silence reign for long enough she would be unable to maintain it. She would talk again soon enough.

In general, though, Brennus was pleased with progress. Despite that their access to the inside of Nidd had not happened again, the regular trading he and Ineda conducted meant they heard a mixture of real news and some misleading rumours. He watched carefully, filtered the gossip, and passed on the important information to Venutius. Though Sorn met regularly with him he had made no better a friend of him moons later. They were in many ways too alike, yet in others too dissimilar. Before Whorl he knew he would have had the impatience of Sorn. Now his former rashness had long since gone, extreme caution replacing it. Not cowardice, merely a sharper vigilance.

More troops from Legio IX had recently arrived at Nidd although some others had left the fort. Whether or not it was some sort of usual exchange process he could not tell. In essence, only the one cohort remained assembled there. Where the other cohorts of the Legio IX were, he had no inkling.

"We are approaching the fort, Ineda. Will you still refuse to talk to me when we get there?"

Success.

She faced him full on, her glare accompanied by little pursed lips. "You know I will not endanger our trade, Bran. I am still very vexed with you but will not let that affect our dealings today. I am correct about the Legio II Adiutrix being raw recruits even if you will not acknowledge that I can find out information just as well as you can. I know it sounds implausible, but it has to be true!"

Time after time he had warned Ineda about the perils of setting up communication lines with Venutius, claiming he could pass on any messages with no risk to her. But Ineda, being the stubborn woman she was, had gone ahead and organised her own courier. Their recent argument had not been about her sending a message to her contact, it had been about the fact that she was not as discerning as he was. In his opinion, the rumour about the inexperience of the II Adiutrix needed to be proven before sending on word to Venutius. Ineda had disagreed, arguing that speed was necessary since it may be useful for the forces of Venutius to attack an untrained force before they could become better trained.

He could not dispute that there had been some dissention at Nidd about new troops who were expected to arrive soon. The soldiers he had heard scoffing and blustering at the fort complained that they had no time to pamper the II Adiutrix who were still garrisoned much further south at Lindum. A visit to Lindum could prove the rumour but it was well to the south, a trek of many days on foot since using a horse to journey with would perhaps make him too observable. He had also heard tell that Cerialis wanted the II Adiutrix to be fully ready for action in the north, before any new battle with the forces of Venutius.

He had argued with Ineda that they needed to first establish if Cerialis was giving the II Adiutrix a different kind of training. She still disagreed with him.

His Brigante king played a waiting game, but that would not last since many northern Celtic tribes had steadily rallied to Venutius and were currently congregated at his Stanwick stronghold. He had a gut feeling the skirmishes that had lately taken place would escalate into a larger scale battle – though not till better weather set in.

It now made sense to him that Cerialis had chosen to split the cohorts of the Legio IX, establishing them at bases around mid-Brigante territory. Rome needed a strong hold across the huge tract of land if there was continued resistance from Venutius.

"Ineda!"

Brennus flicked the rein to slow down the horse when he saw who called out. What he really wanted to do was hurry it along in the opposite direction. Ineda drew an even larger crowd of Roman admirers as their trade continued. Some were immunes, though many were auxiliaries. Their progress to the small market by the bridge was constantly halted by the men wanting to greet Ineda.

"Good day to you, Publius." As always Ineda was pleasant. His argument with her pushed aside as she greeted the Roman.

Brennus hated the grovelling smile on the man's face.

Publius was one of Dulius' little band of soldiers involved in the supplying of the fort. Publius bustled about in an even more haughty way than his superior and croaked like a toad.

"To you likewise, Ineda. We must talk about the amount of leather you are supplying."

"We must?"

Brennus admired that Ineda was careful never to offend anyone as she probed further.

"Why need that be?"

"The leather and wool you supply is very fine though not plentiful enough for our current needs."

Brennus paid more attention. Was Publius saying there was no further need for them to come regularly to the fort? That would not be good news since he was one of the most regular in sending news from the fort to Venutius.

Ineda, as usual, was quick to answer. "We can work harder, Publius. I can get the villages to produce more."

"Yes, yes. I'm sure of it, Ineda. Your tribespeople do very well, and we expect that."

Brennus waited for more information, his control of the horse a distraction he created rather than him being unable to handle it. It was a useful trick as the Romans tended to think he was too busy to listen.

Starved of the sight of a woman Ineda filled Roman eyes pleasantly though she took care to never single out anyone especially. Publius came even closer, his hand resting on the cart next to Ineda's knee. Brennus held his temper in check. *An cù!* If the Roman dung moved the tiniest bit closer he would lose some fingers.

"We need even more than you can produce." Publius' voice dropped as he looked up at Ineda, and then looked askance, quickly and furtively as though he did not wish to be overheard. His words were the merest whisper. "I am tasked with finding supplies for a very large fortress that is planned east of here. More of your excellent leather supplies will be needed."

East? Brennus' ears pricked up. Why would Cerialis want to build a large fort to the east? This definitely required a lot more investigation.

Ineda bent down to whisper in the toad's ear. "I believe we can find more skins if we are able to go further afield and gain supplies from villages at a greater distance than Witton. We would need more freedom to travel at short notice, though. Your local patrols would need to allow our passage beyond their usual perimeters."

They needed to widen the areas they covered to glean more information and legitimate access was necessary for that. Brennus masked a smirk. Ineda was so adept at setting a cunning lure. He swung down from the cart and steadied his now very restless animal. She had the inept man so easily doing her will. He dampened the urge to forbid her from improving her already alluring ways but had no power to do so. That was beyond the role of frustrated foster-brother to a now fully grown woman.

No matter. Sorcha would relieve his frustrations. She was good at that.

AD 72 After Beltane – Quernium

A new fort was built at Quernium, to the north-east of Nidd, though this was not the one Publius had whispered about. It was larger than Nidd, and over the next few moons it became a far more important place to visit. Also manned by the auxiliaries of the Legio IX, organised by a few legionary officers, the design was very similar to Nidd though it was sufficient to quarter at least two cohorts, their tented village having removed itself behind its turf walls till the inner wooden buildings could be constructed.

Trading there took Brennus and Ineda into more northerly territory. Not as far as where Venutius bided his time at

Stanwick, but the first half of the route to Quernium was the same. For some of the treks he alone took the goods for trading, while Ineda organised their supplies from the villagers around Witton. On those trips, when he travelled alone, it was easier to make more regular contact with Sorn. He could exchange messages as soon as he had new information.

Sorn was skilled at appearing in front of him as though having appeared from nowhere; the man being one of the best trackers he had ever encountered. Dropping down from a limb to land right in front of the horse, before nimbly catching the reins to slow it down, was not unusual – though Sorn never did it from the same tree.

"Venutius awaits details of the roll call at Quernium." Sorn's slow drawl did not even seem a hint out of breath.

"No different from our last meeting. Only around half of one cohort is in residence. The same amount of patrols scout to the north-west – as they did on my last visit."

"Two centuries?"

Sorn tested his information at every opportunity. He was never sure if the man held him suspect in some measure. Perhaps even thought he was indeed in the pay of the Romans – both literally for the trading coin and figuratively for trade of two-way information.

"As I told you last time. Only one century has been sent to scout the land. I will repeat what I said last time, though the fort is capable of housing two cohorts it does not yet hold a full complement."

"When do they expect more to arrive?"

"Activity was high today at the food stores. The new grain buildings were being filled at a fast rate. I expect that to mean an imminent arrival of more troops but I did not hear it from any lips."

"You there!" The sound of the barked order from behind made Brennus turn in a flurry. "Get out of the way! You block the road with that paltry vehicle."

Sorn disappeared into the bushes as swiftly as he had arrived. The man wasted no time in pleasantries, his presence not even noticed when Brennus half turned his cart to speak to the Roman who led the small patrol which came trotting along the road.

***

Bran watched for signs of Sorn on the usual stretch of path the next time he travelled, even though the man did not usually declare himself when Ineda accompanied him. They journeyed home in their sturdy new cart designed to seat them both side by side with more space between. They had just had a successful visit to Quernium though he had learned little that was new, and none of that vital. The inside of the fort took shape very quickly, although all he ever saw was through the open gates. Ineda whistled and hummed a merry little tune, happy with herself and was in one of her provocative playful moods.

"What did Lipanus say to you?" he asked her. Lipanus was the Roman scribe that they dealt with at Quernium.

Ineda was not too keen to tell him, the pursing of her lips always such a tease. He waited patiently knowing she would not sustain her silence, she was too excited for that.

"They want double our quantity of cloth next time." Her gleeful smile warmed him deep inside.

The information was mundane though her enthusiasm meant she was withholding something much more relevant. "How do you think to achieve that?"

"You know how it can be achieved. All I need to do is go further west to the villagers of Well and Snape. We have not yet taken cloth from their looms. It is possible and you know it!"

He curbed his temper. She was always so full of ideas but short on a sense of safety. "And when do you plan to do that? Your days are full ensuring our current supply."

He ignored the barb in her now darkened green eyes. "You

always have some excuse, Bran, for not liking my plans. We can go there in two days time and negotiate with those settlers."

"We?"

"Yes. We. You also need to bring more leather and furs to Quernium."

"Since when do I need to do that?" He so enjoyed the colour rising in her pale cheeks.

"Since Lipanus told me just a short while ago. They need more tanned leather, but they also want more furs from us."

"I heard that part. What else did he say?" He kept his tone flat even though her tease was well done, drawing out the real news as long as she could.

Ineda's merry noises accompanied the chirruping birds above. "The Roman Governor is expected to visit Quernium sometime soon. And that is not all. Cerialis plans to build more small forts north-westwards – also very soon."

Though he had not personally heard that part, Brennus was not surprised. He had experienced enough of Roman expansion to see that as soon as a tract of land appeared settled and subdued the Roman boundary moved further out across mid-Brigante territory.

All of what Ineda had just said was useful knowledge to pass on to Venutius but something else caused her excitement to linger. The cart had not travelled much further when she pulled at his sleeve. He slowed the horse. She could barely contain herself, her face so full of excitement he banished the overpowering urge to kiss her.

He pulled his gaze away and studied the surrounding valley. He reminded himself of his latest agreement with her father, Ruarke, as he listened to her prattle.

"Cerialis is expected to go first to Eboracum, to the huge new legionary garrison fortress, the one south-east of Witton. Before the end of the present moon's cycle the Roman Governor expects to meet there with Brigante negotiators. I just heard that some of those negotiators are said to be from Garrigill."

The mention of Garrigill had his blood racing. "And they go to Eboracum?"

Eboracum was the large fort that Publius had whispered about. Brennus was not sure how he felt about the news. He rarely allowed himself to think about his past life and thinking about Garrigill and his family would open hurtful wounds.

"We must make sure to be there when the Garrigill contingent are at Eboracum. Even if you cannot talk to them it would be good to see them, would it not?"

Ineda was so excited about the prospect he knew he had to say something to mollify her. "Ineda. We do not deliver to Eboracum."

He vowed he would go, but he would also be alone on the journey to Eboracum. He wanted to see his brother Lorcan, though it could only happen if his brother never knew anything about it, or the fact that he still lived.

It was a mere three days later when news came via Sorn about the arrival of Cerialis. The Roman Governor had marched north with another cohort of the Legio IX, leaving only two known cohorts of the IX at Lindum, and an unknown amount of II Adiutrix. Cerialis was indeed at Eboracum and had wasted no time in organising meetings with the northern Celtic tribes.

Chapter Thirteen

AD 72 Almost Lughnasad – Witton

"Will you come with me, Bran?" Ineda was certain of his answer but she asked anyway. Bran had made many excuses over the last days, had made many comments about her being able to go to the outlying villages without him.

"You have no need of my company, Ineda. Take your lapdog with you. He will waste no breath denying you anything."

Bran's expression was impassive as usual but she could always detect his annoyance. Any time she mentioned Madeg it seemed inevitable that Bran took the high hand, as an elder brother might do, the draw at the damaged side of his mouth more pronounced when his temper rose. The villages were further west than they usually travelled to. It was a risk she took going there since she knew they were more resistant to trading with Roman scum. In the short time they had been organising their leather, hides and cloth she had learned just which villages had succumbed easily to the idea of trading with the suppressors and which had not. The further west and north-west the less inclined those villagers were to having any connection with the Romans. They still traded some goods as Celt to Celt, but wanted no commerce with anyone else.

"You know they have more goats in those hill settlements, Bran. They can make twice the amount of special wool that our closest villagers produce, and they can likely collect pelts even quicker than our usual hunters do."

"I fear you are coming to like organising this trade more than what you deem your real purpose, Ineda!"

"How can you think that? You know I tolerate the pawing scum, but only to make them impart more of their news."

His jaw firmed as she continued to glare at him. She hated him sometimes, especially at a time like this.

"The trade means nothing to you?"

Restraining the urge to either stomp around, or to whack him across the head, she compromised instead. "I do like the organising of the trade, and I know I am very good at it. Men may know more of hides and leather but they know nothing of the weaving of cloth!"

Since he still looked unperturbed she felt her anger rise even more. "Not many options are available to free a woman from the confines of a hearth, Bran of Garrigill. I have not had the pleasure of being given a warrior woman's training so I will enjoy any reason which allows me free access to journey across our lands."

From the set of Bran's jaw she saw he would not relent. His eyes remained cold as he pointedly looked to the doorway of his roundhouse.

"Take Madeg. He is a fine hunter and will be a good guard for you if he can keep his hands only on his spear."

"What is wrong with you, Bran?" Bile rose in her gorge. "I thought you now favoured Madeg, since both you and my father have had words with him."

"I will repeat. Madeg is a fine hunter. He will negotiate for you and guard you well."

Bran strode to the entranceway and halted, his arms crossed over his brawny chest. He could stride quite well now. His leg had healed as best as it ever would and his limp was not so noticeable since he had worked out ways to compensate for his different leg lengths. The limp was now only produced for effect in front of Roman presence.

She knew what his posture meant: he expected a visit from

Sorcha. A sneer was stifled since Sorcha would not visit him for much longer. Ineda's sweep out through the entrance tunnel was as dignified as she could make it.

AD 72 After Lughnasad – Eboracum

Brennus reached the new road in time to find a place to shelter. He knew Ineda had thought he was expecting a visit from Sorcha but that was not the case. To arrive at Eboracum in time he had had to sneak away immediately after Ineda had flounced off. He knew her moods very well by now. When he thwarted her plans she rarely talked to him for days, save any necessary interaction regarding their trading. They were not expected to deliver to any fort for some days hence, so he had just time enough for a fast gallop to Eboracum.

Such speed had not happened, of course. Unknown to Ineda, he had borrowed a fine mount from the Witton horse handlers but had had to be circumspect about where he rode the horse hard. There were too many Roman patrols to be avoided in some areas. Parts of his journey he was familiar with, but the land covered during the last bit of the ride he had never undertaken before. By the time he got closer to the valley floor where Eboracum was built he feared his desire to remain undetected had cost him too much time. At the last Celtic village he had passed through, the villagers had told him he only had a very short ride to go before he would see the place where two rivers met on the flat plain of the valley, the site of the fortress. He gave thanks to Taranis that their description of the route had been very good.

Coming down a low hill he was now close enough to see the activity at Eboracum in the distance. He dismounted and tethered his horse in a small copse of trees well off the small beaten pathway. Unless anyone entered the copse the horse would remain hidden. He made his way back to the hedgerow bordered road.

He wanted to see, yet not be seen; his height always an impediment in tight spaces. Crouching behind a bush was never the best cover, though he could see well enough through the dense hawthorns. The barbs gouged his hands and face but mattered not a whit as he rearranged the green bratt again to ensure his hair was covered.

All he wanted was a glimpse of his brother.

He settled down to wait.

The cramped captivity was a trial to his Whorl-injured bones before he heard movements. Still out of sight around a bend in the road he estimated there to be a good number of horses trotting his way. The track in front of him was flat, as was the countryside around but the route of the pathway was determined by the proximity of the wider river that harboured the fort of Eboracum. Where he stood the hedgerows grew thickly, protecting the field areas behind him from the breezes off the riverside.

"A short distance only to go now."

Without peering through the foliage he knew the voice must come from a legionary, the Latin sounding fluent with no trace of coarseness, the reply muffled by the hooves of the beasts. Leaning in to the gap between the branches he spied the first bright flashes of metal chest armour as the soldiers rounded the curve. When the file trotted towards him he counted twenty-four legionary soldiers, marching neatly in pairs, behind a centurion. Following them was a sizeable band of straggling mounted Celtic warriors: at least ten. At their rear Brennus guessed was another ten or more Roman auxiliaries. He did not bother to count them, interested only in scanning his fellow Celtic warriors.

The first five or six he had no knowledge of, certain he had never before set eyes on them. Then, unaware of his tense grasp on the closest branch, the clean snap of it surprised him, the blood coursing through his veins like the surge of a river in spate as a small trickle of blood rushed from the sharp tear in his palm.

He blinked the sudden moisture from his eyes, the fierceness of his feelings almost overwhelming. An awkward swallowing was followed by a tight grimace. Sheer will prevented him from blanking out the scene. Painful though it was to stand tight, and not cry out, his grip tightened even more.

Lorcan looked no different from their last meeting. Thanking his god, Taranis, he could see his brother's fine looks had escaped the ravages he himself had suffered. No recent scars marked Lorcan's face, the grim determination he could see there an expression he knew well. He guessed what was going through Lorcan's head. It would not be pleasant thoughts at being so tightly escorted to Eboracum – but the measure would have been accepted as part of the arrangements. Lorcan might not like the Roman tethering, but he was the finest delegate Brennus had ever met.

Blinking back memories of his brother's negotiating skills he looked at the warrior riding alongside Lorcan. At first glance he had thought all the warriors to be men. Not quite; the exception was the woman who was to have been his wife. Riding proudly beside his brother, Nara of Tarras looked very well. She too had escaped injury to her face, her beauty undamaged. In former days he had seen Nara of Tarras wear warrior-maiden clothing. Presently she wore the garb of a princess. A woven circlet held back stray tresses from her forehead. Threads of gold wound through the two side braids that dangled at her jaw line, the remainder of her hair hanging free in a swathe of auburn ripples.

"They may separate you from us on arrival, Nara." Lorcan's tones were low but passing so close that Brennus had no trouble hearing him. "If that is so, I will insist that we do not start any proceedings till you join us. Remember that you are the lips of the Selgovae."

Brennus noted the smile of adoration that passed between

his brother and Nara before she answered, equally circumspect. "If they do, I will not be parted long from you, my husband, though I do also remember where my origins lie."

No more of their conversation was heard as the file trotted past. Brennus took note of only one other Brigante that he recognised. Shea of Ivegill, of the Carvetii tribe, was also a very tough representative. A tight smile slid up his jaw as he imagined the meeting between Governor Cerialis and the Brigante contingent. The Romans might hold the upper hand in the territory around Eboracum but they did not yet hold complete sway in the areas overseen by Shea, or his brother Lorcan.

Before he moved away he closed his eyes and committed to memory the scene that had just passed by. Though he did not know the other Brigantes he could describe them well enough to Sorn. Venutius, naturally, would be well aware of who was in the band of envoys, though the king did not directly deal with Governor Cerialis.

"What are you doing behind his hedge?"

The startled yelp of one of the auxiliaries had him whirling so fast his leg failed him and he stumbled to the ground. His heart thundered, the blood rushing to his head as he looked up.

One of the Romans had slipped through a gap just a little further on to relieve himself. Stuffing himself back into his small clothes the soldier brandished the spear that had been thrust against the foliage and ran towards him.

"Get up!"

When Brennus lumbered to his feet, his practiced blank stare in place, the soldier poked at him with the pilum, hard enough to pierce his clothing. The auxiliary was a small dark little man, speaking a form of language not unlike Brennus' own. He guessed the man was from the Iberian areas where Celtic speech was fairly similar.

He made sure to stutter, his words as though coming from an infant, whilst praying to Taranis that the auxiliary's shout had not been picked up by his companions on the other side of the hedge. The last thing he needed was to have the auxiliary troop push through and discover him.

"I…just…"

He had no visible weapon, his spear still tied to his horse. Even without it he reckoned he could easily tackle the little turd and overpower him, but not the thirty or so others who had passed by and he dared not upset the progress of his brother and the rest of the negotiators to Eboracum. Their purpose was too important. Furthermore, he had no wish to be exposed. Lorcan must not know he had seen him. His mind working furiously he attempted a friendly sort of smile.

"Just like…to see…your shiny…" He pointed to the man's helmet, his head cocked to the side, the sheepish expression of one of dull wit on his face.

The soldier was suspicious. "My helmet?"

Brennus grinned, ensuring the stretching at his scar made his smile even more lopsided than usual, his hand reaching out as though wanting to clap an animal's flank.

The tip of the pilum jabbed right into his palm, the soldier clearly alarmed by his imprudent gestures. Biting down on the pain, as though impervious to its sting Brennus hoped it was so unusual to approach a Roman in such manner.

It worked. The soldier backed away as though frightened by the sight of such a huge imbecile.

"Get back to your village. Go now!"

The pilum repeatedly jabbed at him as Brennus turned and lurched away, making sure his limp was the best he could make it without falling over. The sound of someone calling from over the hedge had sweat pooling down his backbone though he continued to limp away as if he heard nothing.

The soldier on his side shouted back. "It is just…a creature I was deriding. I will not be long."

The soldier could not see Brennus' relieved smiles as he hobbled his way across the field. There was a roundhouse village on the horizon – it seemed the soldier assumed that was where he headed. Only when he had gone a good distance did he turn to look. The soldier had disappeared.

He waited a while before he headed back to his horse, the copse of trees in a different direction from the village. It gave him time to give thanks to Taranis. If the soldier had not been fooled he dreaded to think on what would have happened had the man called out to his centurion. Perhaps being a superstitious Romanised Celt had some advantages. People born genuinely witless were feared by some as being a particularly bad omen.

Wending his way back to Witton, Brennus reflected on the group of Brigante negotiators he had just seen. Though there were many men unknown to him he was confident they would be just as adept as his brother and Shea of Ivegill, and Nara of Tarras had a fine way with words. She would not hold back during the coming to terms. Nara would have made him a very fine wife, a woman any man would be proud to have by his hearthside, but her love had never been for him. From the looks he had just seen exchanged Lorcan had undoubtedly gained that and still retained it.

He resolved to do without a wife. He had no need for one since his sexual needs were fulfilled by Sorcha.

Yet seeing his brother with a loving wife had set a restlessness in him. Perhaps it was time for him to move on with a new part of his life, even though he knew he and Ineda had been regularly sending on valuable information to Venutius. Nothing had been particularly dangerous, save a few moments like the one that had just occurred when they had been asking too many questions. The trading and the message sending was becoming routine.

Maybe he would not remain at Witton for much longer.

Brennus paced around his small roundhouse. Everything about Witton stifled him, now. He had had very little that was new to report on the troop movements at Eboracum and even less about developments at Quernium for days now. The winter season was nigh and the fortresses were settling into what seemed to be the typical over-wintering pattern, as far as he had learned. No new troops had arrived. No exchanges made for others from garrisons elsewhere in Britannia. The harsh winter days were spent training and drilling inside the fortress walls and only on the few occasions during skirmishes – or ambushes to convoys by Celtic tribesmen – had there been much Roman activity outside of those walls.

The lack of action rankled since he had learned that even more supporters of Venutius had been converging at Stanwick, the oppidum of the king, for days now. His gut told him that King Venutius was almost ready to attack – though a winter offensive was never done by Celts either.

"What has kept you?" His comment rattled out after Sorcha entered through the tunnel.

"Nothing that affects you."

Sorcha's tone was just as snippy as his had been. He looked at his sometime lover. The baby she carried made her look tired and worn.

"Will you tell me now? Is this baby mine?"

When he had noticed her change of body some moons ago, Sorcha had been unwilling to tell him, though she had still been eager for him to bed her. He was less keen but could not bring himself to send her away immediately. And now the growing evidence of her motherhood was much advanced. As far as he knew, he had never before sired a baby.

"It is a Celtic warrior's baby and that is all I need to know!"

Sorcha's declaration was not good enough for him. He respected that she was honest but could not continue to have her visit any longer.

"I will acknowledge it if you tell me it is mine." He knew his tone was flat but he could summon little enthusiasm under the circumstances. It seemed likely she would never tell him who the father was.

Sorcha had never been venomous in his presence but she was now. "This baby will be acknowledged by my hearth-husband. Of the five lovers I have taken recently only my hearth-husband loves me and accepts my needs." Her voice grew shrill as she exited. "Encourage a new visitor to your hearthside, Bran, because it will not be me."

Chapter Fourteen

AD 73 One Moon Before Beltane – Witton

"I tell you Madeg is sure of this!"

Bran's sigh drifted to the clouds as he scanned the white wispy traces having laid down the ocarina he had been playing just outside his roundhouse. She knew that he, too, had heard of the new Roman who was fast becoming the most spoken of Legate. This Agricola of Legio XX was said to be much more aggressive than the legion commanders they had prior knowledge of. They had to act soon but Bran was being his usual stubborn self when she presented a new plan to him.

"It is an idea that is fraught with danger, Ineda. We cannot just go south-west to find out if it is accurate news."

She refused to be set aside. Conscious of being like an irritating hound, she persisted. "Once we are beyond the usual western places we normally visit for our trade who is to know we plan to journey further? When we return we can say the horse was lame or…the weather set in too foul to progress with the cart. Our return to Witton has been delayed before and no harm has befallen us because of it."

Bran respected her judgement in many things, however, she knew he thought her still too inclined to be over enthusiastic and without thorough forward planning. She was about to prove him wrong, again.

His one seeing eye fixed on her in an intimidating stare, but she would not be swayed by his tactic. The words spat from his mouth. "The Beltane fires are almost here. The sky gods look favourably on us and the days fare warm and pleasant. What poor weather would prevent us?"

Her scornful return might have impressed Madeg, but not Bran. "We will not journey on with the cart. It will remain hidden in a forest area till we reclaim it on our return."

The beginning of a smirk tipped up one corner of his mouth, a disbelieving twinkle lurking in his blue eye. "You think to ride behind me on our horse?"

He waited for her answer. Their horse was a game little beast but the mare was now far too worn to be carrying two people, especially with one of his size as part of the burden. A smirk of her own won over on caution. Bran had experience of it before and knew she had more to tell. A sense of triumph bubbled inside her.

"On our new horse, yes."

"New?"

***

"Be at rest, Ineda!"

The wind soughing through the trees, the occasional bird call and scuffle of a small animal replaced Ineda's chatter. Brennus hated being irked by her but it seemed to happen regardless of what she did, or he said. And he was much more annoyed with himself, loathed the short temper that constantly sat on his shoulder and nipped at his ear.

One thing he could always rely on was that Ineda knew exactly when he had listened to enough of her mundane updates on people she encountered daily as she went about the business of ensuring the regular supply of cloth, her chatter abruptly halting after his harsh words. Perhaps she had acquired more of a sixth sense from her grandmother, Meaghan, than even she realised.

He had found himself falling in with her plans to travel to

the Setantii, despite the fact that he did not want to be on a journey to anywhere with her. She increasingly became a burden he no longer wanted to shoulder, the pledge made with her father such a trial to keep honoured. Images of her as a lover plagued him daily but Ruarke hinted regularly that Madeg would make a fine son when the time came for Ineda to declare Madeg her hearth-mate. The thought of her sharing a roundhouse with Madeg, or any other man, still infuriated to bubbling point.

It was easier when he avoided seeing her.

Brennus sighed as she shifted her body back towards his on the new horse that had been gifted to them, so close that the silver bangle pressed into his chest. He still wore it though now found it to be encumbrance, his promise to Meaghan difficult to comply with. A constant voice inside told him to just give the ring to Ineda and be done with it since she was the granddaughter Meaghan had referred to, yet Meaghan's other words prevented him from doing that. It was the weak plea in Meaghan's squeezing fingers that stopped him, her old voice assuring him to keep it for the woman who would truly win his heart.

That woman would never be Ineda, not any more. She had grown out of her immature fascination of him and even seemed to loathe him now, all the time finding fault, and was constantly short tempered with him. He had done too well to dissuade her in his role as foster-brother.

He wanted her to choose him at the next Beltane fires, yet knew he would not be her choice. He had recently seen her dally with a number of the young men who lived around Witton, though he had no idea who she would choose. Madeg most likely would be her favoured mate, but not knowing who it would be angered him as much as knowing who it would not be. His head was a muddle. Lust grew daily; other feelings deep inside were something he refused to contemplate.

He had not made love to any woman for moons and

frustration sat tight on him. He had looked at other women around Witton, needing a replacement for Sorcha as a substitute to not having Ineda, but not one single female stirred any interest. No one looked at him with lust in their eyes either. He was tolerated, but he knew his dour attitude tended to dissuade. There was no delusion in him; it was all to do with his temper.

The horse was restless under him, not yet used to two people riding its back. Ineda had acquired the beast through some form of exchange, though he had no desire to know how that exchange had been accomplished. She claimed the gelding was a straight trade that Madeg had organised between her and his villagers. Believing that statement was difficult, though he was sure she had never before lied to him.

Anger burbled. He was sure Madeg had been her lover for a long while. He had no claim to be jealous yet he was. He slid back on his horse when he felt her burrow into him even more, widening his legs across its back to enable him to make space between their lower bodies. What he had no need of was the curves of her buttocks pressing closer. Want warred with denial.

Preoccupied with quashing the frustration that invaded him, the stirring of the hairs at the back of his neck startled him. He knew instinctively they were not caused by the strong breeze that blew from behind, and they were nothing to do with Ineda either. Though he had seen no evidence of anyone around, Roman or Celt, his innate warrior sense of danger was still acute.

Jaw tightened, his words whispered at her blonde tresses, the braids lying tight at her ears. The day was early enough but by dusk much of her wavy hair would have unravelled from the leather restraints. Thick and lush with health and vitality the very strands seemed to crackle at him. "We are approaching the Setantii settlement. Guard well what you say while we are there for we do not know yet if trust is appropriate."

Her teeth-clipped words muffled into his chest when she

squirmed around to answer him, her eyes darting exasperation. "I do not need that advice, Bran. I know well how the negotiating process goes."

Draping his wrists more firmly around her small waist he drew her closer. His feelings could not be paramount: she was in his care.

"Halt and dismount!"

The sudden call from the hedgerow he was ready for. Pulling on the rein to slow the horse a group of warriors disgorged themselves from the bushes, blocking the pathway immediately in front of him. He slid from the gelding, his tight grip at her waist belt remaining firm.

"We have come to talk with Iohan, chief of the settlement of Scortin."

When silence greeted his words he gestured to the leather pouch at his waist, a general one that had no bearing on sheathing his weapons. After a cautious nod from one of the warriors, he extracted a small item and held it flat out on his left palm. "I bring this from our druid leader, Tuathal, but I will place it only into the hands of Iohan himself."

Twisting it around, he clamped it tight between two fingers and held it aloft, in order that the sparkling amber stone should catch the sun's rays. The bratt pin was of a simple interwoven design in silver, but it was the amber stone that had significance. Tuathal's stone carried a message that words could not convey.

Little was said to him as he paced behind the band into the settlement of Iohan, Ineda still on the horse.

Once seated at the hearthside of Iohan, he breathed only a little easier. Their welcome seemed cordial enough but he still had doubts.

"My hearth is yours, Bran of Witton." Iohan was amiable. "And your companion is also most welcome."

Brennus had noted the interest Ineda had produced during their escort to the settlement and pondered over how to introduce her, but found he had no need to since she took the initiative.

"I am Ineda, Bran's foster-sister."

He had to be imagining it, but it seemed the smiles and expressions of awareness on the faces of the warriors around the fireside were even greater than before. Masking his jealous feelings he paid full attention to his host.

"Tell me what you know of the summer plans of Cerialis?" Iohan's tone was demanding. He was almost as large as Brennus was, though many winters older, the greying hair at his temples now in the thinnest of side-braids.

"I know about his determined progress in building small auxiliary run forts all over mid-Brigantia. So far Quernium is the nearest to be built to Venutius' stronghold."

As he added more details his eye scanned the gathering. Some of the warriors around the fireside listened to him but more continued to assess Ineda. It distracted him and he needed to concentrate.

"What of the II Adiutrix?"

Brennus studied Iohan carefully, the chief's tone nearly as abrupt as his own father's had been, his stare intent. Edginess to Iohan's posture made him guess the Setantii leader was not content to sit idle for too long. What he had heard of Iohan had proved the man to be a fierce warrior who would protect his own slice of territory very well – though he had not yet had much interaction with the Roman Army. Total domination of the west coast was still well south of Iohan's small Setantii stronghold of Scortin.

Brennus was careful about the information he shared. "Only three cohorts that I know of from the II Adiutrix have been moved from the garrison fortress at Lindum. One of the cohorts has split into two and they presently occupy the new small forts built in Coritani and Parisi territory to the north-east of Lindum. A second cohort has settled at Eboracum. The third is split into smaller detachments and has been sent to the north-west."

"Did you not already say they have built no new forts near the western coast?"

He tried to force calm to his words. "Aye. There have been no new forts that I know of near the lands of the Setantii, and Carvetii, but I said nothing of Roman encampments. Small exploratores patrols have been seen in many places. Cerialis splits his army very effectively as he widens his claimed territory for Rome. At present they still remain under leather tents but that may change at any moment. They now hold sway over much of the land from around the fort at Nidd to where the Celts fell at Whorl."

"I have heard there has been little resistance and no major attacks by the forces of Venutius."

He kept his temper. The man was becoming deliberately provoking and disrespectful of the Celts of the north. "King Venutius may not have engaged in major battle, recently, but there have been many small skirmishes."

It surprised him when Ineda joined in the conversation since she had been so quiet at his side. He was not sure why since she usually had plenty to add, though the fact that the gathering only included one other woman might be the reason. Or it may be that although many warriors seemed interested in her as a woman there was also a degree of distrust in their glances; even more acute when they regarded him.

Dedication was evident in Ineda's vehement addition. "There are many Brigantes, like us, who do not accept the yolk of Rome, and many who still perish for their fervour."

Iohan's tone was clipped. "Aye. And so it should be. My settlement is vulnerable to attack from more than one Roman force and to prevent total slaughter I must be prepared with the best knowledge of Roman movements."

The conversation continued as they were served food. Brennus brought the talk round to the information he sought from Iohan. "Venutius needs to know much more of this

Roman leader they name Agricola."

"*An cù!*" Iohan spat vehemently into the fire, tossing his well-chewed rib bone at the centre of it. "The Cornovii wish heartily that the man had never set foot on our Celtic soil. Death and destruction follow Agricola. His ruthless attack has decimated the peoples due south of here." Iohan continued for long moments describing the relentless and ruthless strategies of Agricola, Legate of the Legio XX. "No tribe, so far, has prevented his advances. The soldiers under his command are merciless to anyone who opposes their domination."

Brennus felt Ineda's hand clutch his tunic as she leaned forward, now very eager to join the conversation. "What can you tell us of his plans to move northward?"

Iohan fired another bone into the flames, contempt in his face warring with wrath. "The Cornovii are powerless now. The forces of Rome subdue every small skirmish and leave fewer warriors to carry on to the next battle. Agricola has established a large base in mid-Cornovii lands using a fortress that was established by his predecessor and his patrols are relentless in the surrounding areas."

"Will his legion be kept occupied there in that task?" Ineda's voice held the doubt he felt.

"Nay!" Iohan's scoff rumbled deep. "We heard only this morn that he already plans to move north by the new moon. The days are longer now and the walk between camps can be lengthened. Before long his hordes will be well through the lands of the Setantii and then onto the Brigantes."

"So soon?" Ineda was agitated by the news. He guessed what was going through her head – the news had to go to Venutius as soon as possible. The new moon was almost upon them.

As the talk continued Brennus watched the assembled gathering. The Roman named Agricola had ceased to dominate the conversation, the talk more about when Venutius would strike back. No one knew the answer to that, but he hoped the confrontation would not be long in coming. He wanted no more Celtic blood spilled but the situation could not remain the same as it had been for long winters.

"I heard tell you play and tell a good story, Bran of Witton!"

Brennus was surprised out of his distraction by Iohan's statement.

Ineda rushed in. "Bran has a fine voice, too. Have you a favourite song he might amuse you with?"

Though he had only entertained the Witton tribespeople with his ocarina playing he was easily persuaded. During his many lonely eves at his own hearth he had created a few new song tales – one of them about the current Roman advances and the Brigantes triumphs.

"Very heartening!" Iohan's praise was loud. "You must make a new one for the Setantii. We would appreciate that very well!"

A few others around the fireside were persuaded to add their voices; some of the songs lusty ones which gained Ineda renewed admiration. Preventing scowls from forming was a constant ache. She was now enjoying the attention even if he was not. When warriors began to drift away from the fireside he brought his straying thoughts back to what Iohan was saying.

"My roundhouse is not large, as you see. I have only the one stall that is not occupied at present which is available to you, Ineda."

"My thanks, Iohan. I am pleased to accept your hospitality."

Iohan's nod was minimal before he got up from the fireside and walked to the back of the room. Pulling aside a hide curtain he indicated the cot that lay beyond, heaped up with a pile of furs. "You may choose where you wish, Bran – the fireside is also free to you."

Brennus knew what the chief indicated, as did all the warriors still present. If he chose the fireside then Ineda was free to choose to bed down with another warrior from the many who had sent her interested glances.

That, he would never consent to!

"Come, Ineda." If his voice was brusque he did not care,

Ineda might balk at his tone, but she needed to do his bidding.

No black looks and no rancour in her voice was a surprise when she bid the company farewell, before she followed him through the entrance tunnel and outside, as meek as a little lamb. It was suspicious; nonetheless, it was what needed to happen.

A distance away from the chief's home, when no one was near enough to see or hear them she rounded on him her small palm slapping at his chest. Her anger erupted. "You do not trust me, do you?"

Easily snaring her arms he gripped her close to him, pretending innocence. Telling himself he would do better to let her go when her snug little body sagged against him, stirring him even more. "Trust you? Why should I not?"

"You drag me out here as though I am your hearth-wife and not your foster-sister!"

"Ineda." He caught her arm as she made to speed away. "I have a duty to your father to ensure your welfare."

"So, you would bed down alongside me to ensure that no warrior from Scortin can pleasure me?"

He focused on her features, exhaling a tortured breath through his nose, even though the darkness was too deep to see much. There was too much cloud cover for clear moonlight to illuminate the walkway and they were well away now from the torches that flickered and sputtered outside Iohan's roundhouse. His thoughts were just as dark. The idea of lying down beside her was excruciating. To lie near and not take her would be a trial he was beginning to think he could not master. He would not show his feelings though. She could not be encouraged one tiny bit. "If need be."

"Lie on the ground at my feet if you have to, though even my brothers would not have done that. But know this. You will never pleasure me, Bran of Garrigill! You rebuffed my advances many times in the past. I will never have you for my lover, now."

Though his insides shook he gave no answer, could only glare.

When she shrugged him off and stalked off to find the latrine area he let her go. The settlement was not so large and he kept her within his sight.

The night was endless and the earthen floor bumpy. Stretching out on the small stall floor was the only way he could be sure she was alone. Deep sleep was elusive. The whole night long. Sorcha, and past lovers paraded through restless dreams but satisfaction was denied him. When he awakened from a light sleep at dawn his fingers were curled around the bangle which lay exposed at his throat.

Guilt crept over him, but he banished it just as quickly. If Ineda had protested, and demanded he leave her alone to chose one of the warriors of Scortin to bestow her favours on, he would have had to relent. She was now a woman well grown, fully able to make her own choices. That she had mutely accepted his presence was a surprise, but it suited him well, since one night was all they intended at Scortin. He refused to acknowledge the bittersweet feelings she engendered.

It was expected that she did not respond to his morning greetings – though her farewell of Iohan was affable.

Chapter Fifteen

AD 73 One Moon Before Lughnasad – To Quernium

"Rest easy!"

The horse was picking up on Brennus' irritation as he hitched her up to the cart – his mood sour. His mood was always sour. Beltane had come and gone, and so had two more moons. His displeasure came and went too often as well, his bad humour remarked on by many a person at Witton, which he shrugged off, not interested in their opinions.

Ineda had not chosen him at Beltane. Madeg had had that public honour. He told himself he did not care, yet the feelings he constantly repressed belied that.

Lara, the woman who had chosen him at Beltane had not deserved his quick coupling, but he had been unable to banish his errant imaginings. Knowing whom Ineda was with had added a desperate edge, the act over with in haste. He had thought Lara would not seek him out again and was surprised when she had. Only a few times, though. His lack of interest in her was not what she was looking for.

The horse harrumphed in his face as he tightened the traces.

"Easy now!" He rebuked the horse more gently. It was not the mare's fault she was skittish. She was generally a docile and good tempered horse, a happy disposition till she picked up on his displeasure.

Stroking the muzzle settled her down. It settled him down a little, too. "Are you happy now?" He repeated soft encouraging words, pleased that his own annoyance was abating.

Ineda's happy disposition constantly angered him, always pleasant with everyone – except him. Yet, in spite of their unpleasant interaction, she chose to continue the trading with him.

During the summer, many more intense messages passed between Brennus and Venutius at Stanwick as the trading continued. Every trip yielded some little piece of useful information. He was sure that the king of the Brigantes was ready to strike back at the forces of Rome though Governor Cerialis seemed content to oversee land already settled upon with forts and lookout posts, yet no positive word came back to him.

Agricola had battled with some Ordovices using ferocious strength, and steadily claimed more of the western coastal territory. The news that came from Iohan was dire – Agricola was possibly the most brutal of any legate that had come to Britannia. His Legio XX was feared far and wide. The lands of the Setantii were directly threatened now; Roman presence was already encamped on its southern fringes.

Governor Cerialis was well able to send many more troops to northern Brigantia, and to meet Venutius in terrifying huge battle, but for some reason he had not. Brennus wanted no more slaughter of Brigantes; however, the temper of the far northern areas was all but broken. A slow and systematic subjugation of more Celtic villages north and east of Nidd took place, and the resultant localised rebellions continued to be ruthlessly quashed. Patrolling the surrounding areas afterwards was a systematic plan the Emperor's army rigidly adhered to.

"Bran!"

As he loaded up the cart, a breathless Ineda sped towards him.

"I have just met Madeg."

He had no need to know that piece of information but Ineda was animated for some other reason. An excitement, coupled with vehement anger flashed across her expressive green eyes and transferred to him with ease.

"Agricola marches towards us with three cohorts of the Legio XX, a mounted ala leading the way." Her chest heaved with the fast run she had made to reach him. Hands on bent knees her words were stilted, pauses for breath obviously annoying her as her endearingly scrunched-up face looked up at him. "He halts only to rest for the darkest part of the night. Only the simplest of trenches are cut to create the defensive overnight barriers for their camps."

"Has Madeg seen the soldiers of Agricola?" The news was ominous, if true. It could only mean that Cerialis was ready to pounce on all Brigante territory. Why, else, would the Governor have moved Agricola from land that still required constant patrolling?

Ineda rose to full standing, her words scathing. "Nay! He has not been so close yet, but word has arrived from those who have seen Agricola heading up through Setantii lands. Even if you fail to acknowledge Madeg's truth, it still bears investigation. We must warn Venutius that Agricola will attack from the west!" She strode around the cart, in her agitation picking at the pile of leather he had laid down in a tidy pile.

He stilled her rifling, holding her agitated fingers in a loose grasp.

"We need to be sure before we send word." He could not disagree with her assessment but wanted more evidence. If Agricola was expected to arrive from the west then the soldiers at Quernium would be all abuzz with it.

He also could not contemplate her attempting to journey alone.

They had not been to Quernium for many days, their stock of skins very low and not much coming off the local looms. The cart only held a few items of tanned leather; an amount just sufficient to make a trip justifiable to the fort that was closest to the stronghold of Venutius.

The squeeze of her fingers tingled as did her sudden excited kiss at his cheek. "Then let us go now, foster-brother!"

The peck cheered him, the name not much at all.

As they headed towards Quernium Ineda could barely contain her excitement, her speech full of Venutius making a surprise attack since he would be forewarned in time. He had not the heart to dispel her fervour – but she had never witnessed true battle. She had certainly seen death at the hand of the Roman Army, even Celt on Celt, but never a full scale battle. The realities of bloody war he knew only too well.

He did not want to dampen her enthusiasm but felt compelled to give warning.

"Ineda. When Venutius is ready he will attack. Battle will come soon but when it happens you will remain at Witton."

"I will not! I want to see the armies of Cerialis crushed by our mighty Celtic warriors. They can do it, Bran! They are much more battle ready than they were at Whorl. You have heard the news of the training Venutius has overseen himself."

"Witton." He refused to say anything about the Roman training he had not so long ago witnessed and clucked the horse on to a good clip. The warm rapport he had been enjoying was fast disappearing, though her slap at his arm to gain attention was highly amusing.

"You will not force me to remain at Witton! Though I am not fully warrior trained I can wield a knife and swing a sword well enough."

He knew just how well she could wield that sword she spoke about since he had trained her along with some of the young striplings who had begged for some of his advice, there being no champion at Witton any longer. She was determined, and had learned well but her small stature meant she made little impact on larger opponents. Presently, those expressive green eyes of hers sparked fury, the clench at her jaw so tight her cheeks were turning a remarkable purple as she continued to lock gazes with him. Her fierce little face held such an appeal he pulled up on the reins to enjoy her annoyance even more. It had been a while since he had roused her up so much.

He had missed the connection he never felt with any other woman, and she was no longer the innocent young woman who needed time to mature.

Knowledge slammed in. He could resist her no longer. He would not put off his lust any more.

His lopsided grin was untameable, his sigh all show as the horse slowed at his bidding. "Ineda. Deadly engagement is not made with wooden weapons and I have not taught you all. Right this moment though, I need to show you why I must have you safe."

He watched her annoyance turn to shock when he wrapped the reins around his wrist and slowly reached for her. He veiled none of the lust in his expression as his lips sought succour.

Ineda's gasp of sheer surprise was muffled by his mouth, the recognition in her eyes shielded when he closed his own. The sensation of lips on lips almost too perfect for him. Once started he could not stop. Could not get enough of the taste of her. His hands burrowed their way into her braids to pull her even closer till he had to stop for breath.

Ineda pulled slightly away from him, the incredulous gleaming of her darkened eyes showing anticipation as much as surprise. It was she who pulled his face back down and began her own frantic journey, her arms snaking around his neck and all but strangling him in their desperation to get as close to him as possible. The kisses continuing, he wound his arms around her back and settled her so close to his chest the silver armband dug into his skin.

He must give Ineda the ring! The thought whirled but he was far too occupied to declare her the rightful owner.

Focused in such a battle of their own they were unprepared for the noise that had them pulling back in alarm. The rush of Roman soldiers who gushed through a sizeable gap in the hedgerow was upon them before he was able to do any kind of protecting. Three brawny soldiers dragged her from his arms by the hair, her screaming and cursing a match for his own cries.

"Bran!"

"Ineda!"

Before he could jump down the sudden rocking at the back warned him that more troops had joined the fray.

"Leave the woman be!"

The blow to the back of his head slammed him onto his terrified gelding. *An cù!* His last thought was similar to that from some time before. Falling beneath a horse was an occurrence he wished no repeat of.

***

"Let me go! Take you hands from me!"

Ineda's frantic cries muffled into the mail-clad chest of a muscular auxiliary, her writhing around to no avail, her feet kicking out into nothing.

"Bran!"

Dragged behind the hedgerow she had no way of seeing if Bran was alive or dead. The blow to his head had made him drop like a heavy boulder onto the rear of the horse. She had seen no more before groping and grasping hands carried her off.

"Bran!"

Repeated hollering was all she could manage, her attempts to bite her assailants unsuccessful, her head locked into an immovable position. Close by, the three who held her excruciatingly tight by the hair braids and arms made the noise of a whole roundhouse, their cackling and ribbing right in her face as they carried her aloft. The stench of their sweat and unwashed tunics was gagging, no doubt gained from many days on the move. Lust dripped from their eyes and mouths as she continued to spit and kick and scream. Though she understood none of their words she guessed what they meant as they argued.

"*A mhic an uilc!* You evil bastard! Roman turd. Leave me be!"

Her angered cries and protests encouraged them all the more as she was roughly jostled between them. Not even her grandmother had told her what to do in such a situation, but she would not let them assault her without putting up the best fight she had in her. Her arm momentarily freed she managed a poor attack at the face of one soldier, her tightened fist launching wildly.

"Aieee!" The pain was excruciating, the back of her hand having walloped off the soldier's helmet flap as well as his chin.

The jeers and guffaws of the two still binding her rang in her ears, as they laughed at her pathetic attempt, the man she hit rubbing his jaw with a leering grin on his face as he came even closer. The kick to his bare shin was a good one, but did not stop his reeking breath from coming at her mouth, his filthy fingers holding her face in place. She refused to cringe at his garbled words. Struggling her face free of his grasp her eyes lit on the hedge. Bran was beyond but what was happening to him?

On the far side of the hedge men bawled and shouted. The neighing of the horse indicated the animal's terror; the thudding of hooves beating a frantic protest. If Bran was under those hooves he would have no chance.

"Bran!"

She managed only one more plea before a massive fist clamped over her jaw and twisted her cheeks. The agony of it matched the pain at her hairline, the tugging and hauling of her body loosening more than a few strands of her long hair.

One soldier relinquished his grip of her arm, frantically clutching at his tunic, thrusting it aside.

"Nay! Leave me be!"

Asking for Bran to help was futile. There were no yowls that sounded anything like his, though she heard dull thuds that sounded like sandal shod feet kicking bones, accompanied by hollers and curses, in Latin and in another different tongue. They were killing him! The tightness at her chest was agony. She had to get around the hedge to help him.

"Let me go!"

Her squirms and bites and kicks only earned her brutal fists and slaps to subdue her as the soldiers dragged her down onto the tufts of rough grass. One of the men held her down, his full body weight put onto his knee that was slanted across her stomach.

"Lady Rhianna! I beg your help!"

She cursed the fact she had not grown tall and strong like many of her Celtic race; she was an easy capture for three sturdy soldiers. In despair she watched the man whose knee ground into her. Her struggles and rearing did not prevent him from extracting a long knife from the pouch at his belt. He reached to the neck of her dress, the glint of the blade making the breath hitch in her throat. She momentarily closed her eyes, her thoughts frantic. If death was in his hand she would not make it easy for him. Another frenzied wriggle of her body added to the bawl into his face, causing him to start back a little in surprise. Sheer anger joined her fear.

"Meaghan! You did not say I would die at the hands of Roman scum. Help me, now!" She cared not that her spit spotted the man's face.

Her holler made no difference. Recovered, the man grinned at her, his face a hairbreadth away from her chin.

Whatever he growled she had no comprehension of, but knew it was not good. The first flick sliced through her belt. The next flash slit the full way down her dress, exposing her body to the elements. Her angry shrieks earned her another blow to her jaw from the man who held her arm down.

Pain like she had never felt before wracked her body. Another ferocious slap came at her from the opposite side, this time hitting her ear, making her head ring. As she reeled from the blows from the right and then the left, tight fists gripped at her legs and forced them apart. Stinging tears leaked from her eyes and ran rivulets into the shells of her ears. She squeezed her eyes tight to clear her vision and to ward off the agony but also to block out the sight of the third soldier leaning down over her.

The deafening command that superimposed all the other noises startled her eyes open again. Ringed by shining helmet flaps the furious dark eyes that confronted her faded…to blackness.

***

Grit rolled around Brennus' mouth, his face squashed into a rut on the path as he slowly opened his eyes. His blood lurched and bile surged up into his throat.

"Ineda!"

Where was she? Momentary panic flooded till he overcame it, a cool rivulet of fear lingering down his backbone. Quelling it, he knew alarm would be of no help at all to her. Shouting would do no good either; not from his present position, though if the scum had hurt Ineda he would kill them bare handed. He flexed his shoulders the tiniest bit. Pain slammed from his fingers right through his backbone. Ah! Bare handed retaliation would have to wait a while. His hands were bound behind his back, his fingers crushed by what he guessed was the hob-nailed sandal shod foot of a Roman auxiliary. Taking stock of what had happened, any resistance from him seemed pointless. There was no option but to bide his time till he worked out a better plan. From the sounds of the talk around him he was well outnumbered by many Roman soldiers.

By Taranis, he cursed them all.

Except the noises he could hear were not all around him when he really listened. Muffled grunts, and cries, and jeers came from somewhere not too far way. Ineda's sudden squeals of fury startled him. He writhed around, frantic to be free. She was still alive but was being accosted!

"He stirs. Get him to his feet!"

He had learned enough of the tongue of Germania to know what was happening. What seemed like many arms tugged him around before the sharpest of pila poked tiny punctures in his chest, drawing blood. The vicious kicks at his lower legs he ignored as best he could.

"Up!"

Even if he had not learned the word he would have known the intent.

Yanked to an upright position took three of the smaller Roman soldiers, as he felt them heave and tug and shove his resistant weight, their taunts an attempt to belittle him that he would not allow to affect him.

He raised his head at a new noise. A legionary soldier, fully plated and well decorated, pounded into view. It took no effort to guess the other riding behind was his scribe and translator.

Rapid Latin rattled out as they yanked the horses to halt. The translator's tone in rough Brigante was just as harsh as he pulled up his mount close by and slid from the horse.

"The tribune would have you tell him your purpose in this area."

Brennus felt the wind rush from his chest, as one of his restrainers decided he had hesitated too long. As he absorbed the pummelling, the powerful fist in his gut was not much help if they wanted him to give answer.

Hospitable was not how he was feeling. Raising his head again, and shaking off the agony, he glared. The soldier named tribune had dismounted and now stood right in front of him. The man was a good head smaller than him but was fit and muscular. It was the deadly, livid stare he liked the least as the tribune looked around, his cocked head taking in the clamour beyond the hedge, Ineda's fuming squeals undoubtedly feminine. If anything the tribune seemed even angrier at her cries, the flare at his eyes unmistakeable.

Remaining silent, Brennus' single eye searched the area attempting to quell the sheer panic that gripped him. How could he free Ineda? The hands that held him slapped and punched at his tiniest movement.

"Bran!"

More of her muffled, frantic shrieks came from beyond the hedge. By Taranis, he would kill them. The blood inside him surged wildly, his temper at a fever pitch as he thrashed himself free of the grip that held him and surged forwards. He had too good an idea what they were doing to her.

"Let her be! Release her!" The fury that welled inside him spilled over as he head butted the important Roman in the chest, the only recourse since his hands were tied fast.

The sword hilt cracking against his skull sent him sprawling against the scribe, the pain at his forehead from colliding with the tribune's armour sufficient to send him to oblivion without that extra help.

AD 73 One Moon After Lughnasad – Witton

Brennus had little interest in going anywhere but there was really no reason for him to remain at Witton. Farewells were not something he had made too many of in his past at Garrigill but his leave-taking from Ruarke was a painful one, and one he had no desire ever to repeat. His chest felt hollow and yet it was also full of violent angry urges. Every single part of him deplored the Roman scourge on the land and he vowed he would spend every moment of his life doing what he could to thwart Roman domination.

"We do not know for certain that she is dead, Bran." Ruarke made no attempt to disguise his frantic appeal for him to stay.

"A whole moon has already passed. You know your daughter well. If she is alive, she would have got word to us by now. Ineda would not leave us to wonder."

"Your search has been thorough and no trace of her, I know that, but until someone tells me of her remains I will not believe her dead."

"I want her to still be living, Ruarke, but there is more likelihood that the Roman scum used her ill and then left her for dead – as they left me. Rest assured. My enquiries will continue even though I am no longer at Witton. If anyone hears of her fate you know how to find me at the stronghold of Venutius, and if I find her I will bring her back to you."

His true feelings he did not allow freedom. Ineda had been a ray of sunshine he had not properly appreciated and now bitterly regretted the loss. Apart from expressing it in a brotherly fashion to Ruarke, he told none of his misery of heart. That he had only just decided to make love to her before the attack rankled so badly – he had had moons of time and opportunities prior to that but now he had lost her.

His relentless searches for her had been in vain. Back on his feet soon after the beating at the hands of the Roman patrol, he had barely stopped to eat. The ground he had covered encompassed all of the areas they traded with and much further, even though it was extremely dangerous now to venture far from Witton. The forces of Agricola had been just as ferocious in subduing those near Quernium as they had been to the northern Cornovii as they had swept northwards through their lands.

Many villagers near Witton had heard of the surges of the Legio XX in nearby territory but none had heard of any female Celt in their grip. He had not given up, but felt compelled to leave Witton. Ineda had been the reason for him going there and now he found no reason to stay, though the sight of Ruarke's pain cut deep. The older man had settled in well at Witton, and in truth had nowhere else to go.

Ruarke paced around. "I will remain here, but if Venutius lifts arms I will ride north to Stanwick and join my brother Celts in the fray."

"You know you need to stay here at Witton. There will be too few able warriors left here to sustain the settlement. And if Ineda is still alive and gets word to you, you must be here to receive it." There was little point in telling Ruarke he was not fit for battle, or that he now doubted Ineda would send word.

He looked at the older warrior; compassion eating at his gut. The man had been injured before Whorl and had never recovered full fitness: age and lassitude exacting their toll early. Larger scale training of Witton warriors, under the watchful eye of the Romans still encamped nearby, did not happen. The men still occasionally sparred, one to one, but their personal battle lust was largely gone. That was not what the followers of Venutius needed to defeat the powerful strategies of Rome.

Venutius needed a cohesive fighting force of fully fit and supremely trained warriors, like the Roman army, but the king of the Brigantes had nothing like that. Brave warriors were not in question; it was their training as a unit that was doubtful and that fact angered Brennus even more.

Ruarke continued to plead. "Bran, you have not properly recovered yet from the beating you received. If Madeg had not been searching for Ineda you would not have been found."

"I am well enough." His fingers strayed to the arm ring that hung beneath his tunic, as they had done many times during recent days. Regret twisted inside him as though the metal had just come glowing hot off the forge. Ineda should have had the ring from him. She had been more than Meaghan's granddaughter. Too late to proclaim it, she had also been his love. He acknowledged that now. She really had been the one woman who sang to his heart.

Ruarke was difficult to face, yet he had to do it.

"I made a vow to your mother that I would live to thwart the Roman pestilence. I intend to fulfil that vow!"

Whether going to Venutius brought him nearer to death meant nothing to him.

Yet, again, he had survived a severe beating, and he would continue to wear Meaghan's arm ring as a daily reminder of Ineda.

He had more to do.

Chapter Sixteen

AD73 One Moon After Lughnasad – Viroconium Cornoviorum

"Eat!"

Ineda shuffled the food around on the wooden platter, glaring at it. She had no desire to eat anything, and certainly nothing that was given her by Gaius Livanus Valerius. However, somewhere deep inside her, she unwillingly acknowledged that if it had not been for the man now cross-legged opposite her at the low table, she would be dead, or at the very least a broken woman.

"Eat!" The Latin came at her again, though he spoke Brigantian Celt well enough.

She flicked the salted fish around the platter, saying nothing, the food an irritating mess because the scent teased her appetite and willed her to relent. It became increasingly difficult to ignore it because she stared at the food rather than the man. She detested him and could not alter that. She loathed his bland appraisal of her even more. Even after more than a whole moon she preferred to speak only when absolutely necessary to him, or when sorely provoked, which was in fact too often. Her reticence quietly infuriated him; she knew that and intended it to be so. He was the one who kept her prisoner, though not in chains and never beaten or abused at his hands.

A lump of roast venison landed on her platter, the knife flick so deft she would not have been able to grasp the blade even if she had tried to.

"The meat is good. Our venators are skilled huntsmen and use their spears well."

Venators. Another new Latin word.

The man was very persistent in giving her the opportunity to learn more Latin. From beneath her bent head she dared a glance. He picked the bones from the remainder of his fish with commitment and purpose, much like he always seemed; his expression unemotional as he made space for the meat he had piled on his own plate. Even the taste of good food barely registered, he was such a perpetually uncompromising man.

Why he chose to keep her alive she still had not fathomed. Gaius Livanus Valerius she had discovered to be one of the tribunes attached to the Legio XX. The man had a very important function in the legion and had no need to trouble about her plight, yet he had done so.

He caught her staring. His flicking fingers gestured at her food, one eyebrow twitching a command, deep brown eyes boring into her as she sat unmoving.

"I did not save you from the lust of my men in order that you starve yourself to death." His lapse into her Celtic tongue was deliberate. Sometimes he wished for no misunderstanding.

His tone was much as usual but a short-lived glint in his eyes betrayed some inner emotion. Perhaps anger, perhaps frustration, maybe even a touch of guilt? Why that should be so was something she could not work out the cause of. Tribune Valerius, she had learned, was a man of many quiet moods but the most prevalent of these was one of calm, deliberate, focus. His fish all gone he attacked the meat, alternating it with a chunk of fresh flat bread scooped into a dish of oiled olives. A spark of enthusiasm? Though he said nothing she guessed he was actually fond of the slimy green fruits she found difficult to swallow. His stare irritated her so much her vow to remain silent failed.

"Why did you?"

It was a question she had asked before but got no definitive answer to. Perhaps this time she would, since he seemed more mellowed by the meal or by the wine he glugged down between mouthfuls of food? The shrug of his shoulder was encouraging, though she could not say why.

"You were not worth the effort of me having to discipline the men under my command any more severely than they received. Had they violated, or killed you, they would have been discharged from the Legio XX. Orders are to be obeyed. Their punishment was severe enough."

Tribune Valerius' answer was better than she had had before, nonetheless still did not explain. No one told her much of anything.

"What happened to Bran?" She had asked the question repeatedly but he never gave answer.

"Olives?"

She silently pushed the dish away when he held it hovering over her platter. He picked up a few of the green olives and chewed heartily, his eyes rarely straying from her face.

"Has Agricola reached Stanwick yet?"

The silent battle of wills continued. She asked questions – Tribune Valerius either failed to answer or tendered another question instead.

Though she had constantly probed she had been unable to find out if Agricola's army had reached the stronghold of Venutius at Stanwick. No one would tell her if any huge battle had resulted from Agricola's northwards march, and no one would tell her if Bran still lived, though in her heart she willed him living.

Via Tribune Valerius' militis she had heard her three molesters had been demoted to a lower rank and sent to a different cohort. As far as she knew, the men were now somewhere further west in much more hostile Ordovices territory, the small auxiliary fort they were sent to constantly under tribal attack. Their fate may already have been sealed since there had recently been some Roman casualties. If death did not come at the hands of a Celtic sword, they had already paid dearly for their treatment of her since their current circumstances would be less favourable than they had had before the incident with her.

She probed for more, unwilling to keep censure from her tongue. "The soldiers of Rome have molested many Celtic women. Why not me?"

The memory of her attack was still fresh, but beyond opening her eyes when her assailants were forcibly ejected from her body all she really remembered was the widening of Tribune Valerius' eyes when they locked with her own and his rapid hollering to his troops. Although she had been truly terrified about what was happening to her, she had also been raging.

Something about her quandary had made the man intervene, but he would not disclose his reason. In general terms, and in the nature of war, she was just another enemy woman to be dealt with. Why he had saved her, and was determined to keep her prisoner, was a deed she had not fathomed.

"You needed to live."

His blank stare continued but his words were new, and even more confusing.

"Live?" By Rhianna! She did not understand the man.

Reaching for the flask of wine he busied about refilling the deep red liquid into his goblet. She had learned it was the job of a militis to do this but there was no such second-level recruit in her room. The full goblet that had already been poured for her was placed closer to her elbow, Tribune Valerius' expression now more of a question. So far, she had refused to drink the potent brew in his presence, preferring to keep her senses, but he repeated the gesture every time he came to eat with her. Perhaps hoping to change her mind.

"The drink will not harm you."

She knew it would not harm her since he was freely drinking it…but he might. Doubt laced her tone, sarcasm abundant in her spat reply.

"You kept me alive to drink your rich red wine?"

For the first time in more than a moon's worth of nights the man's mask slipped. The smallest of smiles turned up the corners of his lips and his brown eyes sparkled, softening the harsh cut of his shaven jaw.

She remembered little of the ride to his tented camp after her attack, her beaten body limp and drifting in and out of awareness, her low moans and pleas for Bran going unremarked – save that someone told her Bran was long dead. Over the following day the militis who had tended to her scratches and bruising had done his task with little more than basic care. She guessed the young soldier could not understand why Tribune Valerius' had ordered her to be kept alive either.

The idea that Bran had been hacked to death and she had been unable to prevent it had driven her into a spiralling and desperate despair. At times she wanted to join him in the otherworld, fully realising what he had meant to her, knowing her love for him had been deep, even if he could not love her in any other fashion than as foster-sister. Although the memory of those desperate kisses before the attack had changed that perception greatly. Those kisses had been as a lover, not as a brother. At other times, she refused to believe him dead; for surely the great sky god, Taranis, could not treat Meaghan's work so lightly?

After many hopeless days, her recovery slow but sure, she decided to live for Meaghan's sake…and Bran's.

Meaghan – or perhaps her goddess Rhianna – had protected her, though, and she was grateful for that. No bones had been broken, not even at her hand although her wrist had been badly sprained in the struggle, and she had no lingering wounds. The severe bruising that she had received mainly to her face and upper body had gradually receded leaving no lasting marks that she could detect in the small bronze mirror that Tribune Valerius used when he hurriedly shaved himself, eager as he

194

always was to be off somewhere else. Where he went, after his rushed attempts to tidy his person, she did not know and did not care to know, yet noticed all the same.

Presently, the barely concealed mirth she read in his gaze was an irritation she could not thole. The man angered her so much.

"Did you set out to make me some sort of public announcement for all to see?" Her words were out before she took time to caution her bitter tongue.

The momentary widening of his eyes was telling enough, almost as though impressed that she had made a correct assessment of his motives, but his mocking tones belied that fleeting emotion.

"A public announcement?"

Why he had ordered her to be laid on a cot at the front area of his tent had been unfathomable. As tribune, his tented accommodation was spacious but was also at times a very public place, much of the business of the legion conducted there, a steady procession of clerks tripping back and forwards.

When her awareness had properly returned, the morning following her attack, she had been horrified to find she was on a low cot just inside the tent flap, to one side. It had been Tribune Valerius' cry bidding someone enter which had awakened her in the pre-dawn light that filtered through when the tent flap was pushed aside. The blue-pink haze; the fully-armoured legionary bustling his way in; and her sheer astonishment at finding where she lay would be forever in her thoughts. From that moment on it seemed every face that exited strayed towards her after attending Tribune Valerius at his desk, which was centrally positioned and towards the back of the leather enclosure. Embarrassment had been acute till she learned to turn her face away.

Some of the clerks and messengers had looked at her with a tinge of lust, many with cutting derision, but most with insatiable curiosity since they were no longer directly facing their superior officer. An enemy woman paraded in such a position, she guessed, was not usual. During those first healing days in Tribune Valerius' tent she was not certain the presence of his militis at night, lying on the ground alongside her, was in any way usual either.

"Was I some kind of admonishing example?"

He eventually answered a half smile now at those normally stern lips. "In a way."

What could he mean? The words meant nothing to her. At times it seemed Tribune Valerius was flaunting her at all of his fellow soldiers, undeterred by any resistance to his choice.

For nights and days she had endured that public situation as her body healed, seated on the cot by day and not allowed freedom to move. The only good aspect had been that Tribune Valerius had been out of his tent more than in as he went about finding the whereabouts of a delivery of heavy supplies to one of the small forts in the area. During his exchanges with his underlings she had understood the Latin words for iron and wood, used in relation to the building of interior wooden structures in the fortlets. It sounded as though the shipment had been intercepted by a local Celtic tribe and the goods stolen. The idea appealed to her but smiling broadly hurt her face so she smiled inside her head, and willed more successful attacks by the locals.

Sometimes an update on the movement of other goods which were in transit to northern Brigantia set him to his feet and to hurry from the tent, his conversation rushing past her as swiftly as his body exited without looking at her. By deduction, and careful listening between Tribune Valerius and his secretary, she had worked out that he was not happy about being away from the main forces of Agricola at that time, though he seemed to relish his commission of keeping the supplies moving for those Romans who were infiltrating northern areas.

Nonetheless, his stare had always been penetrating when he returned to his base as though checking she still lay there. While he always inquired after her progress, he tended to address the militis in attendance rather than her, and he ensured there always was a militis on guard at the doorway.

"The bread is good. Eat."

He handed her a piece of bread, the half-smile gone again. She had once thought Bran of Garrigill a man who could mask his feelings but Tribune Valerius was much better at the task. His arm gesture urged her to eat.

The smell of the food was tempting, since she had refused more than she had ever eaten in his presence. "If I eat, will you free me from this existence I do not ask for?"

Derision sparked in his dark eyes but no more words passed his lips. His sudden lurch to his feet she did not expect, and was not prepared for it, when he bent over her. Grabbing her chin with one hand he forced her mouth open with the other. A chunk of bread crammed into her mouth, he firmly forced her mouth closed and insisted she eat by manipulating her throat and by pinching her nose.

Gagging on the bread she swallowed hard, angry frustrated tears leaking from her stinging eyes. He stuffed another piece of bread into her mouth and an even larger piece into her hand before he sat down again, his glare one she had seen before. He detested her just as much as she hated him. His meal finished he settled to drinking more wine from the flagon, as though nothing untoward had just occurred, his strong body stretching back to more of a lounging position though she knew he was fully alert to any threat she might make to his person.

"Eat your food. All of it."

She did not even try attack. Never given any knife to eat with her fists were futile.

Defiance would gain her nothing either. Yet, though he had forced her, she knew she would show no bruises come the morrow. He was a man who used his considerable strength with care. She pecked at the food Tribune Valerius continued to push her way, the silence painful. He intended his stares to wear her down, she knew that, but resistance to them was her only recourse. She had no other strategies to free herself. The steady stream of militis who were always in attendance saw to that. She had not been allowed to leave the tent during that first half moon of tented existence, except to use the scrubby bushes that had been her temporary latrine area – and even then the escort remained close by. An embarrassment close by.

"Drink your wine; it will ease the bread in your throat."

He was correct about that; the bread was hard to swallow. She would follow his dictates, she would eat and drink – but he could not know her thoughts. She glared at him and chewed… slowly. He stared at her and sipped more wine.

The same guarding situation had applied during the long trek southwards when Tribune Valerius had been recalled back to his main base at Viroconium Cornoviorum. The auxiliary fortlets, manned by part-cohorts, which they visited during the journey had accommodation and hospitality for him. Naturally, the invitation was not extended to her – she remained in his tent, set outside the turf walls, a constant double guard in attendance. Escape had been futile.

Oh, she had tried, but had failed.

Her prisoner status was the same since her arrival at the garrison fortress of Viro Corno. Viroconium Cornoviorum was too long a mouthful. Tribune Valerius hated it when she shortened it to Viro Corno but to call it thus was one petty rebellion she could win. She had no idea what that Latin meant and did not care. By continuing, he would know that she hated her room at Viro Corno, her captivity, and him.

She silently finished the food and dared a sip at the rich warm wine. Tears of frustration and self-pity were ruthlessly squelched; they would do no good. Meaghan's words rang around her head. Was this what her grandmother had meant when she had said life would hold some very bad times? Looking around the small room she could not truly say her present circumstances were bad. Apart from the low cot at one side, the room only held a low table and some padded cushions. It was very different from a roundhouse, bare of the normal trappings of Celtic living but it was clean, dry and quite warm. Tribune Valerius' militis called it a storage cell but she was all the goods contained in it.

"When will you free me?" she asked, when the food was all consumed, though was certain he would not reply.

A particular twitch passed fleetingly across his features. It was the one she thought meant he would never release her, yet she was sure also meant he had no notion of what to do with her. Dashing the remainder of the flagon of wine over his throat in one gulp, he rose to his feet and left the room still saying nothing.

Ineda flopped back onto the low couch pummelling her fists against the cover and kicking her heels against it. She had never been so frustrated, so confused, or so enraged in her whole life.

"*A mhic a' choin!* You bastard! I hate you, Gaius Livanus Valerius. I have no wish to go to the otherworld any more, but this idle life is almost a death of its own!"

Her screeches would be heard by the fool *tironis*, the first-stage recruit, who stood eternal guard outside the doorway, but she cared not. She did not understand Tribune Valerius at all. He had saved her from violation and likely death but short of forcing her to eat he never laid a finger on her in any other way. He never tried to abuse her like the auxiliary soldiers had attempted.

Not that she wanted him to, but why keep her alive and in such misery?

Chapter Seventeen

AD73 One Moon After Lughnasad – Viroconium Cornoviorum

"I hate you!"

Ineda's words harangued him.

Gaius Livanus Valerius lurched away from Ineda's cell. The fiery brand he had removed from the guard flared in his face, the never ending winds of Britannia gusting it, Ineda's taunts still ringing in his ears. She hated him, and his behaviour encouraged her to despise him even more. A part of him wanted it to be different, but it had been so long since he had had any female regarding him with anything but loathing and he hardly knew how to change that. Was so used to it he was not sure how it could be changed.

"She will not be allowed to die! I forbid her to die!" His mumbles were snatched off in a gust strong enough to make him trip.

The almost full flagon of good strong wine surged to his head as he stumbled back through the walkways of the fortress to his own quarters, his thoughts as dark as the night sky above. No stars to light the night was something he would never get used to, even after his three long terms of office in Britannia. The inhospitable dampness that went along with cloudy skies and biting winds, even at this early harvest season, still had the power to annoy him. He hauled his dark cloak over his chest, the torch flame threatening to set him alight when he turned a corner and moved down the Via Decumana towards the principia, the heart of the fort.

He had ordered Ineda to be installed in a storage room near the Porta Decumana, the rear gate. Well away from his own quarters his intention had been to keep her temptation at bay, though in that he had failed. He was determined to continue to eat his evening meal with her to ensure she did not refuse to eat all food, even though his fellow officers could not understand his conduct, and even though he was building huge resentment. He ate all other meals with them as was expected and that would have to suffice till he was sure Ineda did not starve herself to death as a form of escape from her captivity.

He thoroughly despised himself, reviled the situation he had created in taking Ineda as a captive, but at least his determination not to touch her till more than a moon passed still stood firm. He would not repeat the killing of an innocent ever again, nor did he intend to willingly beget one either and would take the necessary steps to avoid it.

His mood now so sour, he barely acknowledged the soldiers he passed by when they saluted him at his doorway.

Back at his desk he stared at the latest dispatch that had arrived in his absence. The missive unrolled he scanned over it, the content blurring before him. His words muffled as he re-read a second time, more carefully.

"Jupiter! Save me from incompetence." His gaze rolled skywards, met by the flickering shadows on the leather roof.

Needing further fortification before he decided what to do about another Celtic raid on a supply of iron, he shambled to the doorway and thrust out his head.

"Bring me wine!"

A helmeted head nodded nearby. "The good wine or the usual, sir?"

"Usual!"

His head was already wine-muzzled since he had drunk a lot more of the flask than Ineda had, the better quality and less vinegared wine he was able to acquire as an officer, though she never acknowledged that. Naturally, she probably did not know what good quality wine was. He set aside the scroll knowing mistakes could not be tolerated due to drunken reading. The decision would have to wait till dawn.

Now he just needed to get more drunk, to banish his frustrated inclinations, and any wine would do. Drunkenness was rare for him in recent times; he had quaffed enough in his misspent youth. Dedication to his post was too serious for such misconduct on a regular basis, but Ineda tried his patience so sorely.

"Juno? Deliver me from tiresome women!"

He allowed his thumping forehead to rest on the desk for a few moments. What should he do? Forcing her to eat was not what he wanted to do to her but he would not allow her to fade away – like Fulvia had. His groans trickled moisture onto the desk.

"Why does she so resemble Fulvia? Am I always to be punished, Juno?"

He prayed to a goddess he knew did not listen to him. His youthful dalliance with his maternal cousin had cost him dearly, the result of it banishment to the country estate of a very distant relative for five whole seasons, and then a departure to a very junior military post earlier than had been planned by his father. Those days seemed so long ago; the freedom of youth a vague memory. His life of the soldier was now almost as long as when he had been a carefree boy, though much of that time spent in Britannia was of his own volition.

"Shall I pour?"

Opening his eyes he nodded at his militis and then shooed him from the room without properly lifting his head.

Why did Ineda look exactly the way he remembered his cousin?

More moans and spit slithered the desk before he lifted his head. In reality he knew Ineda was not really like Fulvia. The blonde streaked thick hair was similar and the facial features were somewhat alike, but Ineda did not have the deep brown eyes that were common to his family. He gulped down a beaker of wine without drawing breath. Belching at the vinegary taste he did not hesitate about refilling it, and only then wiped the drips from his chin. Toying with the second cup in his hand, he pictured Ineda's startled expression when he had forced the food into her mouth; a very different expression from his very first glimpse of her.

"Spitting little cat!" No one answered. Empty walls surrounded him.

When he had first seen Ineda being primed for violation by the auxiliaries under his command his inclination had been to walk away, even though they were contravening a direct order recently given. The women of Brigantia were to be left alone, except if they were retaliating with weapons, or resisting Roman occupation. He may not have agreed with the ruling laid down by his superiors but commands were to be obeyed. If he had walked away his conscience would have been appeased for she was resisting with all her small might; the small knife at her pouch a puny weapon, but a blade, nonetheless.

All it had taken was one glimpse of Ineda's face, and her slight though well developed womanly body, and he had acted otherwise. Fulvia's image had launched herself at him, though fighting back in such temper had not been in his cousin's nature, and had she lived he did not think she would ever have acquired the spirit that Ineda had.

He had ordered that Ineda be released by his too-eager auxiliaries and he never ever rescinded an order. Once done, he had to live with the consequences. The battered woman could have been left on the ground but her furious eyes had haunted him.

What he had then chosen to do with Ineda was not well received, but he cared not. He had kept her alive and would continue to see that she lived. Keeping a woman at his level of command was not unknown, but it was rare amongst those presently in post around him who were attached to Viroconium Cornoviorum. Rare and enviable.

He stared at the dark blood wine in the cup, attempting to banish the past, then swirled it around slowly.

"One wheedling. Another fiery and defiant!"

His second swirl created a small whirlpool that burst into his mouth and dripped from the edges of his lips when he brought it close. Before the cup was fully drained the rage he held inside burst free. The wooden goblet shattered against the plastered wall, a deep red trickle like a rivulet of his pent up tears, such was the power of his throw.

"Cease to haunt me, Fulvia!" Crumpling to the floor his hands cradled his head. "I have paid my dues to you and more!"

So long ago, yet still so fresh, now that he had Ineda to look upon every single day. Fulvia had been of similar age to Ineda and had been of similar stature and shape. When Fulvia had come to him begging for his help he could not refuse her. They had been more like brother and sister than maternal cousins from the time he had passed twelve winters. Before her arrival to be fostered by his father he had been an only child, his mother's attentions very cloying. Fulvia's sweet nature had changed all that. After her appearance as a ten-year-old, his mother had taken Fulvia under her wing and had showered her with all of her pent up maternal feelings. Gaius had not been neglected, but had in fact been relieved that his cousin made his life easier.

"My father should not have accepted your fostering."

More sips of the wine went down, his eyes screwed tight shut. As he had matured from boy to man he had found Fulvia's proximity just too close, though till she had come begging he had resisted her flirtations.

He glugged even more directly from the flagon, staring at memories.

At sixteen summers he had been sexually experienced, as was expected in Roman society. His consorting with prostitutes, and his regular coupling with his father's chosen female slave, had been happening since the previous summer when his father had declared him ready to be a man.

It had been different of course for Fulvia; she was expected to go to her marriage bed a virgin. They were not of senatorial rank, yet the equestrian blood in their veins demanded they follow society's rules, or their family would lack advancement. Fulvia may have been normally meek and obliging but she had balked against her father's dictates over her marriage.

Fulvia's wheedling words haunted him. When he screwed up his eyes she remained there before him.

"You should not have tempted me so, Fulvia!"

Had the flagon been glass it would have shattered between his flexed fists as he forced more down his gullet, choked on it, a gush of red spattering his tunic. Undeterred by the mess he shook his head to clear his murky thoughts, slurping down the remainder in between his solo conversation.

"Our behaviour did not rate such punishment, Fulvia. Why did you force death?"

Pushing himself upright from the stool, he attempted to stand and then thought better of it, his hands gripping the table edge to allay the wavering of it.

"Your passing was foolish beyond bearing! I have done many things that would rate more highly with Fortuna's judgements."

From somewhere illogical he chuckled and then could not stop the rumbles emitting from deep in his belly. His fingers slipped and re-gripped the edge of the desk bearing his full wilting weight.

"Aye, Marcius. And some of those instances were with your assistance." His youthful best friend had often called him a morose drunk. Marcius was correct in his assessments since they had practised getting drunk often enough back then. "I am a maudlin drunk."

Slumping to the floor, having missed the stool completely, he ignored the hilt of his sheathed knife digging into his back.

No one listened to him, but it had been a very long time since he had talked about Fulvia.

"A hand full of couplings, Fulvia? No more, no less." His fist rose, he splayed open his fingers and waved at the memories.

In truth, he did not remember much of the actual unions. He had taken Fulvia with the desperation of youth, at her wheedling, his shedding of seed fast and furious with no kind of love involved – not even cousinly at those moments. He had been driven by lust, and her availability. What he remembered more of was his imploring Fulvia to find another way out of her predicament before they had embarked on their short-lived affair of two days.

"Old Diodorus would not have been so bad. He would have managed to beget a son you…"

Her wails and cries haunted him. "Gaius, please, please help me? He is repulsive! I can't bear the idea of his gnarled old hands touching me…everywhere." She wanted a younger man to do that first.

He could not exactly remember when his clutch of reassurance had changed to one of lust that first time. Fulvia's little hands had stroked him and he had been lost. She had always been able to twist him round her little finger; he had never been able to deny her anything.

"I should have resisted." His whispers receded into a drunken stupor.

***

"Ineda?"

Ineda had been asleep for some time.

Tribune Valerius had left her chamber earlier when called out by his secutore to sort out some incident and had not returned. She had waited for a while, and then had slipped into bed assuming he would not return. Still heavy with sleep she was startled to hear his voice whisper in her ear, his heavy body pinning her down as he climbed onto the narrow cot. The touch of his hands caressing her face was confusing; gentle and feather-light. His lips feathered at her ears as she came to full awareness.

"I will not hurt you, Ineda, unless you fight me."

"What are you doing?"

Struggling under him, when she realised what was happening, made no difference, he was too strong for her to fight him off. He grasped her hands and pinned them above her head with his forearms, his full weight on top of her. Yelling would do no good, for the only one likely to hear would be the tironis outside her door on overnight guard, and he would not dare to intervene. Instead she spat at his face.

"Let me…go!"

Subsequent breathy pleas whiffed against his cheek as she continued to squirm away from him.

"Leave me be. I do not ask for this."

His low laugh rumbled at her neck, his lips and teeth nibbling the tender flesh below her chin.

"I am no Celt to be encouraged or denied, Ineda. The choice is not yours to make."

Freeing one hand from his tight grasp she pulled at his hair and scratched any part of him that she could reach but that protest lasted only moments. Her fingers were easily recaptured and her whole arm was tucked under her body, trapping it securely under their combined weight.

"Do not fight, Ineda. I will not beat you…but I will have you."

"Leave me be!"

Tears leaked and wet both of their faces as he kissed her lips. Just once. When he gained no response, he cradled her head in a loose grasp with his free hand, his lips soft at her neck and chest. Though she continued to squirm he pinned her down and continued his soft kisses, his aroused body feeling even heavier than before.

"There is no need to worry. I will not hurt you."

In between unremitting gentle pecks he repeated, "Let me love you, Ineda."

Love her?

The very suggestion was horrible! He was Roman. Her enemy. Those things were dreadful, but most of all he was not her choice. He never would be her choice of lover. Wriggling her face away from him, her thoughts whirled.

She had not the strength to keep fighting and would never free herself from him. If she did not submit would he kill her? It was a distinct possibility, and no one would dare to stop him. Yet hating what he was doing was not enough for her to want death to visit her. She could not summon the will to do other than lie limp below him. The man used her body as silently as she silently cursed him.

And she let him.

Though he said he would not beat her, she could not banish the memories of how she had been attacked by the soldiers under his command. The pain of her bruising at their hands was still too fresh. Her body acquiescent under him, her heart bled at her inability to free herself from her circumstances. She had not wanted to die at the brutal soldiers' hands...and she still did not want to die under Tribune Valerius' caressing ones. Firm but not in any way hurting, he ensured that.

But she hated him. How she hated him.

Her eyes closed tight to block the sight of his body above her.

Bran?

Thoughts of Bran filled her head. If it were Bran, she would not be meekly submitting, she would be wholeheartedly participating. She could do nothing about her present physical situation, but imagining Bran making love to her was a solace that got her through the short ordeal.

It seemed only a blink before Tribune Valerius pulled himself free, gasping alongside her ear, his seed spurting at her leg. Afterwards he rolled off and wordlessly left her room.

Her spirit was crushed for such intimate interaction was loathsome – he was Roman scum and she had allowed it. She was not sure if she hated herself more than she hated him. Either way hatred was fierce. Dry tears kept her awake till eventual physical and mental exhaustion made her succumb. Nonetheless, she would never forget the seething abhorrence in her heart.

The night had been bad but the morning following was worse.

Summoned to his quarters she approached the doorway in trepidation. Was her resistance, and then lack of participation, going to be punished? If so, how? He had said he would not beat her though that had been in the dark of night. She detested Tribune Valerius' treatment of her, but she loathed the guard on duty at his door even more. Glaucius' leers set her teeth on edge.

Though she was sure Tribune Valerius would not have made any mention of it, Glaucius seemed to know what had been done to her, no doubt from gossip with her overnight guard. Glaucius' tone was low because his superior officer was within.

"I hear the tribune regards you as a mere prisoner no longer." His jeering laugh made hardly any noise. "Your new whore status suits me. When your master needs a break from your delightful body, I will gladly take over, and believe that I will be much better."

She did not even bother to pretend her situation was unchanged; the slimy guard was not worth the effort, but her rebellious tongue would not stay silent. "If you know so much, then tell me what you would do differently?"

Glaucius' sneering guffaw went right into her face. "I would not have waited till your womanly bleedings had come and gone. Any bastard child you carry will not be acknowledged by me anyway, and I hear our tribune has a severe dislike of babes in the womb."

The guard's words were cut short when Pomponius, Tribune Valerius' secretary, bustled up and urged her to enter.

Pushing past the odious guard she moved on into Tribune Valerius' quarters determined not to let it affect her, yet the information was alarming. She had wondered why he had waited so long but she could not be sure she had understood it all properly, even though Glaucius' remarks had been accompanied by lewd gestures. Was she now to be told she was whore to all the men of the garrison? Terror was added to; a furious anger swelling in her blood.

By Rhianna, she would never let that happen!

Yet, her legs trembled so much she feared breaks at her knees would cripple her forever more as she was bid enter his office. The hint of a smile on his face added confusion to the mix.

Tribune Valerius coupled with her regularly after that first time but never made mention of it during daytime or night time, not a conceited lover like Madeg had been. Reluctant to take her – she sensed that from Valerius' manner – she knew she was not expected to enjoy or make any response, the man giving nothing of his feelings. He never made any sign that he found the act pleasant, or encouraged her to behave alluringly or familiarly. He always seemed still edgy after the act, perhaps even aggrieved, sliding quickly back to his own quarters.

One thing she was fairly sure of, and definitely glad about, was that she was not really likely to bring forth a child. The spilling of his seed was never inside her and after he left her room she cleansed herself of his traces, cursing him all the while for his persistence, yet glad he never abused her in any other way.

So long as she lay unresponsive.

She had wormed information out of Tribune Valerius' militis about women in the fortress. Dismay had settled on her when she learned they were extremely rare. The news that Roman legionary soldiers were forbidden to have wives explained the lack of female presence. The higher echelons were naturally exempt from that general rule but wives were still scarce, and there were only a few of the superior officers who had concubines with them in Britannia. Any women she might see around the fortress were likely to be camp followers – communal slaves of Rome.

At present, by allowing Tribune Valerius to make love to her, she was slave to him only.

Tribune Valerius might use her body, but he could never remove Bran from her thoughts while he did so.

Nonetheless, hatred festered.

Chapter Eighteen

AD 73 Samhain – Stanwick

"Stanwick!"

Venutius was indeed ready for battle when the huge hillfort of Stanwick came into view as Brennus came over the brow of a low hill. The tremendously noisy training ground way ahead looked much like he would have presided over at Garrigill. For a moment his heart leapt in sheer pleasure. But only for a fleeting moment. The old Brennus would have spurred on his horse without hesitation and ridden into the fray. Not so the new Bran. He stopped to really look, his head scanning back and forth, halting and pausing before swivelling further. The surge of blood settled into a dull dread. And a blinding rage. It added to the anger that rarely left him now.

The sight of many warriors training on the flat plain below the ramparts should send any Roman who dared come close a very strong message. But having seen even small amounts of Roman auxiliaries training outside Nidd, and mostly having experienced at first hand the battle at Whorl, the forces of Venutius in front of him lacked a tight fit. The pairs of fighters locked in battle made an impressive sight but that was exactly what it was. Warrior fighting another warrior. No little protective huddles like the Romans got into. The noise from the training ground was tremendous; nevertheless there was no direction to the mock engagement.

"By Taranis! Will they never learn?" His curse floated off in the wind.

He made a slow approach down the hill, his scrutiny a fierce focus. Those warriors of Venutius below him lacked no courage, but they did lack the orders he had heard bellowing forth from the cohort commanders, and centurions, and even the contubernium leaders at Whorl. None of these Celtic warriors, who risked their lives from even a dull blade in the fierce practice, appeared aware of the warriors around him save the one directly engaged with; the customary Celtic warfare still man to man. A neighbouring warrior only impinged if he moved into the fighting area of another.

Nothing of Roman battle tactics seemed to have been learned.

Well before the gates he was intercepted. This time he was fully ready to declare his identity. Having removed the bratt pin from his cloak, he held it aloft.

"Venutius will know me if you say Bran of Witton has come with information and that I bear the stone of Tuathal."

The scathing assessment of some of the guards he ignored. The loss of an eye, or severe scarring did not mean a warrior was unable to function. His limp he controlled the best he could, but the long ride, and nights on the hard earth, had made his back injury return with a vengeance. His sorry state he disregarded and held his head high.

The wait was long. He had no expectation of Venutius giving him an audience immediately so did not anticipate otherwise. He was only one of many warriors in the chain of messaging between Venutius and the outlying Brigantes. Sitting at an outside fire, some distance from the roundhouse of the king, he made desultory conversation with the warriors who came and went around him. Food and ale had been gifted him, he was not ignored, but sheer exhaustion and an inevitable frustrated bleakness enshrouded him. He gave answers and asked questions of others. He was interested, but it was also a ploy to keep awake and alert. What his fireside companions had to tell was not news and he had nothing new either to share with them. They were not the ones who would need to teach new battle tactics.

Thoughts of Ineda plagued him. Whatever had happened to her he still regretted bitterly. Every single day. His trek to Stanwick had been much longer than necessary as he had journeyed further than needed – initially to the west, and then northwards again making fruitless inquiries about her.

The fireside chatter diminished as the warriors settled down for the night. Drifting into a light sleep, his head nodded onto his chin, the sights and sounds and smells around him not mattering till a soft push at his shoulder jolted him awake.

"Venutius will speak with you now."

Some time later he stood looking at the man he called king and had no idea what to answer. Venutius wanted to know what part he wished to play in the impending battle. Was this a test of his loyalty? He did not know whether to be offended, angry, or pleased to be consulted. His answer was careful but firm, the anger and frustration under a tight leash.

"I would join my brother Celts in repelling Cerialis and Agricola from these parts. I made a vow after Whorl that I would thwart the invading Roman scum in every way I can, and I wish to serve you in doing that. I have experience of their battle skills and now know better what we need do to prevent them from being victorious against us."

"You would instruct my right hand warriors who have also experienced bloody battle with the Roman usurpers?"

He tried to ignore the piecing glare of his king; a man who must now be worn and tired of the situation facing the Brigantes, yet the fervour in Venutius' eyes was unmistakeable, the words cuttingly dismissive.

"Whorl was not kind to you, Bran. And neither was it pleasing for many of my warriors who lie outside. My followers will die for me, but they will never imitate the Roman ways of battle. They are Celts at heart and must act as they always have done."

Brennus felt ashamed in the presence of his king. He had had no intention to impugn his Celtic brothers but did not know what to say. "I mean no offence…"

Venutius cut him off with a terse flick of his arm. "You will not be in my front battle lines, Bran of Witton. I need all warriors to rally to my cause, but I also require some of my loyal followers to do tasks other than fight at the forefront of my battle lines. I am told you have the gift of a skilled messenger and that you have a knack for finding out and sending information that others cannot flush out. You must still remain a messenger for me, since I have few who are able to carry out my tasks. Being my envoy carries a great responsibility."

There was little point in protesting. Brennus could see from the firm chin and cast of the king's face that his mind was made up. And from the recent warrior talk it sounded as though Venutius was still not ready to face the Roman Empire in battle. Till then, he may as well remain on messenger duty.

"What would you have me do?"

Venutius was not quite as large as he was, though he was well able to slap an arm around his shoulder and drag him to the hearth.

"My old friend Tuathal told me you sing and play well, and that you have many tales on the tip of your tongue. Just like a bard."

Discomfiture was high. He was here to help his king fight the Romans not discuss his singing prowess.

"My old friend needs you to hone those skills, as do I…"

"I would fight alongside…" Again his words were rebuffed, the king forcing him to sit down.

"Many tasks await you, Bran, but first my old friend Tuathal needs you. We must talk of this."

Chapter Nineteen

AD 73 Samhain – Viroconium Cornoviorum

"Ineda. When I send for you, I expect you to arrive without delay."

Annoyance wrinkled Tribune Valerius' cheeks as he took her arm and drove her forwards into the aedes, the temple area of the fortress. His cornicularius, the younger of his clerks, followed behind with an offering of apples and berry fruits.

"I came quickly!" If he was irritated then she was even more so. She had had no choice; her escort had hurried her along the walkway of the fort, pilum at the ready, as though invaders were at the gates.

How she wished that were true. Bottling up her resentment and hiding true feelings behind a bland half smile she awaited her captor's next instruction. Not that she needed it since it was always the same.

"My time is short. Antonius Pulis awaits me. Where were you?"

Exasperation boiled. Her every movement was monitored so rigidly. "You want dried figs. Your cook sends this fool tironis but he has no idea where to get them! And since he is my constant shadow he drags me around to find them!" She glared at the recruit who stood alongside, his pilum now pointing to the sky, unconcerned by her outburst. Caring not for any repercussion she vented her ire, turning again to make sure he was seeing her displeasure and every movement of her tight lips.

"He will make no militis level, save he try harder. He speaks Latin, but I am the one who knows where to go for the figs. If you gave me some measure of freedom, even if only around the fortress, I would not take so long to acquire things for you."

She had had enough of trying to speak Latin, finishing her berating in Brigante, under her breath, even though Tribune Valerius insisted she try to speak Latin in public when he addressed her. His look of censure remained but she would not hold her tongue. "Your dull raw recruit has been at your beck and call longer than I have. His six moons are almost over but he will never progress to militis rank if he does not look and learn more about his surroundings."

The frustrated grunt that followed was typical. Tribune Valerius was such a conundrum. Sometimes he was deliberately harsh to those inferiors around him, including her, when his mood was dark. At other times he was far too lenient, allowing for mistakes too readily from the youthful tironis under his charge. She knew well that people learn by their errors but felt they should try to avoid repetition of the same error. The foolish recruit was only good for forcing her forward with his sharp blade, and had absorbed nothing of the daily functions of the garrison.

She had learned diligently to tread carefully around the moods of Gaius Livanus Valerius, yet she would not quell her acid tongue for him either.

"Why not make your prayers later when you have more time?"

"Later may well be too late! The Legate Agricola needs my prayers right now."

The ominous cast to his features, and his clear agitation, did not bode a good evening: something bad had changed during the course of the day.

Gnaeus Julius Agricola, the legate of the Legio XX had remained in northern Brigante territory, having kept the bulk of the legionary and auxiliary soldiers of the Legio XX with him.

Although no one would tell her anything of what was happening in Brigantia, an attack on Venutius must be at hand. The excited lurch to her stomach almost made her retch right in front of Tribune Valerius. Venutius must win! So many nights had passed since her capture that her king must have even more Celtic blades beside him, ready for the fray.

Biting her tongue for a while was now the only way to ferret out the reason for the tribune's short temper. If he insisted on squeezing in a visit to the temple it had to be something serious which troubled him. The man was a very dedicated worshipper – Etain, the horse goddess, being his favoured deity – and he paid more frequent visits to her shrine when under strain.

"We will waste no more time!"

The fingers at her elbow nipped hard, right into the soft spots, but she refused to show any pain. Tribune Valerius knew well how strong he was. He was not nearly as tall as Bran but he was solid, with muscles well strengthened by regular training, and though older than Bran he was still a young man.

She had learned his rank of Tribune Angusticlavi tended to be filled by the career soldiers from Rome and did not necessarily demand the same rigours of training as the general legionary, though he chose to fit physical exercise in to his very busy day. His responsibilities as a supplies officer at the fort meant he did administrative duties that saw him, and his scribes, at a desk for much of the day. Though, of all the tribunes of the Legio XX, she guessed that he was probably more active than his counterparts. It had taken no time for her to learn that he preferred to stride around and solve a problem, rather than merely send a minion to do it for him. He could never be said to be in dereliction of his duties, or a lazy officer: his nature was far too driven for that. Though reluctant to acknowledge the man had any positive attributes, she could see he was dedicated to his work.

Unfortunately, he was also dedicated to keeping her as his bed slave.

Inside the wooden temple building were many cubicles separated by simple wooden walls to a little above head height. Ineda had not seen what lay in each niche as Tribune Valerius used only one when he dragged her along. Whether, or not, he prayed to other gods or goddesses when alone she could not say. At present she could detect only the murmurs of a few other worshippers. That seemed to be how he preferred it. For reasons unknown he always waited if the building was full of worshippers. She guessed he wanted his deity to have no confusion over who might make a plea.

"Kneel!"

She knew the drill, could have slipped to the floor, but preferred to make him do the ordering – that way she accommodated her forced capture better.

The niche he had towed her to, dedicated to the goddess Etain, had a small altar just of sufficient height for the average soldier to top when kneeling with bent head. As Tribune Valerius knelt down beside her she could not fail to notice that the bowl set in the stone showed traces of dark brownish-red, indicating a sacrifice had not long since been offered. Attempts had been made to wipe it clear but the smears across the rim, and the drips to the side, coupled with the acrid blood tang that lingered in the air told it was a recent event. It mattered little to her, and did not surprise her; she was now well used to the frequency of the rituals. The aedes was a temple used by the whole garrison, and the altar she faced was only one of many.

"Etain, hear my plea…" Tribune Valerius' words were low; suffused with zeal.

He had never had a sacrifice conducted in her presence, though to her knowledge, his secutore organised it often enough for him. His main scribe, Pomponius, was a bustling little man full of his own importance, yet she knew Gaius Livanus Valerius relied heavily on the man to carry out his duties faithfully and competently. She understood Tribune Valerius' need for privacy at such times but wondered why.

Bloody sacrifice was a ritual she had witnessed often enough to her own goddess Rhianna and to Taranis before battle, the Celts being no stranger to the proceedings. He understood that about her.

Sacrifice was denied her, but in this frequent ritual he now conducted she was included. Roman ways were definitely strange, and the tribune was a very perplexing man.

"Worship, Ineda!"

Fierce. He sounded fiercer than she had ever heard before.

She joined his low mutterings, preying to Etain, the goddess not unfamiliar to her. He murmured feverishly alongside, his pleas louder than hers, never appearing aware of what she always asked for. Her request never varied, but if he ever heard her murmurs he never acknowledged it.

"Freedom, my lady, Etain," she whispered a repeated refrain, "I beg my freedom. I hate him, hate him…" She made her usual pleas though added a new one, whispering it so that it was not overheard. "Give Venutius the might to overcome this Roman dung horde, and make Agricola and Cerialis capitulate like they make the Celts do…and…expel the Roman oppressors from our land!"

She never had anything personal to offer the goddess in turn for the favour, but she prayed, nonetheless.

Directly behind the stone focus of the altar was a representation of the horse goddess in carved wood. It was a crudely made image depicting Etain riding a horse, the beast's forelegs high in the air. Etain was partially naked, breasts proud and bountiful, her open bratt flying wide to her sides. Etain drew her attention for a while.

Tribune Valerius' mutterings grew louder, more harried, too fast for any comprehension.

She allowed her head to dip further, surreptitiously checking to see if the fool tironis remained in place at the door. Too bad that he was; he had no wit to disobey and wander off.

"Etain, lady, hear my pleas…" Tribune Valerius was so

intent.

Ineda scoffed silently. Etain was not heeding any of her pleas for freedom.

His murmurs continued. She knew this bit since he always chanted it very slowly, nearing the end of his ritual. Why he towed her along every now and then to the aedes she had not yet worked out. Perhaps the frenzied part of the prayers concerned her? If so, she never ever detected her name as part of it. To discover all of his ritual she knew she would need to learn a lot more of the Latin tongue, though learning more of the Latin tongue was something she wanted to do anyway – regardless of the tribune's instructions.

As his intonation tapered off, she tried to read the letters that decorated the pedestal but knew only the part which stood for the Legio XX.

He held on to her shoulder as he rose to his feet. Not because he was infirm or incapable: it was more that he claimed her in the sight of his deity. Turning back to his assistant his voice was calm, though she felt a great tension in his fingers as his full weight seemed to fall on her through his heavy squeeze.

"The herbs."

Tribune Valerius gathered the bunch proffered by his secutore. Splitting the greenery to each side of the focus he went on to the next part of his ritual, the conclusion.

The mumbling coming from behind her was usual as his scribe made his own prayers.

"Come!"

Monosyllabic orders from Tribune Valerius were the norm in the aedes.

Towing after him, she side-stepped the scribe who went to lay down an apple to each side of the stone basin before kneeling at the altar. The underling always produced something of his own for the focus but only after his superior officer was completely finished.

"Take her back to my quarters!"

The tironis outside the door acknowledged the order accordingly before Tribune Valerius turned away from her without any further speech. Deep, deep anger simmered. Ignoring her as though her value was again redundant was a habit she could well do without, his treatment constantly exasperating her. Desperation to escape surfaced to swamping level at such times as these. She sensed Tribune Valerius was desperate to get to Antonius Pulis, Praefectus Castrorum – the camp commandant, who was the third most senior soldier at the garrison fortress and a man who did not like to be held up. She had seen him before and he was a formidable old soldier. Not one she would want to cross – except if it gained her the freedom she sought every single day.

Though in Tribune Valerius' present mood she was happier to be out of his sight. Trudging in front of the tironis – his name was Zosimus, though she refused to name him so – she resolved to find out why her captor was in such an incommunicative ill-temper.

Stopping short at the end of the principia entrance she looked over her shoulder. She knew Zosimus was literally on her heels but liked to annoy.

Staring up at him because she knew it discomfited the boy she growled, "Figs. Remember? We go for the figs first."

Turning left she walked along the pathway named the Via Principalis to go around the corner and head back to the main storage buildings. Escaping from Zosimus would be easy enough, for the boy lacked full wit, but escaping the hundreds of Romans at the garrison was not yet something she had worked out how to do. Until she could formulate a successful escape her life as a female slave of Tribune Valerius was better than being totally imprisoned. Tribune Valerius was not the ugliest man she had ever seen, though his appearance was not anything she placed importance on.

Her escape attempts had been rare. Not because she wanted to stay encamped with a legion of Roman soldiers; more that it was impossible to flee. The times she had tried had been at the beginning of her imprisonment, when they had been in the tented accommodation. Her only freedom was when she had been allowed access to the temporary latrine areas, though the guard was always close by. After her third or perhaps fourth escape attempt – she had not got more than a few strides – she was hauled back to Tribune Valerius who had railed and ranted at her.

"I do not keep you alive to be killed by a guard who halts your escape! If you flee another time they now have orders to kill you."

She believed him, had heard him give the orders to that effect.

Since she had arrived at the huge garrison fortress of Viroconium Cornoviorum her security was always vigilant, and the guards at all the entrance gates constantly watchful of all movements. She knew that because she had contrived on many occasions to walk past and survey the area as she was presently doing. Stopping short at the end of the street facing the Porta Principalis Sinistra, the eastern gate, she waited for the pilum to gently poke into her back. Zosimus was so predictable.

"Stop that! I am thinking of which way to go." Knowing well which route to take she liked to draw out the time she spent outside in the fresh air. Observing any traffic at the eastern gate was also very useful since there was always troop movement of some kind.

"Move on!"

Zosimus' orders made her grin down into her bratt; the boy always sounded so pathetically dull.

Turning left she headed up towards the Retentura, the back part of the fortress, the paved walkway she trod on fairly busy as it was a main route around the perimeter of the buildings. It never failed to amuse her that no matter how many people used the path the open space alongside remained empty. In her belligerent way she always tried to annoy Zosimus. She had only taken a couple of steps off the pathway when the pilum waved at her side.

"Step back onto the walkway!" Zosimus' order barked out, far louder than was necessary, but the fool was so assiduous about appearing to all and sundry as the dedicated guard.

Sliding the pilum away from her clothing Ineda moved back onto the busy area. "I do not see why I must walk where it is busy. That space is empty. Why cannot I walk there?"

As usual the answer was no answer. "We walk on the path."

What she called the 'empty area' under the fort walls, the part they named the intervallum, was almost deserted, save a few guards who hovered near the guard posts at the side entrance to the fort. Sometimes troops marched along the wide space but not presently. She had confirmed her guess that the space was there for defensive reasons and not because it had yet to be built upon. Any missiles that might land over the walls would not strike any buildings because they were set far enough back, and the only people who might be hurt would be soldiers who had strayed into range of weapons if under attack.

Despondency had almost been overwhelming when she had seen the wide areas those first times. Escape over the walls was not possible. Flight through the gates impossible too, unless the fort was abandoned by every single Roman soldier.

For the present she had accepted her incarceration, deciding that without major changes to her circumstances she could do no other. A guard was continually posted outside her room, and the few places she was allowed to venture to, in order to keep Tribune Valerius' table supplied, were always under escort.

Since becoming his bed slave her situation was marginally better, in that Tribune Valerius had ordered that she could walk about the fortress for exercise and fresh air, though not alone. She never failed to do that several times a day. Whether the wind howled, or the rain pelted down, she walked around to keep boredom at bay and to absorb what was around her.

If she could establish a link with the Celts outside the walls she knew, just knew, she would be able to ferret out useful information to send to Venutius. Even if she could not escape over those walls herself.

"This way!" She did not even bother to look at the fool who guarded her as she changed direction through the Retentura.

Trudging alongside the tironis past the storage buildings she paid no heed if anyone around heard her dire mutterings.

"Ignorant turds!"

Though they were well aware of her female presence none of the soldiers passing by returned her greetings, friendly or otherwise. The knowledge that she was Tribune Valerius' slave woman was enough to keep them all at bay. Women inside the garrison were not plentiful, but neither was she unique. She had been told who some of the inevitable female camp followers were, but there were also a few women of slightly higher status – concubines who had come to Britannia to live alongside their higher-ranking soldiers. Though none of those soldiers were the other tribunes. Rare glimpses were all she had had of those concubines and she was never allowed close enough to speak to them.

"Almost three moons I have been kept prisoner!" she griped as she entered the area where fresh produce was delivered. "Samhain fast approaches and I am still here."

Zosimus grunted behind her.

She had cried, she had railed and ranted at Tribune Valerius. Her pleas for release had gone unmarked. She had remained silent; she had purposely talked all the time in the languages she now knew a little more of. The words she spouted in the tongue of Germania she was sure were ill words but no one had dared give her translation. Nothing had made the slightest change to Tribune Valerius' stance. She had moved from being his prisoner to his bed slave who had her own tiny room.

Chapter Twenty

"Dried figs!"

The stallholder's eyes widened at her vehemence. She was not normally so abrupt in his presence for the man was affable enough.

"How many does the tribune wish for?"

The trader held some out for her to sniff. She may not ever have seen the fruit before meeting the tribune, but she had quickly learned which were well preserved, and which not. The tribune's personal cook had seen to that.

The cook was another who hated her and deeply resented her presence. It was hard to fathom his hostility at first but through time Ineda had worked out why. It still amazed her that a Roman soldier serving in Britannia would have his own cook, who in turn had his own slaves to do his bidding. It made a sort of sense to find out that the cook was also a soldier, an immune who could bear arms as well as any other soldier when necessary, and that the man was part of Tribune Valerius' permanent staff who followed him wherever he was posted.

When she felt at her most unforgiving Ineda scoffed that the cook had an easy task since the tribune often dined with the others of the legion who had as high a command as he had. At such times the tribune's cook was redundant. But that was where the antagonism came in. The tribune had issued orders that even if he was not dining in his quarters Ineda still had to be fed. On the first occasions she had not been given anything like the tribune would have expected – that was until Tribune Valerius found out.

Though Ineda felt she had nothing to do with the orders she bore the brunt of the cook's scorn, insults and antagonism. Though she trod warily around the man, he was inadvertently contributing to her learning new aspects of Roman daily living.

The vendor now knew not to sell bad goods to her.

Naming a quantity, she inspected some of the spices he sold. She had never seen or used them before coming to the garrison, but in her inquisitive way she had learned which gave the tastes she preferred. Tribune Valerius seemed little moved by any of his food so it was a little petty rebellion of hers to ensure that the cook made food she liked to eat. She smirked at the thought of what might pass her lips that evening, fingering some of the tiny black cloves that gave a nip to the food. Indicating she would have some of those too, the vendor added them to the basket.

Coin never needed to change hands, Tribune Valerius always honouring any purchases she made on his behalf. Accepting the laden basket she nodded at the trader and attempted a smile, though knew it came out as more grimace, her words bitter. "It seems that acquiring figs is all I am good for!"

Tramping doggedly to the doorway of Tribune Valerius' quarters her mood was angry. It got even worse when she saw who stood on guard. Glaucius always made some kind of comment about her person, sneered about her association with the tribune, and bragged about his sexual prowess often enough. He was an arrogant fool, tongue-ready and too inclined to be insolent about his superior officer when out of earshot. She may hate her captivity but the tribune did not deserve such insubordination. Yet how to tell him about Glaucius' attitude was not something she had tackled, though she often wanted to.

"The tribune is agitated today." Glaucius prevented her

entering with his spear, a tactic he used often, knowing it enraged her.

She refused to answer, waiting for him to say his spiel and be done. Confrontation had gained her nothing in the past. Zosimus cleared his throat awkwardly behind her, unwilling to make any challenge to anyone of higher rank.

"Have you put the mood upon him? Or could it be that events have unfolded which might alter your whore slave status?"

Glaucius' slur on the word whore enraged her, but she had no idea what he talked about. The man always toyed with her, his foul, garlic-laden breath filling her nostrils, so close was he leaning in towards her, his whisper and assessing stare designed to tease her even more. His eyebrows rose as he delivered more information. "There will be much celebration and feasting in the garrison this eve, as we rejoice in a great victory. A major defeat of the Celts of Britannia tends to lead to that."

She squirmed out of his reach, refusing to respond to his suggestive leer.

"If the tribune is not man enough to bed you this victorious night, send word to me. I will see that your last night here is a good one." His sneering comments over, he raised his spear tip and stared ahead as though the conversation had never taken place.

Irate at the man's insolence her tongue lashed. "The tribune will grace my bed as he has done countless times already!"

Glaucius' ugly sneer cut deep, the snarl even worse though she would not show how it affected her.

"You think yourself out of the ordinary? He is too fussy to consort with camp followers who give their bodies to all and sundry. To mate with only one woman till he returns to Rome, and to his long-waiting betrothed, avoids that."

Betrothed?

Walking inside Tribune Valerius' quarters to find the cook a dread coursed through her, even though she tried to ignore

Glaucius' taunts. It was a bitter thing to swallow but explained why she was not allowed any freedom at all. That the tribune bedded only her was no comfort.

And what did Glaucius mean by her last night? Could Venutius really have been vanquished? The Roman Army not repelled by the northern Celts? The idea was so horrendous she did not want to contemplate it. Did Glaucius mean that she would be killed because her fellow Brigantes were dead, or now under Roman conquest?

It took all her strength to keep moving, her legs not as steady as she willed them to be. Forcing down all panic, she persuaded herself to carry on till all was revealed, determined not to show any concern.

Zosimus at her heels, she delivered the goods to the cook. Though simple, it was a task she had earned and would not relinquish – not for Glaucius or anyone else. That little bit of freedom to make a decision about her life she had earned with her body. She might not like it but it was a fact she was learning to live with.

Shivering with dread for what the eve might bring she drew her bratt tighter around her, her hatred for Tribune Valerius and her present life deep. Yet, if death was to visit her that night she would not go down without a fight. Of that she was sure. She had not fulfilled her purpose of thwarting the Roman scum. Her life had to be more meaningful.

Was this what Meaghan meant when she mentioned she would wear two bratts?

***

"You will leave at dawn, Gaius Livanus Valerius. Since Tribune Marcellus and his First Cohort are still battling with the Ordovices, none of them can accompany you. Instead, a small mounted detachment and some scouts will go with you as far as the encampment at Deva. Make decisions with the agrimensors and the architecti about the supplies for the new fortress. Is all clear to you?"

Gaius accepted his orders and exited the office of the Praefectus, suppressing an unaccustomed urge to grin. He had been waiting for this moment for a long time, forced to remain in the garrison at Viroconium Cornoviorum since the short foray when he had encountered Ineda. The new orders suited his need for action. He liked being out of the fortress and the notion of going to the new forts in the north appealed to his mood, even though the winter chill had already descended upon them.

The news just relayed was excellent. The inhospitable weather had not stopped the Roman Empire from vanquishing Venutius of the Brigantes near his stronghold at Stanwick. The Celts of the north had been slaughtered, few of them left to scatter and flee. All of northern Brigantia would be under complete and total Roman domination before long and the process of fort building would be more effective without the constant raids that had been occurring before Venutius' defeat.

"Tribune!" He accepted the salute of the guard at the door, not even trying to hide his smile.

That the Legate Agricola would not be returning to Deva, or Viroconium Cornoviorum, was not really unexpected. Agricola was a very ambitious man and his recall to an administrative post in Rome had been likely even before the man had gone north to vanquish the northern Celts along with Governor Cerialis and the troops of the IX and II Adiutrix. He wished Agricola well. He had not liked all of the man's methods but Agricola had been a formidable leader of the Legio XX, a man he had great respect for even if he would never be a true friend.

Outside the office of the Praefectus a full blown grin broke free. His secutore picked up pace alongside him, having been denied entrance to the office. "Your new orders please you, Tribune Valerius?"

"Most certainly, Pomponius."

Striding ahead to his quarters he ignored the attempts by his secretary to find out more information. He had much to think on about his two new sets of instructions.

There had been unrest for too long. Encouraging better harmony amongst the troops was exactly the sort of task at which he now excelled. He knew it, and so did his superiors.

His new promotion pleased him greatly, though it was nothing like the passage back to Rome that Pomponius, and his father, hoped for. It was in fact the opposite and would keep him in Britannia for some further winters to come – but that was exactly what he wanted.

His father would be angered to learn he had accepted a further extension to his time away from Rome, but his father's ambitions and plans held no interest for him. The more idle life of an elevated clerk in Rome, even though of high equestrian status, was something he wished to avoid. Marriage to the high-born lady chosen by his father he likewise wanted to evade.

He did not even want to think about what his mother's opinion would be of the new extension to his military service. She hated him and had stated she always would while he thwarted her ambitions to rise in status in Rome. Her venom had been so profound he believed it, her lack of contact with him further testimonial of her feelings. And naturally, the females in his family sided with his mother, all blaming him for Fulvia's self-induced starvation. His cousin had done all too well at blaming him for the seduction, and she had been believed. The loathing in everyone's eyes had remained an abiding memory during his years in exile, even before his father had purchased his first military commission.

"Will your new orders mean major changes, sir?" Pomponius continued to burble.

He decided to take pity on the man who exasperated him, but who generally did an admirable job. "They will."

His secretary's beaming smile had to be quickly dispelled. Though Pomponius's less than subtle wheedling about advancement annoyed him, he wanted no illusions and no disappointment. Stopping abruptly at the corner of the Via Principalis he faced the clerk. "My new instructions will not lead me back to Rome. My new task pleases me very well, Pomponius, and will keep me in Britannia for many winters to come."

Though his secretary tried to mask his disappointment it was impossible to miss the flash of it in the man's eyes as he forced a small smile.

"The task will often take me to hostile territory, Pomponius, but it will be a challenge I shall relish. If you do not wish to remain my secretary, we can come to some other arrangement for you?"

"Oh, no, sir! I do not wish to leave your employment."

As they walked on he outlined his new instructions, Pomponius's head nodding in agreement, though Gaius was sure the man felt daunted by the new commission.

Promotion to superior officer for the acquisition and transportation of iron, lead and other metal supplies to the builders of the smaller forts in the northern territories satisfied him very much. It was a task he had lately assumed more responsibility for since the return to Rome of the previous senior commander, though his focus had been on supplying only for the troops of the Legio XX. His new commission would mean much more co-ordination with the other three legions in Britannia since he was now to also oversee the stocks of lead that would be produced from the Brigantian mines.

Each fortlet and small auxiliary fort required a large amount of metal goods and the movement of them around the north was a troublesome task. Metals were not only heavy to transport, deliveries were prone to attack from the local Celts since the metals were commodities they could easily use for weapon making. In Roman terms no iron meant no nails, and no interior building within the forts. Lead was needed for plumbing and other pipe work. Other metals and ores were mixed to shape many tools and goods.

Short forays into northern Brigante territory, by engineering scouts, had established raw iron supplies could be sourced locally – though some of those areas had not yet been settled properly by Roman presence. Until that happened native stocks of iron ore were not readily available in the north, but he needed to be closer to the mines when the surroundings were secured. Till then, all of the heavy supplies still had to be transported from the south.

Pomponius dribbled along at his side jabbering at his ear. "My congratulations, Tribune Valerius. This is the perfect situation for your further advancement. You have all the skills learned from your current post."

Gaius accepted the acknowledgement with a nod, a small smile leaking to emphasise his next words. "That is not my entire new task, Pomponius. I am also given new instructions that will mean some possible displeasure." He knew his smile caused confusion. After outlining his secondary task he watched Pomponius' expression brighten to a full beaming grin.

"That is to be congratulated even more, sir. You have noted how the Legate Agricola worked to quell any disturbance. Utilise his methods and you cannot fail to succeed. Before long, I predict, you will be back in Rome!"

Gaius silently snorted, but even if it had been loud Pomponius would not have noticed. The man's ambitions could not be repressed for long. His continued drivel was punctuated by his loud inhalations of breath as he struggled to keep up. A small man with short legs, Pomponius' stride was half as long as his. The man could be a sycophantic toad but Gaius knew the worth of his secutore. The man used his stylus faster than he did, and had an unfailing memory for facts and figures. However, the gibbering tongue was something he could manage without.

"If I employ Agricola's methods at the forts north of Deva they will no longer have enough soldiers for them to function.

233

There are not enough men in them to discipline in the way Agricola would have done." His answered bark set Pomponius to grovel even further.

Seeing his mistake, the secutore backtracked. "Well, I don't quite mean disembowel them all. Just the ringleaders."

Gaius had reached the end of his patience as well as his door. "Our respected departing legate had no qualms about stamping out the insurrection of the ringleaders and everyone associated with it. I will use some of his methods, Pomponius, but I will not condemn all at these forts without listening to them first."

Agricola's methods of command were legendary, and not all brutal, but he had been known to act precipitately. That mattered little if dealing with marauding Celts but was critical, in Gaius' opinion, if dealing with Roman troops.

"It has to be the fault of the II Adiutrix; they do not yet work as a cohesive unit. Their training has been lax." Pomponius' certainty was unmistakeable in his expressions and tetchy tone.

"That may be true, Pomponius, but I will hear no more of your theories just now. Find me all you can on the II Adiutrix, and especially about those troops who barrack at our new fort of Nidd. Anything else about their presence in the northern areas, as well. I want details immediately."

Dismissed so abruptly Pomponius huffed off in the opposite direction from which they had come. Gaius was not concerned. He knew his secutore would go off to probe particulars from the clerks of the other tribunes, one of whom he knew had served a short term at Lindum. The II Adiutrix had been at the Lindum garrison for quite some time before Cerialis had sent some of them to the north. The clerk would likely have useful information, and one thing Pomponius could be relied upon to know was how to garner valuable morsels.

He had plenty to think on, but Ineda had to be dealt with first. She was both burden and blessing since he had taken her prisoner. He had only just begun to seek her out at night and was not sure he wanted that to stop so soon. Under no illusion, she only acquiesced and accepted his advances because he gave her no choice. He knew she blocked the act from her mind in some way, her passive inaction a good indicator of that. That did not matter. What mattered was that he still wanted her even if she hated him. It made no sense to him, she was an enemy woman, yet he craved her body more and more and he intended to use her till he tired of her.

Having her accompany him to the north was possible, but it would take her closer to the territory she had come from and he was not convinced that was a good idea. Her acceptance of captivity, and her role as his slave, he knew was only because of her good sense and because she had realised escape from the garrison was impossible. Tolerance of him was all she could manage; any tasks she undertook for him not out of any fond regard. If they were on the move, encamped before they eventually reached the fort at Nidd, she would try to escape.

Doing without her for the coming days was the only viable option. A deep sigh showed what he thought of that. He also knew she would need to be continually guarded to keep her safe from the men of the garrison. None had countermanded his orders regarding her while he was there, but when he was out of the fort he was less sure of continued adherence to those commands.

"Tribune!"

The salute drew his thoughts back to his present situation, Glaucius on duty at the doorway to his quarters.

"Have Ineda brought here immediately."

Gaius guessed the man would be smirking as he wheeled about and walked away, having seen enough smirks masked on previous occasions. Though attached to his personal guard the man was not one he could befriend; there was something about his manner which always irked. Glaucius always kept on the right side of obedience, though, so there was no legitimate reason to replace him with another.

One thing was definite. Glaucius could not be left at the garrison, he could not be left in a position to seduce Ineda whether she would want the man's advances or not.

Chapter Twenty-One

AD 73 One Moon After Samhain – Scortin

"Venutius has come to a mighty defeat! All is lost!"

The warrior of Scortin was exhausted, bedraggled and bloody as he slumped down close to the low burning logs. His limp body had been supported through the roundhouse entranceway, the man's strength all but drained. Those around Brennus at the fireside had jumped to their feet on hearing the commotion the man had made outside. Utter dread flashed across old faces. Iohan's wife's lips trembled, her hands wringing in misery across her cheeks before she dropped to her haunches. Wailing at the prostrate warrior, Lara's words were muffled.

"Where is Iohan?"

The room was in panic. Everyone wanting to ask their own questions.

"The king?" Tuathal's old voice still held sway.

"Gone! Most likely dead, but his body has not been recovered yet. Most senior warriors of Brigantia, also. Mown down. In huge numbers."

Brennus lifted an ale jug and poured some of the liquid into a wooden cup. Passing it carefully into the shaking warrior's hand he did not relinquish it till the man's chest ceased to heave. Maintaining calm he did not feel his question was a repetition. "What of Iohan?"

He had only recently arrived at the lands of the Setantii, his last days having been spent in Cornovii territory with Tuathal.

King Venutius had sent him south to aid the old druid whose mortal nights were numbered, his old bones exacting a toll, yet the old man continued his tasks of information gathering and druid rituals. Venutius had confided that he needed a trusted warrior to support his old and faithful friend, worried that the druid would fall into the hands of the Roman patrols. Venutius also gave him the charge that in due time he should assume the role of official messenger after Tuathal's death.

Tuathal had been determined to say his farewells to the hillforts and settlements he had frequented for many winters. As he journeyed with the old man Brennus made acquaintance of the warriors who formed the messenger link to the king, established his own contacts for future times and sometimes even had fun entertaining – Tuathal adding to his repertoire.

All areas of the Cornovii and the Setantii were under total Roman control but discrete travel was still possible. Two men moving from village to village were not considered a danger, not enough to cause any significant revolt. Not especially one so old and decrepit and the other a limping maimed warrior. When they encountered Roman patrols Brennus made his infirmities seem much more hampering than they now were, making them work in his favour, and he always ensured some valid reason for moving from place to place.

Scortin was Tuathal's last stop. The old man's vigour was waning fast and a few more nights might be all he would have left in his mortal shell. His thready voice took precedence though, since he was the most senior person seated in the roundhouse. "How bad?"

The Scortin warrior flopped down even further, his head hanging low between his knees, the words muffled. "Iohan is dead." The man lifted his head and sought Lara. "Your stripling son lives."

Her wail echoed around the roundhouse. Whether it was joy at hearing her son lived, or sorrow her hearth-husband was dead

Brennus could not be sure, but the woman was distraught.

The warrior continued. "Your son returns with those who were lightly wounded. He brings back his father's sword and bratt pin." The man stopped to look around the gathering, to explain his motives. "I volunteered to come on ahead. We had no mounts and the way back is long. Though there are few left in the line of warriors, they need help with the more severely wounded."

It was not Brennus' place to take charge, not his settlement, but the warriors left around the fireside seemed too old to make snap decisions. Stepping to the door he bid the young guard rouse help. His orders were met with no resistance, the lad rushing off doing some hollering of his own.

"Bran? See to Tuathal!"

He turned at Lara's shout. The old druid's knees had buckled, his body contorting into a rickle of bones as he slipped to the packed earth.

Holding Tuathal's hand as Lara straightened out his body the druid's eyes fluttered before closing. Coming to himself a few moments later, Brennus watched the life drain from the man who had lately been more than a just a travelling companion. Tuathal's old rheumy eyes flickered, his words the tiniest broken croak as he issued a string of last commands. "Continue to ensure that messages are carried, Bran. Use that fine voice of yours to win the people over to our mutual cause. Let your stories of Rome be the exchange for their hospitality. Our line of contacts will need to be extended to all Celts north of here. The chain must not be broken. Your part will be to know which chief will work for the cause of all of us."

"Rest easy, old man." He sought to make the old druid comfortable but Tuathal was desperate to speak.

"Nothing will prevent the Romans building their forts in northern reaches of Brigantia. You must now warn the settlers who live over the high hills of the Roman arrival to their territory. Find a way to bring our Celtic brothers together. They will resist you and want to fight for their own territory but that will never work. Persist. You must persist and never relent, even to the furthest areas of Celtic terrain."

To mollify a dying man, he nodded his agreement. "I vow I will persevere, Tuathal. I will warn all Celts of impending danger, journeying on as far as I need to. On that you have my word."

Weak fingers squeezed his own. "My flute."

"You want it now?" It was a strange request, but he knew what the small bone flute meant to the old man.

"It is yours now. I know what you will say – that you cannot play this instrument with two fingers. Believe that you can! But you must learn the movements with your left hand and play it as well as you formerly wielded your broadsword."

He fetched the ancient flute from Tuathal's bag and pressed it into the old man's hand. Tuathal's fingers pushed the bone instrument back into his grasp.

"Use this flute as your rallying call, as you will your ocarina! Find your own words of warning for it and teach those who will unite to it. Be the call of the far north."

Realising he had no time for lengthy explanation he sought to clarify Tuathal's words. "My understanding is poor. Are you saying I must be the one to rally the Celts together? I can not be that man, Tuathal."

"Nay! Not you. But you will be an instrument to that man. Return to Garrigill first, but do not tarry there. Seek a leader from the tribes north of the Selgovae, even though it will be a difficult task. He will be a charismatic man who will gain many followers, but he will still need time to be awakened to the threat of Rome." Tuathal's voice lapsed into silence, the old man's breathing very shallow, his eyes closed.

Brennus waited, his confusion still great. Tuathal's words made little sense. A small eye flicker indicated the old man was not yet gone. When the old druid did talk it was so faint he had to bend close.

"I cannot see where he dwells. The Caledons of the mountains may know. Find him."

"You have my word." He squeezed the old man's cool fingers.

"I have great faith in you, Brennus of Garrigill." The last word was a hiss as the breath in Tuathal ceased.

Any momentary dismay on Brennus' face he hoped would be put down to his grief at the old man's passing. He hoped he could live up to Tuathal's confidence since he was not so certain he was the man to find such a great leader.

He now had four precious items. The bone flute joined the arm ring thong that lay around his neck, the ocarina was safe in the pouch at his waist, and the bratt pin was displayed for all to see.

Another new phase of his life seemed about to begin.

To be continued in

After Whorl: Donning Double Cloaks

Glossary

Gaelic terms:

Fóghnaidh mi dhut! – I will finish you!
Diùbhadh! – Scum!
A ghlaoic! – You fool!
An cù! – The bastard!
Ciamar a tha thu? – How are you?
Madainn mhath! – Good morning!
Tapadh leat. – Thank you.
Mar sin leibh! – Farewell!
Dé thu a déanamh? – What are you doing?
An cù! – The pig! / The bastard!
Màthair – Mother
Ceigean Ròmanach! – Roman turds!
Buachar each! – You piece of horse shit / dung!
A mhic an uilc! – You evil bastard! (to a man)
A mhic a' choin! – You bastard!

Latin terms:

A – agrimensor (engineer/land surveyor); aedes (temple of worship); auxiliary (soldier with no Roman status); architecti [plural] architectus [singular] (architects); ala: mounted force
B – basilica (great hall)
C – contubernium (group of 8); centurion (in charge of 80+ men); centuries (80 men); cohort (480 soldiers); cornicularius (clerk to tribune)
D – decanus (in charge of contubernium)
F – focus (bowl in altar)
G – gladius (sword)
I – immunes (non-combatant workforce); IX (Ninth legion); II Adiutrix (new auxiliary legion given to Cerialis in Britannia);

Intervallum (vacant ground behind fort walls set to beyond the maximum distance within which a missile could land)

L – Legio (legion); legionary (soldier of Roman status); Legate (Commander of legion)

M – militis (level above tirone, 2nd from bottom)

P – pila [plural], pilum [singular] (spear); principia (central marshalling area in fort); Praefectus Castrorum (camp commandant 3rd in charge of legion); pugiones [plural], pugio [singular] (dagger); Porta Decumana (rear gate); Porta Principalis Sinistra (eastern gate)

R – Retentura (back part of the fort)

S – secutore (secretary/scribe); scribe (office assistant); stylus (writing implement); standard (insignia of legion held aloft on a high pole)

T – tribunal (raised platform for the legate to announce from); tribune (officer – one of 5 to a legion); tironis (raw recruit – served 6mths at the stage); Tribuni Angusticlavii [plural] Tribunus Angusticlavius [singular] ("narrow striped" officers/ equestrian legionary officers/five to each legion)

V – venator (hunter); Via Decumana (street leading to the rear of the fort)

Dating terms:

Time mainly in moons before or after...
Imbolc – Feb 1st
Beltane – May 1st
Lughnasadh – Aug 1st
Samhain – Oct 31st
Summer Solstice – June 21st
Winter Solstice – December 21st

Roman Legions mentioned:

Legio IX
Legio XX
Legio II Adiutrix (new auxiliary legion given to Cerialis in Britannia)
Legio II Augusta

Tribes mentioned:

Fantastic Books
Great Authors

CROOKED CAT

Meet our authors and discover our exciting range:

Thank you for buying my novel.

If you enjoyed reading this book please consider writing a short review (a few sentences will do) and post it on Amazon or email me your thoughts. It really helps to get the honest feedback and also increases the popularity of the book.

Kind regards
Nancy Jardine

it
icals

Children's

oks.com

Lightning Source UK Ltd.
Milton Keynes UK
UKOW03f0944120314

227990UK00001B/3/P